MENAGERIE OF SHADOW

The Collector #3

MATHIAS G. B. COLWELL

Copyright © 2017 by Mathias G. B. Colwell

ISBN: 978-1-68046-517-4

Melange Books, LLC
White Bear Lake, MN 55110
www.melange-books.com

Published in the United States of America.

Cover Design by Ashley Redbird Designs

For Rose. Maybe you will grow up to love fantasy and will one day read this book. Or maybe not. Who knows? Either way, this is for you.

CHAPTER ONE

THE CROSSBOW BOLT FIZZED THROUGH THE AIR. ALAYNA ADJUSTED her body ever so slightly, enough so that the projectile missed but not enough to unsettle her balance on the eaves of the abandoned house. As it passed, the bolt sliced free a lock of her strawberry-blonde hair. Momentarily distracted by the striking contrast of the floating, red-gold hair framed against the austere, snowy ground, Alayna was almost struck by another bolt from the assailant. She saw it at the last moment and dodged again, this time with a bit more force. She jumped and then slid on the frosty ledge to avoid the bolt. The jolt of fear that trilled through her body was familiar by this time—it was a well-known accompaniment to battle. A year ago, the human version of herself would have been so terrified she likely would have frozen as stiff as the icy roof on which she perched so precariously. A year ago, she would have been paralyzed with fear. Not anymore. The Elfas in her, and perhaps the fact that she'd fought more times in the last half year of her life than she would have in many lifetimes as a human, was enough to keep her moving and dodging. Enough to keep her alive.

Returning fire with one of her own miniature crossbows, Alayna leapt with grace from the eaves of one frosty roof to that of another building, sliding again as she landed. Skidding with an intended elegance, she freed another crossbow from the clip on her hip and fired two bolts in quick succession. Her aim was true and the Collector below doubled over with a grunt as the two projectiles pierced his black cloak—one in the gut and the other in the shoulder —sending him spinning to the ground, dead.

Alayna didn't even pause to think of the life she had just taken. This abandoned village in Romania was crawling with Collectors, and there was no time to waste on ethical quandaries. Besides, there wasn't really a dilemma at all. It was kill or be killed. That was her reality now. Alayna reloaded her two crossbows and held them at the ready as she slunk quickly across the rooftops of the town. She was the eyes and ears in the air. The graceful one. Philip was likely in the midst of a brawl by this point. In fact, she could hear the clatter and creak of shattering wood made all the louder by the freezing tempera-tures. Philip had no doubt tossed someone through a beam, aided as he was by his troll blood. She flipped her fur-lined hood up against the cold as she moved and kept her weapons trained on the ground.

Another Collector stalked quietly through an alleyway beneath her. She dispatched him with a bolt in the back and reloaded. She heard a scream from the outskirts of town—a piercing cry—and then a muffled moan as the scream quickly subsided. That was likely Beathan doing his work around the edges. They had a system following months of being tracked and hunted, months of fighting and battles. After the first few hectic fights, they had needed to figure out a method. The strategy they had settled on for their skirmishes was fairly simple. Wherever the fight took place, Philip—the strongest and most resilient of their company with his enhanced healing—always took up the middle or center of the fight, drawing the most attention and distracting notice from the others as much as possible. He was the target, after all. Beathan always flanked the enemy. He utilized his half-fairy speed and crafty powers, which Alayna was still trying to understand; it was nearly impossible to get a straight answer out of him about anything, let alone about something so personal as his supernatural abilities. Alayna with her agility, her Elfas affinity for trees and heights, along with her increasingly good aim with crossbows, took up whatever high ground was available and provided aerial cover—just as she was doing now.

More screams echoed through the village, and Alayna hurried toward their source. Philip would need her above him to provide cover. That was always the plan, only this time their personal fights had pushed them in opposite directions. She prowled stealthily across the rooftops under a troubled, grey sky with darkly encroaching clouds. The first few flakes of snow began to drift down, swirling around her, making the footing even slicker, if that were possible. Alayna leapt lithely to another rooftop, crossing the narrow gap between buildings as if it were two feet instead of six. She crested the steep roof and slid down the other side, stopping herself at the gutter, and found herself looking down at a scene of mayhem.

There he was—her everything. Alayna's true heart. His hair had grown even more in the last six months, and it hung wild and free just above his shoulders. It swirled with his movements as he fought, caught up in the icy breeze. Philip wore his usual sleeveless tunic, unlaced at the neck, and slim breeches tucked into black boots. He fought like a madman, like a tavern brawler possessed by a demon. He felled a Collector with his fist and turned to fight the next in line. He kicked out kneecaps and shattered forearms, leaving behind a wake of mangled bodies. But he was outnumbered and had taken a variety of wounds in the process. He needed her, just like he always did. He might be a hybrid, but he was still just one person.

Without delay, Alayna sighted her targets and began picking off their enemies. She winged the first Collector at which she aimed, but the bolt to his shoulder was enough to force him to fall back for a moment. Only five surrounded Philip right now. Her next bolt took a Collector between the shoulder blades, and he keeled over dead. Philip flashed a fierce grin of thanks in her direction and kept fighting. Kneeling on the eaves of the building, she reloaded. Alayna was just sighting her next target when she heard the crunch of frost above and behind her. Cursing, she swung around, arms aiming both small crossbows upward. She loosed both bolts as a dark form leapt down toward her from the top of the roof. One bolt flew high and wide, rushed as she was. The other grazed her enemy, but not enough to stop him from colliding with her, sending the two of them spinning off the roof into empty air.

Alayna landed with a shock of pain, one shoulder bearing the brunt of the fall. It twisted under her in agony as she fought to gain air in her lungs and purchase on the ground under her feet. Stumbling, she clawed her way to her feet and fumbled with cold fingers to reload the one crossbow she had managed to retain. Up high, she was calm and composed. Here on the ground, in the thick of it all, she was less so. Oh, she was more dangerous and qualified to fight than she had been a half year back when the three of them had fled St. Thomas after rescuing Beathan, but she still didn't possess the extent of battle experience of either Philip or the fairy.

The sounds of the fray surrounded her. There were grunts, cries of pain, as well as shouts of plans and strategies as the Collectors fought to subdue Philip. The Collector who had snuck up on her and knocked her from her perch struggled to his feet, too. He looked a little less dazed than Alayna felt after the fall. He pulled a knife and a wooden stake from his belt. Alayna was no vampire, but vampires were dangerous enough that all Guild members in the field always kept a stake on hand. It was a standard part of every Collector's arsenal. Alayna's assailant grinned menacingly when he saw the flash of uncertainty in her eyes as she became aware of her vulnerable position on the ground. The man casually flicked the wooden stake into the air in a small toss, caught it, and hurled it with precision in Alayna's direction. She arched her body to one side and let the stake fly past her. The Collector's face darkened in fury at his miss. Alayna steeled herself and charged him with a curse of half-fury, half-fear. They came together with a clash of bodies and then spun apart, raining blows upon each other. The Collector slashed at her face with his knife, and Alayna's dark cloak billowed as she twirled away, all grace and elegance. Her own belt knife came freely to her hand, replacing the crossbow she had dropped before attacking. She whipped in close and ducked under another slash, slicing her own blade against her enemy's outer thigh. The Collector grunted in pain and stumbled. Their momentum carried them apart before they spun around to face each other again.

Alayna saw respect in the Collector's eyes now, a wary fear of his opponent. She felt a savage surge of satisfaction. Perhaps she was right where she belonged, here in the thick of things. Maybe all her training with Philip had paid off more than she had thought. She pressed her advantage and darted in close again. This time the enemy's knife slashed her shoulder, but it was a calculated wound and not too deep. She took the injury but was now within his barriers. Close as she was, she buried her blade in his chest with the speed of an Elfas. Up close and personal, she saw the light fade from his eyes as the glaze of death overtook him. Suddenly, the savagery and satisfaction she had felt was gone. Death was just death. It was a great, dark, blackness that took them all at one point or another. There was no joy in sending any soul there sooner than was necessary. But it *was* necessary. She heard Philip cry out in pain and turned to see him clasping his shoulder, blood seeping out from between his fingers.

Alayna shook away her morbid thoughts. She leapt and slid across the frozen ground to where her crossbows lay discarded from the fall and the fight. She loaded with the speed of practice and spun around, sighting and loosing all in one fevered motion. Her bolts flew true and parted around Philip, missing her lover by inches before burying themselves in the throats of his assailants. Philip shook off his injury and advanced on the final attacker. The Collector backed away warily but hopelessly. He knew it was over now, as much as Philip and Alayna did. Even injured as Philip was, the lone Collector stood no chance against a hybrid half-man filled with the strength and power of troll blood. Philip closed the distance and finished the man quickly with a blow to the face followed by a savage but ultimately merciful twist of the neck.

The heat of battle gone, a chill wind played around Philip and Alayna as they stared searchingly into each other's eyes. Alayna watched the passion and battle fury—the wildness of Philip's non-human side—fade from his eyes to be replaced by sadness. It was not remorse. Philip understood just as she did that survival took precedence. But she saw the sadness in his eyes all the same at having to kill so many of his former brothers. This was by far the biggest band of Collectors that had been sent after them yet. At least ten were dead by Philip and Alayna's hands, and who knew how many Beathan had killed on the flanks.

Philip gazed at her with a deep look through eyes that drank in her soul.

"Thanks," he said simply and without further ado. "It would have been difficult without you at my back."

"You're damned right it would have been," she answered, joking, and then closed the distance between them, hands caressing his injured arm. His grin turned to a wince as she began to prod.

"Easy," he muttered. "It'll heal just fine. You don't have to stick your fingers in it."

Alayna grimaced in annoyance and prodded once more just for

good measure before kissing him. His hands slipped inside her hood to find the sides of her face and press her elegantly tipped ears against her head. They kissed fiercely for a moment in the way that could only be experienced post-battle—the celebration of life and survival. They kissed for a lost-in-time moment, and Alayna wrapped her arms around him, wishing that she could somehow pull him so close that it would fuse their bodies together. She wished the cursed Collectors Guild would stop hunting them long enough for their bodies to heal from one attack before the next began. But that would never happen. Philip had not only taken up arms against his former employers but he had led an attack on St. Thomas Prison, one of the Guild's bastions of power. An affront like that by a former Guild member could not be ignored, and so they had used their Blood Mages to activate the trace that had been placed in Philip's blood so many years ago when he had first sworn his oath. That trace allowed them to follow him wherever he went. There was nowhere safe to hide.

"Interruptin', am I?" The lilting, Irish brogue caused Philip and Alayna to pull apart.

Alayna quirked a haughty eyebrow at the half-fairy. "So, I see you've survived yet again, Beathan."

"Tough t' kill, I am." The gypsy gave a half bow and a quick jig. "Shall we get out o' here, or would the two o' you rather keep kissin'?"

Philip smiled, but then his mirth faded. "We can't leave yet. There's work to be done."

Beathan shook his head. "Ya' can't be serious, mate. Not again. The ground's frozen solid."

"They were good men. They deserve a proper burial." His face was a stony mask of implacable resolve.

Alayna shrugged. "They did just try to kill us, love."

"And we killed them instead. I know what happened, Alayna, but they were following orders. It's not their fault they were sent on a suicide mission. We bury them. Besides, there are far worse types than Collectors in this world."

"Is there even a shovel, mate?" Beathan tilted his head to the side, clearly still hoping to get out of ditch duty.

Philip stared at his best friend. There was a coldness in his eyes that hadn't always been there. Alayna could see that killing Guild members for the last half year had taken its toll on him.

"Fine, search the buildings. Romanians need to dig just like anyone else. Maybe someone left a shovel around here." Philip turned and began lining up the dead, closing their eyes almost tenderly.

Alayna felt a familiar ache as she watched him bid farewell to more of his one-time brothers, just as she had so often done these last few months.

They searched the buildings and, in a surprisingly short time, they found one shovel and an old pickax. They took turns hollowing out the icy ground and finally laid each dead warrior to rest in a shallow, foreign grave.

"Do ya' want to say a few words?" Beathan asked Philip, sincerity in his voice.

Philip paused, thinking the question over. "I was once their brother, but I'm no priest. I wouldn't know what to say. A burial is enough." Then he heaped the last shovel of dirt over the final grave. Alayna watched as he slammed the flat of the shovel to pat down the frosty earth. It was an unnecessary action. She saw the unspoken curse in his eyes as he stared at the graves, knew that he was cursing his old masters for sending more men to their needless deaths.

She took his hand, and he grasped it tighter than she expected. The coldness of their skin in the late winter air forced them to let go sooner than she would have liked, forced them to tuck their hands back into the relative warmth of their cloaks—well, it forced her. Philip could endure much more of the cold than she.

Alayna leaned against him and sent her consciousness into his, spoke to his mind with hers the way her people often could to those with whom they shared a deep intimacy. *I'm sorry, love. I am so sorry that we had to do this again.* She put her head on his shoulder as her words effortlessly penetrated his mind. He looked down and smiled his thanks at her concern, but there was a tight pain in his eyes that did not release.

"Where to?" Alayna asked him out loud, ending their private communication. She and Beathan waited for a response.

Philip ran his hands tiredly through his long, road-weary, unwashed hair. "I'm so tired. Tired of it all, of the killing and fighting. We have to find a way to get this godforsaken trace out of my blood. If only I could change it!" he practically expelled the last bit of the statement in a shout.

"How?" she asked.

Philip turned to look at her, the pain in his eyes sending an aching sensation into the pit of her stomach. "I have no idea."

"The two o' ya' might not, but *I* may have an idea." Alayna and Philip's heads whipped around toward Beathan in surprise.

"You do?" they both asked in unison.

CHAPTER TWO

"You have an idea?" Philip heard the hope in Alayna's voice and couldn't help the stir of hope that he felt as well. Nobody had had a solution worth proposing in months.

"I do," Beathan said. "A dangerous one. An' possibly a bad one. But an idea all the same, assumin' you're desperate enough."

Philip grimaced in frustration. "You know I'm desperate," he said, ignoring the look Alayna shot him. "If you've had an idea, why have you waited six months to bring it up?"

The half-fairy shrugged. "Only just came t' me, mate."

"Just now?" he asked the gypsy, dubiously. "Out of nowhere?"

Beathan shrugged again, his dirty-blond hair swaying around his ears and neck as he did so. His hooked nose and middle-aged features twisted apologetically yet did not quite manage to banish the effervescent mirth and mischief that could always be found twinkling in his eyes just below the surface.

"So, what brought on this sudden idea?" Alayna's cool, calm voice interposed.

"Well, when rolly-trolly over here mentioned 'changing it', the idea sort o' just popped into me head, magical-like." Beathan winked at her.

"What do you mean?" Philip asked.

Beathan stared at him seriously now, mirth receding far into the background. "I know a man. Not the type o' character one mixes with lightly. But he's in the business o' changin' things."

Philip groaned inwardly. If Beathan felt this cautious about his own idea, it did not bode well. The hybrid fairy was reckless to the point of extreme self-endangerment. Philip had learned to watch for cues such at this to know when to tread lightly when moving forward into territory that Beathan deemed dangerous.

"And you really think this person can somehow fix the problem of my trace? You know, the Blood Mages claim that once they place the trace in a man's blood it is there forever. What makes you think this person can 'change' that?"

"Don't rightly know if he can, but it couldn't hurt just to speak to him, could it? Well, actually, it could," Beathan answered his own rhetorical question, "but who are we if we aren't those who take a few risks?"

"He's that dangerous, this acquaintance of yours?" Alayna asked. The cautionary look she shot Philip said it all. She was not in favor of this idea. She would be content to run and hide and keep fighting forever. She didn't know what Philip knew, that the Guild would never, ever stop. Alayna still held out hope that if they could stay alive for a year or two, if they could get far enough away, maybe the Guild would forget about them. Philip knew from firsthand experience that that wasn't the case. Collectors who went rogue were captured and treated more harshly than any of their usual prey.

"Aye, Alayna, he is. The type o' man I'd not tangle with lightly. But there are ways to his heart, just like there are ways t' any man's heart." Beathan winked again.

Alayna just shook her head. "Quit winking at me! Can't you ever hold a serious conversation?"

"Right now, 'tis 'bout as serious as I ever get, lass."

Philip was used to their typical banter—it had been just so for the last few months. It was how they hid the genuine care they felt for one another. Right now, though, it set his nerves on edge, especially given where they were. He turned his head to stare morosely at the line of frozen graves. Unnecessary graves. Philip lost his line of thought for a moment as he stared at the death he had once again caused. His two companions kept up their bickering, but it faded to the periphery of his focus as he regained his line of thought. More Collectors would come. They would always come, now until forever.

He had to get rid of the trace. If Beathan had an idea, it was at least worth exploring. No final decisions need be made just yet.

"Enough." Philip held up his hand to stop their bickering. "Is this really the place to be holding an argument?" He indicated the line of mounds.

Alayna sobered up more quickly than Beathan. The fairy just looked at him quizzically with a tweaked eyebrow and a dispassionate look in his eye.

"They made their own choices, mate. I'll not feel guilty for defendin' meself."

Philip sighed. "Nor should you, but can we at least hold the rest of this conversation on the road? I can't help but feel frivolous when speaking of such things in front of the dead."

"The dead are dead, Philip, no more no less. They cannot judge ya' now," the fairy responded.

"Be that as it may, shall we move out?"

"Move where?" Alayna asked.

Philip looked questioningly at Beathan. Only he knew where to go.

The half-fairy looked south. "South and east into the mountains. The man I know keeps himself deep in the heart o' Transylvania."

"Transylvania! This is a bad idea, love."

Philip put a hand to Alayna's cheek. "No doubt this acquaintance of Beathan's had the same idea that we did. After all, why did we decide to head to Romanian territory? Because we hoped the land and its various inhabitants would deter pursuit." Collectors were wary of this region of the world. Vampires were abundant. During the Great Transformation—when, inexplicably, the world birthed thousands of new supernatural creatures overnight without any of the usual methods necessary for transitioning from human into something other—vampires had dented nearly a quarter of the Guilds fighting men when Collectors had arrived to subdue the area. It was one of the bloodiest eras in Guild history.

"We are already on the outskirts of Transylvania anyway, Alayna. We might as well push on a bit further," Philip concluded.

"I still think this is a bad idea." Alayna was stubborn, and when she set her mind there was just no changing it. Still, they stuck together no matter what.

Philip couldn't really disagree. To be completely honest with himself, he was leery of traveling further into dangerous territory. But they had no other choices, at least none that provided any hope of a solution to the problem. *He* was the problem. Philip grimaced at the thought. They might both be better off if he were just dead, though he'd never voice that thought aloud. Alayna might well eviscerate him if he said that. She was growing very good with that knife at her belt.

Alayna wasn't done objecting. "Are you even listening to me, Philip? I said this is an unnecessary, unwarranted risk. We don't even know if there's something to gain."

"I happen to be an accomplished risk-taker meself, a bit o' a gamblin' man, if ya' will," Beathan said, "an' I am rather good at it—gamblin', that is. I say we go."

Alayna snorted. "You'd advocate strolling into a Fomorian's lair."

"Well, we can't stay here," Philip said. "For now, we follow Beathan's course. We can talk more on the way. The Guild leaders—Lady Helmsted in particular—will have had more than one crew in the area to follow us. It would be best if we tarried here no longer."

"Who's this?" Alayna asked. "You've never mentioned her before."

"Aye, who is this mystery member?" Suddenly, Beathan and Alayna had aligned in their interests.

Philip shrugged. "The Guild is ruled by a council. Equal say to leading members from different parts of the world. However, theory does not always meet reality. The truth is that the council exists, but it tends to follow the lead of a few individuals—Lady Helmsted is one of these. What she says is practically law. She is committed to the suppression of supernatural creatures and is adamantly against traitors. We should leave now, before a secondary unit of Collectors finds us. And believe me, there is bound to be a secondary unit close by. I know, because Lady Helmsted has bases of operation in the east of the continent not far from this region."

Alayna and Beathan rolled their shoulders uncomfortably and began peering around, casting glances into the darkened alleys of the abandoned town, no doubt deserted for its close proximity to the infamous Transylvanian region, an area Philip was now actively choosing to enter.

"Fine, south and east it is," Alayna acquiesced. "For now. This discussion isn't over." Philip nodded.

They grabbed what little gear and packs they had. Alayna kept the fur-lined hood of her cloak turned up against the pervasive chill of late winter in this part of the world. Beathan pulled his cloak close. Even Philip slipped back into a cloak, although for him it was more for a matter of appearance than anything else. Cold didn't touch him the way it once had. The troll blood flowing in his veins allowed him to survive in much colder climes than once would have been possible. In fact, Philip enjoyed the frosty landscape around them. However, he needed to avoid attracting notice, and a man wearing a sleeveless tunic would stand out in people's memory and leave a clear trail for pursuers to follow.

They quickly made their way out of town, edging their way through the narrow streets and alleys between buildings with steep roofs slanted sharply so as to not cave in under the weight of a dense snow. Before long they were past the village limits and into the rolling hills of the countryside. The hills were populated by copses of trees, but not continuous—not yet. The forest could be seen on the horizon, as could the range of peaks as they headed toward the Carpathian Mountains.

There wasn't much talk as they traveled. It seemed that, despite appearances, Alayna and even Beathan were eager to leave the scene of death behind them. After some hours under the dark, rumbling sky, the few snowflakes from earlier began to drift down in greater numbers.

"We'll need cover," Philip grunted as they crested a small hill.

"You don't, but thanks for thinking of us, love." Alayna smiled the smile she'd reserved only for him. He answered in kind.

Beathan clutched his cloak around him and turned up his nose in disgust. "Me isle is wet and damp, but not this bone-chillin' cold. I'll be glad t' be free o' this region o' the world when it's time t' leave."

Alayna shook her head. "And yet you're the one leading us deeper and deeper into it, gypsy."

Philip put a quelling hand on her shoulder. "Leave it, love. We don't need to get into it again. Not right now."

"But we do, Philip. We don't even know where we're going, really, or who we are looking for. He's used to being so damned mysterious all the time that he forgot to tell us, and you never even asked. One of us has to be practical." The frustration and accusation in her voice startled him but made sense. He turned to look at the fairy.

"It's true. You never even said what this acquaintance of yours does. So?"

Beathan stared blankly at Philip. "So what, Mr. One-Time-Collector?"

"So *what* type of creature or man are we looking for?"

"Ah, right. Well, t' answer that question of yours, we are lookin' for a man, not a beastie. A man o' chemicals and dark transfigurations. A man o' dangerous enigma." Beathan wiggled his fingers as a small smile played at the corner of his mouth.

"Enough theatrics, Beathan. Out with it." Alayna was in no mood for games.

He sighed. "Fair enough. We are looking for The Alchemist."

CHAPTER THREE

"An alchemist?" Alayna said incredulously. "How will turning things into gold help?"

"I didn't say *an* alchemist. I said *The* Alchemist. Anyone in this region o' the world knows him. He dabbles in much more than just turnin' things t' gold an' back again," Beathan responded calmly. For all the changes in her nature, the Elfas still thought like a human in many ways. That would pass eventually, but for now her mind was still a mix, and humans never paid attention to details. He conveniently forgot that he was half human, himself.

Beathan watched the recognition register on Philip's face. It went from curious to dark in a heartbeat. The fairy held up a hand to forestall his friend's inevitable objections.

"Now, now, mate. None o' that."

Philip grimaced. "None of what, Fairy?"

Beathan flashed his quicksilver smile. "Ya' know what. None o' those declarations that this is too dangerous or whatever ya' typically say."

"But it *is* too dangerous. I will not take Alayna to meet with the likes of The Alchemist."

"Ah, so ya've heard o' the man."

Beathan's companion nodded carefully. "By reputation only."

"And...?" Alayna always hated feeling left out of a conversation and, right now, Beathan could tell that was exactly how she felt.

Philip turned his attention back to the Elfas. "And the only reason he hasn't ended up in one of the cells below St. Thomas or another of our prisons is because technically he *is* a man. But that was only just barely enough to protect him."

"That bad?" Alayna's query sounded more like a thoughtful statement.

"*Our* prisons? Is it still a *we*?" Beathan asked what he thought was the more pertinent question.

Philip rolled his eyes. "You know what I mean, Beathan. And yes, Alayna, *that* bad."

Beathan debated more for the fun of it than out of any real disagreement. He did have principles and a reputation to uphold, after all. Besides, he figured The Alchemist was the only idea for fixing Philip's bloody problem that any of them had proposed in weeks. "Well, good an' bad, right an' wrong, light an' evil; they're all just a wee bit subjective, don't ya' think? I mean, what's wrong to some might be right t' others. Seems a tad harsh to judge The Alchemist without hearin' his side o' things."

He smiled at the annoyance that flashed across Philip's face. He knew just how to strike a nerve with him after months spent together and countless skirmishes fought. Yes, he knew his friend well.

"You cannot really believe that," Philip began. "There is clearly good and evil, and—," he broke off when he saw the smirk forming on the half-fairy's face.

Beathan couldn't hold back a chuckle.

"Right, you're just getting a rise out of me," Philip muttered.

Beathan shrugged his shoulders and flashed that crooked grin he always displayed when trying to win an argument. "That I am, Philip. But," he held up a finger before continuing, "the point remains. We should at least have a chat with The Alchemist. If he can help ya', who are we to snub our noses at him?"

"I agree," Alayna chimed in.

Both men slowly turned their heads to stare at the Elfas in surprise. Her agreeing with the fairy in general matters was nothing of note. In fact, she and Beathn got on quite well. He could safely say that he liked her far more than he did most of her kind. Not that he had a particular dislike of Elfas—Alderfolk and fairy-kind had always maintained cordial relations—but the gypsy in him sometimes found Elfas decidedly dull. They would often rather sit around, drink honey mead, and play their wooden instruments than engage in actual entertainment. He preferred a good bit of danger and excitement. He'd rather a wager to make or a pocket to pick over a tree to climb any day. No, it wasn't her general agreeable attitude that had shocked Philip and Beathan; it was the fact that she was agreeing with him on this particular point.

Beathan scratched his head idly as he cocked it to one side and stared at Alayna. On matters of ethics and morality, she usually came down hard on the side of absolutes. In many ways, she embraced even less of the grey area than Philip. But not today, it seemed.

"An' can I ask ya' why you're sidin' with me today, darlin'?" he asked his friend's lover.

"Yes," Philip said somewhat more slowly and cautiously, "I must admit that I'd not have guessed you'd want to associate with someone with a reputation like The Alchemist's." They both stared at the strawberry-blonde willow before them.

Snow sifted down lightly and dusted the shoulders of Alayna's dark cloak, clinging to the fringes of fur around the face of her hood. She stared them down, looking at them as if they were mad.

"Why shouldn't we gamble? We've been chased for months without a chance to stop and gather our strength, without hope of reprieve." She turned to face Philip. "You'll be hunted your entire life if we don't fix this. *Forever*," she punctuated the statement by drawing out that last word.

"It's bound to be dangerous..." Philip began.

She snorted. "Like we didn't just face down a whole cohort of your former brothers."

Beathan winked at her and she flashed him a quick smile. They both knew that she was wearing Philip down. His arguments wouldn't hold out much longer.

He resorted to bluntness. "He's a bad man, Alayna. One of the worst I've heard of." His appeal fell short, though.

Alayna shook her head. "I may not enjoy the company of the morally ambiguous, love, but in this case, I think I'll make an exception."

Beathan felt the thrill he always experienced when he embarked upon some less-than-safe course of action. His grin widened. "Well, like me ma' always used t' say—'Lady Chance favors the bold, an' who doesn't risk grows bored'."

Philip shot him a poisonous glance. "I'm sick of your quips and half-breed proverbs. Could you at least try to look a little less pleased that we're about to visit someone like The Alchemist?"

Beathan shrugged again with a whimsical grin. "What can I say? I've killed a few too many Collectors lately. It'll do me good t' test me wits and abilities against something other than them."

"So, you do admit that we may very well have to fight him?"

"Oh, aye mate. 'tis about as likely as any other outcome, I reckon." He switched to a more serious note. "But, like your sweet ladykins, I can think o' no other option. Right now, it seems the choice we have ahead o' us is either a wee slice o' danger with the possibility of a favorable outcome, or a perennial pursuit." He spread his hands wide.

"We have to at least try and speak with him, Philip. Just see what he says." As always, Alayna's voice was the one to get Philip to see reason. *Or*, Beathan thought quizzically, *possibly the one to get him to abandon reason.* There was no denying that The Alchemist was a mercurial man, and the outcome of their meeting could depend quite simply upon whatever mood the man was in when they found him.

Philip sighed and then nodded. "All right. Lead on, Fairy."

———

THEY PUSHED FURTHER INTO TRANSYLVANIA—DAYS of travel which were less than pleasant. Beathan, being from Ireland, was used to chill weather and a damp climate. However, he didn't enjoy snow. And snow was what they got. The white fell increasingly hard over the next few days. It built into drifts as they slogged their way through on tired legs. In the distance, the Carpathian Mountains rose grim and resolute against the horizon. Somewhere in those dark peaks lived The Alchemist. Or, at least, he had some years ago on the only occasion that Beathan had met him.

"How do you know The Alchemist?" Philip asked, echoing the fairy's thoughts.

"Little o' this, little o' that," he responded noncommittally.

"No, I mean it. I'm curious."

Alayna also turned her head his way. "Yes, perhaps a tale will distract me enough to ward away this cold." She shivered as she spoke.

"Doubtful, Alayna, but I suppose I can try anyway. At the very least, it will pass the time until we make our next stop." He glanced at the darkening sky and the snow falling around them. "Which, by the looks of things, should not be far off. We'll want t' find a place with shelter soon, t' stop for the night."

Philip muttered his agreement as he and Alayna peered expectantly at Beathan to begin.

The fairy obliged. "Well now, here's the run o' how things went. Some years ago, there was a certain man who ran afoul of a lycan an' was bitten. He became a werewolf himself. An' credit to him, he had the presence o' mind to realize he could be with his ladylove no longer. Enter yours truly." Beathan swirled his hands theatrically inward to indicate himself. Philip rolled his eyes, but Beathan caught Alayna stifling a smirk. She wasn't quite the prude Philip was.

He continued in rather succinct fashion, "The aforementioned lady an' I met an' struck each other's fancy. T'wasn't long before I began to court her."

"You, court?" Philip interjected incredulously.

"True, perhaps courtship is a bit o' an overstatement. Let's just say we had ourselves some fun. Well, unbeknownst to me, the wolf-man was still keepin' an eye on his lost love an' for reasons unclear he took an immediate dislike of me." He paused to shrug his shoulders innocently and this time elicited a giggle from the Elfas. "So there I was, through no fault o' me own, with a bit of a werewolf problem an' no silver blades to defend meself. Well, had I been further from where we are now then perhaps I mighta nicked me a silver knife or two from our dear Philip here, or maybe one of his old brothers. Wouldn't have been too hard. But I wasn't. I was near where we are now, an' I'd heard the rumors o' The Alchemist, so I thought I'd pay him a visit, see if he couldn't fix me up with a solution to me quandary."

He turned a silent eye on his companions as they continued to slog their way through the piling drifts.

"And?" Philip asked.

"An' what?"

"What happened next?"

Beathan shrugged again. This conversation had gone on long enough—it was beginning to bore him. Plus, they were headed in a direction that Philip likely wouldn't want to hear. Best keep that to himself for now. The half-breed feigned extreme indifference.

Philip wouldn't be deterred. "How did your encounter go? Did The Alchemist help you?"

Beathan slipped a sly wink their way. "I'm still livin' an' breathin', aren't I?"

"You're impossible." Philip gave up and turned back to watching his feet trudging through the drifts filling up the road.

"We gypsy-fairies are world renowned for being the flightiest o' flighty, mate."

Alayna giggled again. If there was one thing the Elfas seemed to love about Beathan, it was his ability to needle her often-too-somber lover without quite pushing him past his limits. And, in turn, it was one of the things Beathan liked most about her—her ability to appreciate his teasing. He turned Alayna's way and they shared a private smile. It was an unspoken agreement between the two of them, stretching as far back as London where they had stopped briefly after leaving St. Thomas. They both took it upon themselves to make sure that their former Collector and current companion didn't take himself—or life—too seriously.

Quiet stretched for a time after Beathan finished his tale. There would be time to talk more about The Alchemist later. Maybe. For now, they pulled up their hoods and bore down, leaning into the wind that was picking up.

After walking for some hours, they followed the narrow track as it passed through a copse of trees that had kept all but a light dusting of snow from settling on the ground. They paused for a moment to rest in the relative protection. The ground had risen slightly, and the copse was situated on the crest of a small hill. They gazed forward and could see a village in the distance.

"If we push, we can make it by nightfall," Philip said.

"It's a long way still, love."

He turned grimly to his partner. "Maybe, but there's no cover between here and there. We either push hard to make it or we huddle up for the night here in the cold, under the flimsy protection of these few trees. Not a good option."

"Ever the optimist, I am." Beathan grinned. "We'll make it, Alayna. Me bones weren't meant for a night so cold as this one."

"Speaking of bones," Philip changed the course of the conversation with a nod of his head toward a skeleton on the ground near a tree some few feet away. The snow had dusted the skull and sifted through the crevices of the ribs.

Alayna shuddered, and Beathan didn't blame her. There was something unsettling about a skeleton. A body was meant to be buried. Or burned—that was fine, too. Either a hot funeral or a cold, earthy burial, but a person's remains shouldn't be left for the living world to see in such a way.

"Why weren't they buried?" Alayna asked in a hushed voice, the quiet tone magnified by the matching swirl of snowy flakes falling around her.

Philip shrugged. "Any manner of reasons."

"'tis the region," Beathan interjected. He motioned all around them, freeing a hand from the interior of his cloak and immediately wishing he hadn't as he felt the chill seep into his flesh. He hurriedly tucked the hand back inside.

Alayna cast an inquiring eye his way and the fairy continued, "This part o' the world don't look too kindly upon the dead, lass."

"Could be they died alone. Or, could be their companions were in a hurry to reach the village before nightfall when they passed." Philip picked up where Beathan left off. The former Collector spoke solemnly. "See how it's dismembered?" He reached a hand to indicate how the skull had been separated and sat a few inches farther from the body than it should have. He showed no susceptibility to the cold in the way that his companions did. It wasn't often that Beathan felt jealous—generally speaking, he was happy with who and what he was —but right now he wouldn't mind a touch of Philip's trollish imperviousness to the icy temperature.

"Why would they cut off its head?" Alayna asked.

"Might be they were killed that way, but not likely, seeing as when a person's dismembered in battle the head usually flies a bit further than when someone chops the head off a corpse. No, this was likely done post-mortem." Beathan could hear Philip slip back into his

Collector voice, all business and professional, assessing a scene, determining scenarios and outcomes.

Beathan chimed in himself: "We walk through Transylvania, Alayna. 'tis the homeland for quite a few dark creatures, not the least o' which are vampires, not unlike our one-time and short-lived comrade, Azir."

Alayna almost blushed, looking worriedly over at her lover. Philip shot Beathan a dark look for even mentioning the hybrid Elfas-vampire's name, but he ignored the stare. Philip could be touchy at times, especially regarding Azir and the strange connection he had with Alayna. But sometimes one had to just bull through and ignore a person's delicacies, so Beathan pressed on, "Vampires are universally feared but nowhere more so than in Transylvania. Durin' the Great Transformation, when supernatural beings multiplied overnight an' seemin'ly without cause, Transylvania was literally awash with newbie nightwalkers. They practically overran this region."

"The Collectors Guild lost nearly a quarter of its fighting force just in Transylvania trying to suppress the overflow of vampires. It took us—them—decades to recover their strength and global reach as a guild," Philip chimed in.

Alayna pursed her lips. "You still haven't answered my questions. Why didn't they bury the body, and why was it beheaded?"

"Gettin' to it, lass. Just tryin' to set the scene." Beathan grinned at her impatience. "What me an' your long-haired lover are tryin' to explain is that people here fear nightwalkers more than just about anythin' else. Yet, they don't really understand them. Most people that see a vampire wind up dead. Eaten. Not a pretty way to go, I might add. So they don't really know how the transition works."

Again, Philip took over: "To become a vampire, one has to accept the bite mentally, internally. You have to *choose* to become a vampire. It's not like a werewolf bite which can turn anyone. Vampires can always kill you if they suck you dry or bite you enough, but there's no guarantee they'll turn you. You have to want to be one of them."

Beathan watched Alayna shudder. "Why would someone want to be a vampire?" Her question carried a hint of genuine interest in the subject despite her obvious discomfort.

"Lots o' reasons. But the one that comes to mind first—fear o' death. When a person faces death or the prospect o' becomin' a nightwalker, many choose to live, whatever the price they must pay."

"Anyway, because of the misunderstandings in this area regarding vampires, at some point people began to believe that a headless corpse couldn't reanimate into a vampire. They didn't know how the transition worked. So, most of the dead are beheaded. Likely they just didn't bury this one because they wanted to make the village by nightfall—like us." With that final description, Philip rose from his crouched position near the corpse and began walking down the slight slope and on toward the town. Beathan and Alayna followed.

"They still should have buried it," Alayna muttered stoutly. "They could have come back during the day."

"Aye, they could've. But it's a harsh land, an' a harsh people survive in it. Besides, might be it was a stranger or a robber, someone not deemed worthy o' the effort o' burial."

"Is anyone really unworthy of a final send off?" Alayna inquired softly, almost to herself. Her eyes had a faraway look, and Beathan had the uncanny feeling that he knew what she was thinking about— or who, more like.

"'tis a good point ya' make, Alayna. Even those who are mostly bad are not wholly evil."

"I'm not sure Philip sees it that way," she responded. Their conversation was mostly whispered now as they walked a few paces behind the man in question.

"That's because his objections to a certain hybrid vampire stem more from personal rather'n philosophical reasons. He hates Azir personal-like, not out o' principle."

"I'm not talking about Azir," Alayna said in a rushed voice. This time the fairy could see a faint blush tint her cheeks even rosier than the cold had.

"Sure ya' were, lass. I'm older than I look, an' I'm not stupid."

"I don't love him or anything. I don't even really like him. But there's this residue, this connection in my mind from that first contact in Trondheim when he was captured with you. I know he's not *good*, but he helped us escape. He isn't horrible."

Beathan felt a flicker of a rather uncommon emotion. Guilt. It was his fault the vampire had contacted Alayna mind-to-mind. "An' what would ya' have me say to ya'?"

Alayna shook her head and lifted her shoulders in a light shrug. "I don't know. Nothing, I guess. I think I just don't want to believe that there is someone stuck inside my head—however minimally he's still there, always—who is pure evil. It would make me feel better to think that perhaps Azir is redeemable."

"No one is pure evil, Alayna, not even the worst o' the worst. The world isn't built on such absolutes."

She flashed him a grateful smile and they slogged faster to catch up with Philip. They still had a long way to go before nightfall, and only one of them could spend a night in the open snow without freezing.

CHAPTER FOUR

THEY MADE IT TO THE VILLAGE NOT LONG AFTER THE SUN SET. Full darkness had not been present long before they strode wearily among the cozy cottages and buildings. It was actually more of a town than a village, being slightly larger than it had appeared from far away. They made their way to the only building in town from which they could hear any noise. Inns were usually the only place to gather after dark in a settlement of this size. Philip opened the door and stepped into the warmth, followed by Alayna and Beathan. All noise stopped and every eye turned their way.

Philip had been in and out of similar towns all along his old Atlantic route with his previous partner, James. They were often small enough for everyone to know one another but large enough to have an inn that could still make a little bit of extra money off the few visitors and wayfarers who might pass through.

He ducked his head to the meager crowd of people. Disheveled and all around rough looking, they were the sort who carved an existence out of the land, lived and died by the seasons, and survived by whatever camaraderie they managed to share with their neighbors. They were not easily trusting of outsiders, as their hard eyes portrayed.

"We're just looking for a room for the night. By tomorrow morning, we will be gone. Take our coin and send us on our way quickly."

Philip knew that often the best way to allay these types of people's fears was to reassure them that you would not long remain in their presence.

"And where might you be headed?" A wide man with an apron stepped through the crowd and made his way in their direction. Bald and wiping his hands on a rag, he was no doubt the innkeeper.

Philip leaned down to whisper in the gypsy's ear, "Where, exactly, might we be headed, Beathan?"

"Ah well, ya' know, south an' east-like for a time. With a few twists an' turns along the way," Beathan whispered back.

Philip cleared his throat and relayed the information. "South and east."

A few dark looks were cast in their direction. Philip distinctly heard the angry rumblings and mutterings of the crowd commenting on their heading in the general direction of the mountains. The Carpathian range was not well trusted by those outside its borders, not by humble folk such as these.

"You will not be here for long, you say?" the innkeeper inquired.

"No more than a night."

"And you've no horses that need tending to? No pack animals to consume what little stores I have left for my own stock?"

Again, Philip put the man at ease. "None. We're more of the walking type." That was an understatement. Alayna was Elfas. Her kind, lithe and quick, never rode. Neither did fairy folk, and Beathan was distinctly uncomfortable on anything other than his own two feet. It was Philip himself who was most opposed to riding. His strange tendency to prefer his own feet to animal transportation could be linked to his hybrid nature. The more he embraced the troll blood flowing through his veins, the less he desired to ride. Even with that inclination, though, he often found himself battling the impracticality of walking when riding would be easier. Nonetheless, they had all three decided under the pretense of security that it would be safer to walk. People remembered travelers with the means to afford horses. Nobody gave a second glance to another weary straggler walking the many roads of this earth. Or so they told themselves.

Philip's words were enough to dispel the innkeeper's worries. Mistrustful murmurings could still be heard, but the innkeeper cut through them. "Good enough for me. There're three rooms available upstairs and a hot supper waiting. Mind you, I'll not haggle over the price. You'll take what you get, you hear?"

"And we would not think to argue, my good sir. However, only two rooms will be necessary." Alayna's silky voice silenced the mumblings of the crowd. Her Elfas tone had a slightly lyric quality to it that sometimes had a quieting effect on unsuspecting people. The men looked eager, the women jealous. Alayna pressed her hand into Philip's as she spoke.

The innkeeper nodded. "Well and good. My man will take you up. Once you're settled, come back down and I'll feed you. You look like you could use it."

Alayna smiled her thanks and turned with Philip and Beathan to follow the shuffling figure that emerged from behind the innkeeper. The innkeeper's man was really no more than a boy, maybe sixteen years of age. The early growth of his first whiskers was still on his chin. He led them up the stairs and to their rooms. All of Alayna's attempts at friendly conversation were impossible, as the boy could barely speak and cast awestruck looks at her out of the corner of his eye. Philip supposed that even after months on the road and even with her ears carefully concealed beneath the folds of her golden-red hair, she was still a sight to see for someone from a small, back corner town such as this—especially since she was a female yet obviously armed. One crossbow hung at her belt and the other was a lump ill-hidden by her cloak.

The boy took his leave as awkwardly as he had led them, and Philip and Alayna settled into their room while Beathan did likewise in his. It didn't take long; they traveled sparsely. It was only a matter of dropping their twin packs on the floor and sitting for a long, tired moment on the lumpy, straw mattress before they gathered their energy to go back downstairs. The sooner they ate the sooner they could be back up here to sleep. He said as much to Alayna.

She whispered wickedly, "We've been making camp with Beathan for the last few weeks. I can't remember the last time we had a room to ourselves, and I have no intentions of letting sleep be the only thing we do after dinner." She nipped his ear playfully to punctuate the comment.

Her words sent a thrill through his body and a smile to his face. Suddenly he wasn't so tired. "Why wait?" he murmured and pulled her close for a kiss. They shared warmth, shared existence for one long, drawn-out moment, their lips and souls pressed together before Alayna put two hands on his chest and managed to push him away with a silver tinkle of laughter.

"I'm looking forward to it, love, but not quite so much as I'm looking forward to a hot meal first." She blew on her hands to warm them. Philip clasped one and felt the chill that was still soaked deeply into her bones. A chill he no longer felt, at least not the way a human did.

Nevertheless, he put on his best hurt expression and responded teasingly, "What? First you say you can't wait and now you say you can? Enough to drive me crazy."

This drew another loving peal of laughter from Alayna. She kissed him again, stood, and pulled him to his feet. "Come on Philip, I'm famished—in more than one way. And as soon as we deal with one of those hungers, the sooner we can get to the other!" She winked and led him from the room. He grinned and followed.

They made their way downstairs and found Beathan already at a table waiting for them. The fairy was idly twisting one of the rings on his finger. He stopped when he saw them and started fidgeting with one of his bracelets instead. Philip shook his head. The half-breed was always fiddling with one of his jangles, or so he liked to think of the many pieces of jewelry that adorned his friend's wrists, hands, neck, and ears. Some of those jangles bore charmed properties, others were for nothing more than show.

"Took ya' two long enough. I was beginnin' t' wonder if perhaps ya' nipped off for a wee spell o' fun. If ya' catch me meanin'." He grinned impudently.

Philip gave him a flat stare. He didn't really mind the fairy's teasing, but he would never admit to it. He did have a reputation to uphold. "We know what you mean, Beathan. And no, we didn't 'nip off' for anything." His flat stare did nothing to discourage the impish smile on the gypsy's face.

Alayna could care less about the joke and grinned back at Beathan wickedly. "Later, maybe." She winked his way before looking back at Philip. He sighed. He hated it when Alayna and Beathan talked like this. He wasn't a prude, exactly, but personal matters should remain personal.

He cleared his throat. "Anyway, how much farther until we reach The Alchemist?"

Beathan shrugged the way he often did when asked a question. Other times he answered with a riddle, or a proverb, or some other useless piece of information. Only very occasionally could one manage to secure a direct answer.

"Been a while since I passed this way, mate. Don't rightly remember the specifics." Beathan looked at him shrewdly over his beak-like nose, dirty blond hair framing his face. Philip knew that he was appraising how he would handle this ambiguity. Philip had told him on more than one occasion how much he enjoyed details. The half-fairy was always testing to see how he would react to little incidents like this. At first, Philip had been annoyed, thinking that the fairy was weighing him, measuring him. But after it had gone on for long enough he had begun to realize that the little tests were often for nothing more than entertainment. Beathan was easily bored and often looked for any way possible to liven things up.

Philip ignored the ambiguity of his friend's answer and dropped the issue for now. Their food arrived, so they ate their meal and talked of trivial matters. It was a good feeling to speak of the simple things in life rather than the present reality and their dire mission.

The meal was solid, good food—dark bread and a hearty stew with mostly vegetables, roots, and a few small but savory chunks of meat. They washed it down with ale. All in all, Philip hadn't had a meal quite so good in weeks.

When it was over, he leaned back against the wall. "Well, shall we then?" He turned to look at Alayna as he asked the question.

Her eyes smoldered. "We shall indeed."

"I think I'll stay down here for a while," Beathan muttered as he gazed hungrily at the small crowd of people in the common room.

"Beathan..." Philip began cautiously.

"Oh, come now, mate, what harm can befall me in a simple place such as this?" The fairy swept a hand grandiosely around the room.

"Don't. Cause. Any. Trouble." Philip said each word slowly and carefully to imbue as much force as he could into every syllable. "You haven't stolen anything in weeks. It's been a welcome relief from your usual antics."

"Exactly, partner. I haven't. An' that means I'm out o' practice. Gotta keep me wits an' fingers sharp." The fairy's fingers practically quivered in anticipation as he spoke.

Philip sighed. "Seriously. If I wake up in the night with a knife at my throat from some angry townsperson, I'll kill you."

"If ya' wake up in such a manner, then I'm likely to already be dead. Although, that entire scenario's rather unlikely. We both know I never get caught." The glee in the gypsy's eyes lit up his face.

Alayna tugged Philip away. "You can't change a person's nature, love. Besides, he usually puts back the things he takes." She had no compunctions about the way Beathan comported himself. She had many fewer reservations than Philip. He wondered if perhaps it was because she was no longer human, whereas he was still half a man.

He let her lead him away, casting one last, worried look over his shoulder at the fairy who was scanning the room with an avid eye. Beathan disappeared from sight as they turned the corner and climbed the stairs. They reached their room, and all worry left Philip's mind. In fact, everything left his mind except for Alayna. She filled his every sense, as she had a way of doing. They lost themselves for a time in one another, and Philip forgot everything. He forgot what it was he'd forgotten. He forgot himself in the pure enjoyment of the Elfas with whom he was lucky enough to share his life. His blood, the trace, their goals, everything faded away, lost in the swirl of strawberry hair and the lean, limber body that tangled with his own.

TRUE TO THEIR WORD, they were gone by first light. The innkeeper bade them a quick but polite farewell and graciously sent them on their way with a loaf of the dark brown bread. They ate it at midday, stopping briefly to rest. Before long, though, they were back on their feet and striding southeast. Not long after midday, the terrain began to give way to hilly forestland. Trees began to cluster together and block out the light. Shadows crept longer and longer the deeper the sun sank until the gloom began to eclipse the light entirely.

"We should make camp," Beathan suggested.

"So early? It's not even full night yet," Alayna responded.

Philip felt similarly to Alayna. He hated the idea of wasting any more time. However, sensibility won out.

"Beathan's right, love. We've come far enough for today. It would be safer to start a fire and make camp."

"Aye, night's not the sort o' time a body wants t' be wanderin' about in this particular region. Strange an' terrible things have a way o' happenin' hereabouts."

"What do you mean?" Alayna asked, ever-inquisitive.

"I mean, lass, there's a reason the people decapitate their dead. Silly solution it may be, but the superstition is not misplaced. This here's Transylvania, an' it's home to worse than ya' can imagine." Beathan winked at her.

Philip smiled. If there was one thing he admired about his fairy friend, it was the way he managed to somehow speak so nonchalantly of danger. Philip was no stranger to risk or death, as it had been a part of his life for over a decade. But the fairy somehow made it seem as if danger was one great adventure, an exciting joke to be enjoyed. It was that very same trait that made Philip question the half-breed's sanity at times, but he admired him all the same.

They set up camp quickly. They had done this for months now and knew their jobs well. Philips used his strength to tear a few slender limbs from nearby trees. He wove the pliable branches into a semblance of shelter and then laid ferns and foliage over it to complete his construction. Beathan gathered wood for a fire while Alayna dug out a small fire pit and ringed it with stones. It all only took a matter of a few minutes. Soon, they were sitting around a small but crackling fire that Alayna had started. The trees blotted out much of the night sky, and only a few stray stars and part of the moon could be seen through the branches obscuring what was above. That same foliage also prevented much of the snow from falling to the ground. A few patches dusted the ground here and there, but much of the snow was stuck to the branches and leaves above. It was not so miserable as some of their open-air camps had been on previous nights of their journey. Perhaps the snow was letting up a little bit, as well. All factors had combined to make it a chilly yet altogether more pleasant night than they'd had in quite some days.

Alayna huddled near to Philip. He took off his cloak and wrapped it around her shoulders; he had no need for it. She shuddered and gratefully clasped it closer to her body. Her smile was warmer than a summer night. It almost seemed out of place there in the foothills of such a wintery mountainscape.

"Maybe I should be the one courtin' ya'. If I did, perhaps I'd be a tad bit warmer t'night. Eh, mate?" Beathan winked at Philip.

It drew a smile from him and a giggle from Alayna. She wrapped her arms around Philip even more tightly. "Sorry, Beathan. He's taken."

"Well, a body can hope, right?" He sighed theatrically.

A sound registered in the distance, and suddenly Philip's instincts sharpened. His body tensed with his nerves.

Alayna felt him tighten up, coiled to spring into action. "What is it?"

"Shush." He gently put a finger to her lips, the moist heat of her mouth threatening to send his mind spiraling in a less focused direction.

Beathan and Alayna fell silent and waited while Philip cocked his ear and listened. Nothing. The silence stretched. An owl cried in the distance, but it was an entirely normal sound, different from the noise Philip had heard. Gradually, his muscles loosened. He rolled his shoulders slightly to ease the tension.

"Must've been nothing," he said after a few long moments of quiet.

"Ya' sure, mate?"

"I'm rarely fully certain of anything," Philip retorted obliquely to the half-fairy.

"We'll set a watch tonight," Alayna declared softly. Philip nodded. They did that most nights anyway, but he had a feeling that doing so would be particularly necessary in these woods.

This place had a different feel to it. Darker, and brooding. It felt nothing like the crisp mountain slopes of Norway. Those peaks might have possessed wild dangers like wights and trolls, yet there was a beastly danger to a troll. Philip's ancient kin were more like animals than people in more ways than one. They were fearsome predators, terrifying and dangerous, yet hardly what one would call sinister. This forest practically crawled with the feeling of dread, and that sensation only increased the farther into night's darkness they went. Philip had learned to trust his intuition about such matters during his long years as a Collector, hunting creatures and monsters through the shadows of nearly every land. Those instincts told him that this was not a place in which to drop one's guard.

They passed the rest of the evening with the light banter that somehow always seemed to find its way into existence given Beathan's presence. The fairy could start or diffuse an argument with hardly more than a word. They laughed and talked, but all the while Philip could feel the foreboding nature of the woods around them. He found himself frequently checking over his shoulder. Idly, he picked up one of the firmer logs, just small enough to fit in the grasp of one of his hands, and began to whittle.

As they talked, he carved without paying any real attention to what he was doing. It was more the motion of the action that he desired without needing to focus on what it was he was creating. When he was finally done, Alayna pulled his creation from his hands.

"What did you make, love?" Her smile died on her face as she held in her hands a freshly crafted stake. Apparently, his subconscious was listening to his intuition. Transylvania—their location was not to be ignored.

"Nothing more than a precaution." Philip tried to shrug off his whittled creation. There was no need to worry Alayna more than was necessary.

She stared at him somberly. "A wise creation," she murmured. Then her mood changed slightly and, with a smirk, she tucked it in her belt.

"What, so I make it and you keep it?" he asked indignantly.

"That's the way of it. I'm surprised you haven't figured that out yet." She somehow combined her most winning and most impudent smiles into one devastating show of persuasion.

Philip had no choice but to join in with the already chuckling Beathan. He pulled another stake from his belt; a remnant of a decade spent Collecting. "Well, seeing as I've already got one, I guess the least I can do is share."

"The least indeed." She leaned in close and kissed him.

The remainder of the evening was relatively uneventful, and by the time it was the hour to turn in, Philip was ready for sleep. Still, he volunteered to take the first watch. His two companions acquiesced, and he watched them repair to the shelter. He sat with his back against a tree, straining his ears and eyes into the surrounding night. The cold air prickling his bare, sleeveless arms felt merely cool to him. Pleasant. If only he could shake the perennial sense of menace he felt from the land around him. He resolved to keep a close watch. Transylvania would not catch him unawares.

CHAPTER FIVE

ALAYNA FOUND HERSELF TWIRLING THE NEWLY CARVED STAKE between her fingers. It was still rough, not yet worn smooth by sanding or by the oils of hands and use. If she were to fight with it, it would likely leave her with a hundred tiny splinters.

She took the middle watch. Philip had gently shaken her awake with a regretful look upon his face. Even he had to sleep, he'd said, to which she'd quietly responded with affirmation. Only he would think to say that as if it were in question. He was a hybrid, stronger than just about anyone she had ever met, and she didn't just mean physically—although the strength afforded him by his trollish heritage was indeed impressive. No, Philip had more than that. He had something that was hard to find in most people: resolve. That resolve might change, but he was the kind of person who put himself fully into whatever task lay ahead of him, and that type of commitment and action lead to results. It was why he'd been such an effective Collector, why his friends appreciated his support and his enemies feared him. It was even why he'd probably been so successful in their early courtship, Alayna thought with a rueful smile. Apart from being charming, the simple fact that he had continued to visit her was one of the things that had been so appealing to her. Resolve. Philip definitely had it.

However, sometimes that resolve coupled with his newfound

acceptance of his hybrid nature left Philip thinking he could do more than he actually could, like having to state the obvious fact that even he needed sleep. Alayna snorted. Sometimes even he could be foolish.

Something rustled in the forest, and she froze. It had been a small sound, but it had definitely been there. A hare, perhaps? Or a fox out for a midnight hunt? She slowly pulled the hair back from the side of her head to reveal delicately pointed ears. She waited, but there was almost no sound to hear. After that one tiny whisper of noise the forest had gone silent. A quiet, thin blanket of white coated the branches and leaves, dusting the ground and the roof of their makeshift shelter. It muffled the forest into a strange, almost under-water-like locale. Not quite, but almost. It was like the chill of the season was enough to freeze time and slow down the pulsing world just like cold could slow a person's blood in their veins. But the world wouldn't stay sluggish forever. Even now, amidst a late winter flurry of cold weather, Alayna could almost taste the imminent spring in the air. Perhaps it was because of her nature as an Elfas. A part of her doubted that Philip or Beathan could sense the changing seasons the way she could. Well, perhaps the fairy could to a certain extent. His kind bore a passing resemblance to hers. Still, they were both half human, and in many ways, they still thought like men. The days when Alayna thought like a woman were fading with a rapidity that told her sooner than later they would be nothing but memory.

She waited for more sound, anything to betray what might have caused the noise from a moment earlier, but though she peered about with her keen eyes, she could see no sign of movement. She was just about to return to the lean-to and wake Beathan for the final watch when everything happened at once. A form dropped silently from the tree above, landing in a crouch atop the snow. Before she could shout the alarm, another and another dropped down from above. Foolish! She should have thought to look up after hearing that first noise. Before she could berate herself further or make any kind of sound, the dark form in front of her smashed a lightning-quick fist into her face. Alayna hit the ground and turned the force of the blow into a roll, coming up with snow coating her clothes.

"Philip!" she cried out.

It was enough. Out of the corner of her eye, she saw both Philip and Beathan stir in the shelter. There was no time to pay any more attention to them, because the form in front of her pressed the attack. The person, whoever it was, fought with speed and agility, striking blows that Alayna was hard-pressed to block despite all of her training these recent months. One fist caught her in the mouth and she tasted her own blood. She spat some onto the snow as the two of them circled each other, the sounds of fighting surrounding them. As soon as she spat, her opponent stiffened slightly, ever so quickly, and drew in a long breath before exhaling almost ecstatically. Alayna didn't bother waiting for an answer as to why that was. She leapt into action. Pressing whatever advantage she possessed, she closed the distance between them and landed blows of her own. She spun and landed a heeled kick to the side of the face, and her attacker went down and hit the ground in a patch of moonlight. The blow from her foot had knocked the hood from her opponent's head, and Alayna saw pale, elegant features framed by a shock of straight, dark hair. The creature's features curled up into a sneer as she pulled herself up to a crouching position. Alayna felt the thrill of fear as she saw two fangs, small but definitive, protruding from her enemy's mouth.

"Vampire," Alayna breathed out almost involuntarily. In a flash, the stake was in her hand. A flicker of fear crossed the vampire's face, but only for an instant. Still, that instant sent a surge of satisfaction through Alayna. She was an Elfas—not the most warlike of races, yet she was quick, agile, and limber. Most importantly, she had been trained by one of the most dangerous Collectors—not just that, one of the most dangerous *people*—she knew. Philip.

Alayna's face curled into a snarl of her own, and she spat contemptuously at the vampire's feet. The sound of fighting still raged around her, but she focused on her opponent. Her blood steamed in the snow. "You thought to have me for supper, vampire?"

"I had considered it." The voice was silky and dead.

"Well, that's all the supper you'll get, bitch!" Alayna thrust her chin at the bloody mark in the snow in front of the vampire's feet.

The creature lightly touched a finger to the red spot illuminated in a shaft of moonlight and then raised it delicately to her tongue. She shivered at the taste. "I haven't had an Elfas before. All there is to eat around here are humans. They can be quite tasty, but there's no substitute for variety." Her voice carried the accent of the East.

Just like *his* had. The thought came unbidden to Alayna's mind and she forced it away. She stepped forward and raised the stake into a fighting stance the way Philip had taught her. Wounding a vampire could slow it down, but a stake to the heart was the surest way to dispatch one of these creatures.

"No, no, no, my little dove. You don't want to be doing that. Put that nasty wooden toy down." The vampire's voice caressed her mind.

Alayna's hand began to drop involuntarily. Why was she holding a stake? How repulsive. A wooden object intended for killing was not something that she wanted to hold. The thought was coupled with the vampire's smiling face, and the creature stepped forward.

No! Alayna's subconscious fought to burst through the haze. Something was wrong. She raised the stake again. Why was she holding a stake? Waves of confusion crashed through her mind. *Why* was she confused about holding a stake?

Alayna shook her head and forced the cobwebs away. "I'll not be toyed with like that," she said through gritted teeth. "You'll have to try harder."

"I suppose I will," the vampire replied, and Alayna could hear the frustration framed by her full, pale red lips. The vampire leapt into the attack again, having been unable to subdue Alayna with the force of her predatory mind. They clashed. Alayna blocked a blow and swung the stake toward the creature's heart with all the force she possessed. The vampire deflected the stake with her arm. It was no longer a killing blow, but Alayna could hear the piercing shriek of pain as the wooden weapon bit into her opponent's flesh.

The vampire backed away, baring her teeth in a wordless snarl. "Volri, Mina, enough!" And with that, the vampire turned and dashed away through the trees followed by two more of her kind. Alayna did not pursue. She turned back to see Philip pulling a stake from a dead vampire's heart. Beathan was cut and bleeding, but there was a vicious gleam in his eye.

The fairy smiled thinly. "Not a bad fight."

"They got more than they bargained for," Philip said grimly as he wiped his stake off on the vampire's chest. He then grabbed a fistful of snow and began rubbing the weapon down to clean it further before slipping it back into the leather sheath at his hip.

"We are not the easy prey they expected," Alayna agreed with a trill of satisfaction.

"You were not." Philip smiled at her. "I haven't even had time to teach you to fight the crooning of a vampire—the way they hypnotize and control the minds of their victims. Yet you fought it off with ease!"

Alayna felt the warmth of his approval, could see the pride glowing in his eyes. It was practically all she needed in life, to see that fierce look of love on his face. "I almost didn't fight it off. I *barely* did. Besides, you and Beathan must have done it, too."

"I've had years of training, love."

Beathan chimed in, "An' I as well've had many years t' practice the art. After all, I am a wee few years older'n I look."

Alayna shrugged uncomfortably. "Perhaps I was lucky."

"No, I don't think so," Philip said slowly, thoughtfully. "I wonder if maybe it has something to do with your kind. There are some inherent mental qualities to the Elfas nature—mind-to-mind contact, the gestalt consciousness. It could be that you are more naturally suited to the defense of your own mind than we half-breeds are," he finished with a smile.

"Well, whatever the reason, I'm glad of it. For a moment there it felt like I was about to drop the stake and offer up whatever vein she wanted." Alayna shivered slightly at the thought.

"But you didn't," Philip responded firmly.

"What do you think they were after?" she asked.

"This is their land an' we the strangers. I suspect they were simply after a bite to eat an' found us less of an easy meal than they bargained for." Alayna watched Philip nod along to Beathan's explanation.

"So they really were just after a meal?"

"That, and vampires are notoriously territorial," Philip added.

"So, what do we do now?" she asked.

"I'll take my watch an' the two o' ya can get some shut-eye." Beathan spoke in a matter-of-fact voice.

It was one thing Alayna hadn't quite mastered yet. She'd been training with weapons and hand-to-hand combat, but she had yet to get the hang of how Beathan and especially Philip could go from battle and then back to normal in a heartbeat.

"I doubt I'll sleep," she muttered.

"At least try." Philip squeezed her shoulder as he led her toward the shelter. Beathan kicked the dead vampire and plopped himself down against the bole of a tree.

Alayna allowed herself to be guided back to the lean-to. Philip tended briefly to a few abrasions she'd sustained on her face before she curled up with her back to his chest and let him wrap his cloak and his arm around her. He was hot. Like always. Philip was as good as a fire to keep her warm, yet sleep eluded her. She lay awake until the sun's grey light heralded the arrival of morning. Thoughts of winding up as someone's dinner made it hard to nod off. Where was Beathan taking them? Was this a fool's errand destined to get them killed?

Alayna forced the thought away. No, they needed to free Philip from the trace. Otherwise he—and, by extension, she—would spend the rest of his life running. She wrapped herself in that thought, armored her logic with it. It was the only thing that could make this all worthwhile.

CHAPTER SIX

BEATHAN SHIFTED HIS PACK ON HIS SHOULDERS. IT WAS BEGINNING to grow uncomfortable after a day of walking. They were deep into the Carpathian range now. He followed the various markers that were lodged in his memory: A peak that stuck up just so there. A gnarled, twisted tree that signaled him to take the left path at the next fork. He muttered a charm and flicked one of the jangles around his wrist. This particular bracelet possessed a rare ability, allowing the wearer to recall memory as if it were present. It was not the most often used of his charms, nor the most practical. Indeed, the stone ring with a defensive charm which he had stolen just before his capture and imprisonment in St. Thomas Prison had turned out to be much more useful over the past few months of running from and fighting pursuing Collectors. Still, when the memory bracelet was called upon for use, it could prove very valuable.

With the bracelet's aid, the spell coalesced, and it was like seeing his memory almost in the form of a map in his mind. Not flat and lacking dimension like a paper map, but living with full color and depth created from what he remembered of this place.

Beathan led the way, his friends following. "This way," the fairy muttered as they reached the fork in the trail. "We go left." His companions continued to follow without hesitation. They either trusted him or they didn't—at this point, they could be of no help to him in finding The Alchemist.

As they walked, his fingers practically itched. Beathan was a fairy, so he loved the wild. He felt kinship with the land, with all life forms, yet fairies also had a distinctly rapscallion nature. The thief in him had been too long from civilization. The other night at the inn, Beathan had assuaged some of his impulses by lifting an item or two here and there before slipping them back amongst the owner's companions. That night, he had specially tasked himself to return each item he stole but to return it to the person sitting to the left of the owner. The little bit of added mayhem it had caused when a few rings and a money purse were discovered in the pockets of the owner's neighbor had been almost more fun to observe than the stealing itself. Almost. Still, it was not enough. Beathan thrived on mischief, and it was a bit hard to *cause* mischief with only the trees as companions. Oh, there was excitement to be had, that was certain. The attack last night by the vampires, their course toward The Alchemist; these things boded well for one who wished for adventure. But they were not a part of the calculated chaos which he enjoyed so very much. He'd be glad when they eventually made their way through a city again.

"How much farther?" Philip asked tersely. His eyes shifted as they walked. Beathan would probably never be able to look at him without being reminded of a soldier. It was ingrained in his partner's nature.

"It shouldn't be much longer now."

"Any more specifics?" Philip asked in that half-exasperated voice he often resorted to with Beathan.

He just ignored him, more for fun than for lack of information. The fairy grinned inwardly. Sometimes he felt like half the fun of traveling with Philip was doing everything in his power to vex him—and the man was easily vexed. The other half of him enjoyed the journey. There was rarely a dull moment around Philip. Events just seemed to have a way of happening.

They traveled the rest of the day until the shadows lengthened again. The lower the sun sank, the more all three of them watched the surrounding gloom. It was likely still too light for vampires, but one could never be too cautious. Besides, at the seat of a race's power the rules did not always apply in the same fashion as they did the farther one traveled from their homeland. Beathan had heard ugly rumors of what vampires were capable of here in Transylvania, much of it likely exaggerated...but perhaps not all of it. It was best to be careful. After all, as his ma used to say, "Carelessness kills more often than a determined enemy." He held the charm for his defensive ring ready in his mind to protect himself and the group in a flash should it become necessary.

The path began to climb. They had already been moving steadily upward from the rolling plains where the inn was situated, each day of travel leading them deeper into the woods and higher into the heart of the mountains. But their path had recently switched from a steady to sharp incline. Beathan focused on the charm that made his memory real before him. According to what he remembered, they would briefly climb in this fashion before leveling out onto a high valley. That was where The Alchemist would be. That was, if nothing had changed in the last few years.

As they walked, he began to worry slightly. His last meeting with The Alchemist had not been the greatest. Beathan had come away with what he needed, but he hadn't left on the best of terms. Come to think of it, Beathan wasn't sure when the last time was that he had parted with someone on good terms—apart from Philip. He shrugged away the thought.

The climbing trail leveled off and they again began walking through forest rather than the more exposed cliffside on which they'd been traveling. Wind whistled through the trees—a tense sounding wind, nothing like the gentle breezes of his Emerald Isle. This wind wanted to howl, wanted to rage, but it wasn't quite strong enough yet. Perhaps by tonight it would be. That meant it would be a miserable night to be caught without shelter.

"We must be close," Philip stated. He bent down and picked up what appeared to be a discarded or forgotten empty flask of some kind.

"Does this look familiar?" Alayna directed her question toward Beathan.

"Aye, we're nearly there."

At Beathan's admission, Philip drew his belt knife and gripped it tightly at the ready. Alayna pulled one of her miniature crossbows free and loaded a bolt. Beathan tensed, as well. They were a nervous lot. Months of constant pursuit and skirmishes had created within them a certain level of vigilance.

They proceeded onward along the trail until the trees thinned and a small vale opened up to them. Shrouded by steep mountains, the valley was little more than a spacious gorge—a big gulley that would have likely been covered with green grass in the spring and summer but was now dotted by piles of unmelted snow and a thin coating of frost wherever the snow did not lie.

"There." Beathan pointed across the small valley. A tiny little cottage—*well, more of a cabin, really*, Beathan amended to himself—abutted the mountainside. A larger building had been erected right next to the cabin.

Their footsteps crunched on the frosty, dead grass as they made their way nearer to the cottage. A thin plume of smoke signaled that it was clearly occupied. The moon was starting to rise over one of the slopes; twilight was upon them. Not utter darkness, but in these regions, there was not much difference. It tended to carry the same dangers.

As they drew closer to the cabin, Philip took the lead by habit. They closed the distance and Philip stepped forward toward the door. Just as he raised his hand to knock, three shadowy figures slunk around the corner of the cabin and into the moonlight.

"You!" Beathan heard Alayna say in shock.

"None other." The vampire's elegant features contorted into a smirk beneath her straight, black hair. Two other vampires flanked her.

Beathan tensed. He saw Philip draw a stake in his free hand, holding that and his blade at the ready. Beathan drew his own knife and readied the defensive charm.

"I believe we have a score to settle," the vampire intoned, her voice a hissing whisper across the night landscape, her penetrating black eyes locked on Alayna's face.

Beathan readied himself for hell to break loose.

CHAPTER SEVEN

PHILIP STEPPED CLOSER TO ALAYNA AND BEATHAN. THREE AGAINST three. The numbers might have seemed even, but Philip had spent too many years as a Collector to view vampires as anything less than extremely dangerous, especially at night. When the moon and stars were in the sky, vampires usually had the advantage. He and his two companions stood back to back to back as their enemies circled. Even though the vampires' eyes were black, they seemed to glow in the darkness the way a raven's feathers carried a glossy sheen.

The three vampires circled wordlessly until at last they attacked in unison. In a burst of energy, they darted forward, fangs out, almost-clawed fingernails at the ready. This was it.

Philip tensed himself, coiled to spring into action. He gripped the stake tight and cocked his arm slightly back, ready to thrust upward, ready to try and bury his wooden weapon into one of the vampires' hearts. In the space of a second, the creatures had rushed forward and collided with an unseen wall.

Beathan. He must have activated his defensive charm. Handy spell, that was. He could hear the fairy breathing heavily. It was a powerful spell but a difficult one. He would not be able to hold it forever.

The vampires thrashed against the invisible barrier again and again. They screamed in rage inches away from their prey and unable to take a single bite, unable to taste what they longed to taste. Philip assumed his most contemptuous smile.

"Poor little vampire. She's so hungry, but she can't get a single bite." It never hurt to taunt one's opponent into recklessness. Any edge was better than none.

The vampire practically screeched in frustration, her voice now nothing like the crooning web of silk Philip had overheard her use in an effort ensnare Alayna the previous night.

"Do you know who I am?" the vampire spat. "I am emissary to the One Who Rules this land—rules in truth." Her voice was not rough, exactly—it was proper, belonging to that of an eastern courtesan, but it was not so smooth now that she was no longer attempting to will-bend.

"Rules the night, you mean. Until the sun rises and you cower away in your holes," Philip taunted again.

"Take down this wall and see who is cowering." Her voice dropped to a dangerously quiet tone as she snarled, "I will show you pain."

Philip smiled. "I don't think you really want that."

He didn't feel fear quite the way he used to when he was a Collector, when he'd repressed all of his abilities other than strength. He was stronger now. Maybe vampires didn't quite have the edge on him that they used to. A part of him longed to test himself, wanted to order Beathan to drop the charm, to let them come. He suppressed it. Whether or not he had an advantage, Alayna likely would not. It was an unnecessary risk.

The vampires bashed into the invisible barrier for a few more moments before Philip heard the latch on the cabin door click and saw the golden light of a fire creeping out of the cracked opening.

The door opened fully, and Philip could make out the silhouette of a man. "Who is it?" The voice sounded cantankerous.

The man walked out into the darkness holding aloft a lit lantern. It cast a torchy light across the ground in front of his cabin. Philip felt Alayna and Beathan shift their bodies to face the newcomer.

"Keep the barrier up," Philip whispered.

"D'ya' take me for a fool?" Beathan responded.

The three vampires sidled around and formed up to one side of Philip's party. The man peered through the vaguely illuminated gloom. "Is that you, Salynksa?"

The vampire Philip had seen confront Alayna last night—and

himself just a moment ago—stepped forward. "Alchemist." She said it like a title.

"Damn it, Salynksa, I'll have no more of this nonsense. Take your fighting elsewhere."

Salynksa drifted forward with the effortless grace only a vampire at night could embody, menace and beauty, darkness and pale regality wrapped up in one. "You would do well to speak more respectfully, human."

The Alchemist's face twisted into a grimace of disdain. "I'm not afraid of you."

"You should be."

"No, I think not. Not so long as you serve the One Who Rules. And you will *always* serve the One Who Rules."

"You sound awfully certain, Alchemist. Such certainties in life are often rewarded with disappointment." She licked her bared fangs.

This time, The Alchemist actually laughed. "He needs me, and you fear him. That's a simple equation."

"For now," she responded dismissively.

"Yes, for now." The Alchemist spoke the words as if they really meant 'forever'.

He turned his head to look at Philip and his companions. He stepped forward slowly, walking with a cane even though he didn't seem old enough to really merit the necessity of a cane. Was it an affectation? A weapon? Or simple misdirection?

When The Alchemist's eyes landed on Beathan, his face twisted into a look of disgust. "You again."

"None other!" Beathan responded cheerfully.

Their brief interaction gave Philip a sinking feeling. Could the fairy *never* make a good impression?

The Alchemist rapped the tip of his cane against the barrier. "You can take this down. There will be no more fighting here tonight." He shot a warning look at Salynksa and her comrades until the vampire bowed her head marginally in acquiescence.

"You are certain?" Philip asked.

"My cabin is a neutral zone. Or, at least, it is supposed to be." He shot another disdainful glance at the vampires.

"And how did you secure that arrangement?" Alayna asked.

The Alchemist gave them a toothy grin, and all of a sudden Philip felt as though he was looking at someone altogether more dangerous than the creatures that had been so bent on attacking them just moments ago.

"The One Who Rules enjoys my services. We have an arrangement of sorts. I work for him when he desires and, in turn, I am left alone to live here and to conduct my business with whomever ventures across my path—with whomever is brave enough to seek me out."

"And who is this 'One Who Rules' that you and the vampires keep referring to?" Alayna asked.

The Alchemist looked at her out of the corner of his eye as he turned to walk back into the cabin. "The One Who Rules is Dracula."

———

"I THOUGHT HE WAS JUST A MYTH!" Alayna whispered to Philip as Beathan dropped the barrier and they moved to follow The Alchemist into the cabin.

"Well, Dracula *is* real, but he's far exaggerated by legend. Dracula is really more of a title. It's kind of like the 'King of the Vampires'," Philip did his best to answer.

They passed the cluster of vampires. "What? You lot aren't comin'?" Beathan asked with an impudent grin.

Salynksa stared at them flatly. "We will return another time to do business. I would not want to break the agreement even further. I do not know if I can control Volri and Mina." The two vampires at her side—one male and one female—glared malevolently at them. They held each other's gazes for a long moment until the vampires whisked around and sprinted off in a flash of speed.

Philip kept a tight grip on his stake until he was absolutely sure that they were gone.

"So, this Dracula isn't really anything special, then?" Alayna pressed. Beathan and Philip shared a look.

"Not exactly, lass," Beathan said tentatively.

"But you just said—"

"What I said was that the rumors were exaggerated, not that none of them are true. It takes an extraordinary vampire to rise to the top of their race. This particular Dracula has been in power for quite some time, as well. No one has unseated him in...how long?" Philip turned his head to inquire of Beathan.

The fairy shrugged. "Word is this Dracula's been a wee lordling for nigh on three hundred fifty years now. Longest reign in quite some time."

Alayna stared at them in astonishment. Before she could say anything else, The Alchemist stuck his head back out the door. "Are you coming or not? I'll not let all the warm air out. I assume you are here for business, yes?" He was clearly not the most patient of men.

Inside the cabin, it was a stark contrast to the outside chill. A fire burned almost merrily in the hearth. By the flickering light, Philip was able to appraise The Alchemist's features for the first time. He was maybe a decade older than himself, certainly not old enough to need the cane for everyday use. However, he did have black hair that was greying in patches. It stuck out strangely like the wind had blown it this way and that and it had never been smoothed down afterwards. He had thick, bushy eyebrows, one of which looked like it might have been singed recently. There were smile wrinkles on the man's face, lines that indicated mirth—but Philip had long ago learned that not all mirth was innocent. The Alchemist was thin, but he looked strong enough with the body of an aging man who stayed active. All in all, there was not much to concern him. Except for the eyes.

Piercing, brown eyes gazed hawkishly at them from the other side of a wood-slabbed kitchen table. The Alchemist stood with his back to the hearth and laid the cane along with the flats of his palms upon the table. But those eyes. There was a cold curiosity to them that sent a shiver through Philip. They were eyes that had seen things, eyes that had marked the passage of time by knowledge acquired, and somehow Philip was sure that much of that knowledge had been gained in a sinister fashion. Their host shifted his gaze to rest wholly upon Philip, and they looked at each other for a long moment. He somehow knew that this was not a man to cross lightly.

"So, you're The Alchemist," he said, finally breaking the silence.

"And you are a Collector, if I am not mistaken."

"You are mistaken."

The Alchemist tilted his head and narrowed his eyes, questioning the forthrightness of Philip's statement. Then understanding blossomed. "Ah, so *you* are the one."

"The one what?"

The older man smiled a small, knowing smile. "The Collector who disappeared, then reappeared, and then disappeared again." He tilted his head once more and murmured astutely, "Although, perhaps not quite so disappeared as I had been led to believe."

Alayna and Beathan remained silent through the back-and-forth exchange. Philip was glad for it. They were here for him, to fix his blood, but he needed to do this his way.

"I wouldn't have thought the Guild would want that to be public knowledge," Philip said.

"But of course they don't. However, whispers have a way of traveling, do they not? After all, it was not only you three who escaped the prison. There was another, no?"

Philip was shoulder to shoulder with Alayna, and he could feel her tense involuntarily at the mention of Azir.

"Yes, you would know about whispers and rumors, Alchemist," Philip answered. "You have quite the reputation yourself."

The Alchemist turned to a pot that hung over the fire and stirred it with a long, wooden spoon. Though his back was to them, he continued to speak: "My reputation has served me well over the years. It tends to sift out the weak of will and stop the unresolved from visiting me. Those who are left are usually the truly...desperate. Other than the vampires, of course." He turned back toward them and put on another of those knowing smiles of his. He knew that they needed him, needed him badly or they wouldn't be here—here in the heart of vampire territory right under the nose of Dracula. Philip immediately hated the fact that The Alchemist had read the situation so well.

"You assume correctly. We—I—am in need of your help." He saw no reason to avoid what The Alchemist already so obviously knew.

"We," Alayna amended his statement. She slipped her fingers through his.

The Alchemist's hard eyes shifted to stare at Beathan. "And yet you bring him with you." The distaste was apparent.

Beathan grinned widely, smiling his most winning smile. It had no apparent effect on the man before them. When it was clear that the smile was gaining no favor, he responded, "Oh, come now, mate. I wasn't that bad, was I?"

"My cabin door was broken down by the time you left. Worse, my workshop was half destroyed. You left me to face an enraged werewolf that was only here because it had followed you!"

Philip groaned inwardly. This wasn't going well. He saw the calculated look of hurt on Beathan's face, the look he gave when he was gearing up to tell either one of his most outrageous lies or was about to try and garner support for a particular action that was almost impossible to justify.

"Mr. Alchemist, I swear I had no idea he was followin' me."

The Alchemist shook his bushy head disgustedly. "You were with me in the house and then we fled to the workshop together. You knew it was here."

"I thought me fleein' would lead it away from ya'."

"Do not play games with me, Fairy. We both know that we shut it up in the workshop and were planning to regroup and plan a strategy to rid ourselves of it. Only, you abandoned me at the first chance to deal with it myself, taking with you the only silver knives on hand."

Beathan sighed, giving up at last. "Well, I s'pose ya' caught me. I was thinkin' o' meself, like I always do. That's why I've survived this long in me line o' work."

"And what line of work is that?" The Alchemist still looked angry, but Philip could tell that something Beathan had said piqued his curiosity.

"Thievin' an' all around general rabble rousin'." Beathan capered slightly and gave a half bow.

The Alchemist snorted. He looked to have lost interest as soon as he'd gained it. He opened his mouth to speak, and Philip was almost certain that he was about to tell them to disappear on account of his dislike for Beathan when the fairy cut him off.

"Come now, Mr. Alchemist. It seems ya' handled yourself fairly well. After all, the werewolf wasn't enough to deal ya' any lastin' damage, not to a formidable man such as yourself."

"Flattery won't work, fairy." Yet the look on his face said that, in a way, it had. His features softened slightly. He turned his gaze away from Beathan and back to Philip and Alayna, the former breathing a sigh of relief.

"So you need my help, then." It was a statement.

"We do," Philip said simply.

"And our request, what we need, has nothing to do with gold or silver," Alayna volunteered. There was a hint of skepticism in her voice.

The Alchemist focused on her. "You would be surprised how little of the requests that I deal with have anything to do with precious metals, girl. Not all alchemists are preoccupied with the search for gold."

"No?" she countered.

"No," he answered definitively. "There are far more interesting pursuits in the field of transformation than gold." The glint in his eyes hinted that those pursuits were dark in nature.

Philip felt Alayna shiver slightly at his side. She sensed it, too; this was a man of whom to be wary. "All right, then. You can do more than transform things into metal."

The Alchemist smiled thinly at her. "That I can. And you would do well to remember it."

CHAPTER EIGHT

"So, what exactly do you need?" The Alchemist prompted with a no-nonsense expression.

Alayna and Beathan both turned to Philip, allowing for him to explain. It was his predicament, after all. He gathered his thoughts and spoke.

"You already know who I am. I was a Collector for many years, working for the Guild with perfect loyalty. I rarely questioned orders or Guild practices. That is partially what puts me in this unfortunate position today."

The Alchemist peered at him keenly. "And what position is that?"

"You have heard of Blood Mages, I assume?"

"What do you take me for, Collector? Some common scholar who's never seen the outside of his tiny, hometown library? I've criss-crossed the continent studying things you've never even heard of! Of course I know what Blood Mages are. Nasty business. All sorts of tricks they can play on a person."

Philip grimaced. He could not disagree with that statement. "Well, since I do not have to explain to you what they are, I will simply state that they are the source of my dilemma."

The Alchemist gave an exasperated sigh. "Get to the point; what dilemma is that?"

"I have a trace in my blood," Philip said simply, assuming that if

The Alchemist was familiar with Blood Mages, then he would also be familiar with what traces were.

"Stupid thing, that, allowing them to put a trace in your blood. Why ever would you let them do such a thing to you?" He snorted derisively.

Again, Philip grimaced, his mouth puckering up as if tasting something sour. Neither Beathan nor Alayna spoke up to his defense. This was his past to explain. Besides, neither of them fully understood his former loyalty to the Guild.

He shook his head. "I was young. I was naively fighting for a cause in which I believed, a rationale into which I'd been indoctrinated from a very young age." Philip thought of his former helper and boy, Stephen. He hoped the lad would find a way out before it was too late, before the only way to leave was as a renegade.

The Alchemist grunted. "That's not really an explanation, but all right."

"The trace is required of all those transitioning from apprenticeship into full Collector status. I had no reason to question it at the time—at least no reasons upon which I allowed myself to dwell. It was either accept the trace or leave the Guild. My parents were Guild to their core, so all I *knew* was the Guild. It never even crossed my mind to refuse."

It was The Alchemist's turn to shake his head. "That's the problem with people today. Nobody thinks for themselves. People just accept what they're told and what they're told to do."

Again, Philip did not disagree, although he would have preferred to avoid the look of scorn on the scientist's face. "Can you help me get rid of it?"

"What, the trace?" The Alchemist exclaimed. "I suppose I could try."

The answer did not sound particularly convincing. Alayna must not have thought so, either, because she finally entered into the conversation. "You'll try? We've come miles to see you, and that's the best answer you can give?"

Philip put a comforting hand on her shoulder, gently restraining her. She shrugged off his hand in annoyance but quieted.

"Would you prefer I lied to you, girl? Made something up, some false promise of success?" The Alchemist stared at her shrewdly, and Philip watched some of her anger wither under his stare.

"I suppose not," she muttered finally.

Her opposition quelled, the scientist resumed his thoughtful expression. "There might be ways to remove the trace, but it will be difficult. Difficult..." He was half mumbling to himself as he stared beyond their three faces into the dimness of the room beyond the fire-lit kitchen. Abruptly, he grabbed a lantern and began walking toward the front door of the cabin. "Come with me," he said without preamble. They had no choice but to follow him out into the darkness of the Transylvanian night.

Snow and frost coated the ground in patches. Chill air nipped at exposed flesh, and after the warmth of the hearth it was an unwelcome change to all except Philip. He breathed in the crispness. He would choose the cold any day over the stuffy interior of a human home.

Without speaking, The Alchemist led them to the next building. This was also built from logs, like the cabin, but it was larger—maybe twice the size. He fumbled with a key until he got it into the lock and Philip heard it click. The older man swung open the door and entered the building. He was closely followed by Philip, Alayna, and Beathan.

"My workshop," he said expansively, waving a hand in an arc around the room in front of them. He still held his cane, making the motion slightly awkward.

The workshop was one large room, indeed much bigger than the cabin in which he lived. There were numerous tables scattered with various contraptions and half-finished projects. Glass beakers were filled with liquids of all colors—potions and elixirs, Philip had no doubt. If the man's reputation were even half true, Philip had no desire to know what those potions were or what they did.

They gazed in silence for a moment. Another hearth, larger in order to fill a bigger space with sufficient warmth, remained unlit. "My pride and joy," The Alchemist murmured, again seemingly speaking to himself as much as to the three of them.

"Quite the spot ya' got here," Beathan quipped, his gaze drifting hungrily around the room.

The Alchemist turned his attention to the fairy. An ugly, possessive expression filled his face. "You'll keep your greedy hands to yourself. Thieves find themselves missing fingers or worse when they try to steal from me." His menacing threat seemed to slide right off Beathan who put on his most innocent face.

"Wouldn't dream o' thievin' nothin' from the man who we've come to for help."

The Alchemist grunted suspiciously but seemed mollified enough to let the moment pass. He walked around the workshop, puttering as he spoke. "I have an idea. It'll be difficult, as I said, but I think it could work. Possibly. But then you'll already have expected danger, won't you?"

Philip didn't know if he was supposed to answer or not, so he stayed silent, waiting for the scientist to say something that required a response. Beathan and Alayna followed his lead. The lantern barely emitted enough light to illuminate the workshop, and it created as many shadows as it dispelled.

The Alchemist continued his muttering, "Yes, yes, my reputation will have had you expecting danger. But this will be a particularly nasty procedure. Which one of you had the idea to come to me?" His eyes glinted in the dark as he looked at them from across the room.

Beathan held his gaze but didn't speak up. It was enough of an answer.

"Ah yes, of course. How very like a fairy to be willing to risk the life of his companion."

That statement got Alayna's attention. "Risk whose life? Philip's?" She cast a worried look at her lover. He echoed her question to the scientist who was now making his way back across the room toward them, weaving his way between work tables and alchemical apparatuses.

The Alchemist ignored their questions and stopped right in front of them. "There will need to be payment, of course. No work without pay." He leered at them.

"We don't even know if you can help me yet," Philip returned. "I'm not convinced you'll be able to get rid of the trace."

Beathan silenced him with a look. "He wouldn't be askin' payment if he didn't think he had a plan, mate. I know how he works."

Philip narrowed his eyes. "What is your proposal for how to rid my blood of the trace?"

"Payment. Let's talk of how you're going to compensate me first."

He sighed in frustration. "Fine."

The Alchemist gave him a toothy grin. "Blood for blood. If I fix your blood, you'll give me yours." There was a sinister cast to his face as he said the words, and Philip was distinctly aware of how little good there was to say of this man based on his reputation.

"Out of the question!" he snapped. "I'll not have my blood fixed only to deliver it into the hands of another. You could use it against me somehow."

The Alchemist put on his nicest mask. "Come now, I'm not a magician. The things I can do with a person's blood have little effect on them once it's left their body. A little of your blood won't kill you. In fact, it might very well save your life. That trace is a beacon after which the Guild will send company after company of Collectors. Sooner or later, they'll send enough soldiers to finish you off. At worst, I'll sell it to the vampires and some blood sucker will get a taste of you to no great harm."

Philip didn't answer, but he remembered the Deadbloods they had faced at St. Thomas. He knew The Alchemist was right, but he just didn't want to admit it.

Still, The Alchemist sensed his reluctance and spoke in an almost chatty voice as he said, "I live in the heart of vampire territory, you know. I *wanted* to live here. Fewer people pass through to bother me. Certainly, the Guild's reach, as well as the reach of any others who might hinder me, is far from strong in Transylvania. Yes, this place has its benefits, but it also has its costs. I made a deal with The One Who Rules. I do what he asks of me and in return he allows me safe haven and the ability to set my own rules with his subjects." He stared hard at Philip now, the conversational tone disappearing as he continued, "Sometimes we have to deal with demons to get what we want."

"How much?" Philip finally grated out through clenched teeth. He hated being held over a barrel.

"Three vials each."

"Out of the question. Three of mine and none of theirs," he fired back.

"What is life without variety?" The Alchemist countered. "Two vials from all three of you."

"One from each of us."

"Only if I can test them first," The Alchemist said.

"Fine," Philip agreed.

"Done!"

Philip shared a look with his two companions, asking the

unspoken question about whether either of them had any objections. Beathan looked grim. He knew the power of blood. No fairy in his right mind would want to just hand over a vial of his blood, but he stayed silent. Philip felt an overwhelming sense of gratitude that he had friends willing to risk their lives for him. His gaze swept across Alayna. She was silent, as he'd expected. She would do anything for him, whether he wished her to or not. Their eyes met and the resolve he saw in her eyes reassured him. Pay the price and be rid of this trace once and for all. He could deal with whatever consequences came next. *They* would deal with it, he corrected himself. He was not alone.

The Alchemist had bustled away and was now walking back toward them with a scalpel in one hand along with a few empty vials. He approached Philip first. "Which vein would you like?"

Philip silently held out his wrist. In the half-lit darkness of the room, The Alchemist nicked his skin. Not enough to cause any damage, but enough to get a steady flow. The red liquid dropped steadily into the vial until it filled to the brim. Adeptly, the scientist corked it and handed a piece of cloth bandage to Philip. The man moved on to Beathan next.

The fairy grudgingly held out his wrist, as well. A smile of delight played across The Alchemist's features: satisfaction. He knew that the fairy would not want this, but he also knew that he had all the leverage. They needed his help, and this was the only way to secure it. Philip hated that he had put the fairy in this position. Vial full, the scientist moved on to Alayna.

"I don't remember the last time I drew Elfas blood," he murmured. He sounded positively excited by the prospect. He repeated the procedure with Alayna and then wrapped her wrist deli-cately after having corked the vial with her blood.

"There, done," he proclaimed. "Now I will analyze them, and if they are sufficient we will proceed."

"*If* they are sufficient?" Philip asked angrily. First the man had strong-armed them into giving up their blood, now he intimated that it might not be good enough. This time it was Alayna's restraining hand upon his shoulder instead of the other way around. He let her, but a smolder burned in his chest.

The Alchemist carried the three vials to a nearby table and set them in a stand to keep them from falling and breaking. He grasped a beaker of greenish liquid from one of the apparatuses on the table and poured a portion of the potion into another small vial. "Easier to decant," he spoke to himself again as he held the small vial of green liquid, his eyes never leaving his work. The Alchemist uncorked the three upright vials of their blood and left them on the small stand, hovering over them with his vial of green solution.

Finally, he looked up. "One drop of this in each vial will be sufficient to analyze them, I think." And with that, The Alchemist meticulously dribbled one tiny drop of the green potion into each of the three vials. He poured the remainder of the potion back into the beaker and then sat down to wait.

There was no visible change in the three vials of blood, at least not to Philip's eye, but the scientist seemed pleased with whatever was occurring. He even dipped his little finger delicately into each vial before touching it to his lips.

"Human—gypsy, I imagine. Fairy. And do I detect leprechaun?"

"Ya' do, indeed. Got a wee bit o' leprechaun from way, way back on me ma's side o' the family," Beathan responded.

"That must be quite the story." The Alchemist grinned pleasantly and moved his finger to the next vial. His little finger hovered over Philip's blood. A tiny dip followed by a meager taste.

His eyes widened in surprise. "So. No wonder you left the Guild. Did they know you were a hybrid? With the blood of the North, no less. How very rare!" The greedy satisfaction on his face was enough to make Philip want to end the deal right at that very moment. He forced himself to stay silent, to ignore the gloating face before him as he held his finger over the final vial—Alayna's. Dip. Taste. The shock on his face followed by the obvious rush of covetous glee was almost too much for Philip to take.

"My, my, my, my, my..." The Alchemist seemed almost at a loss for words. "This blood is positively...fresh," he practically purred with elation. "Not bred like the fairy or hybridized like the Collector. No... you, my dear Elfas, were transformed, were you not? The likes of which we have not seen since The Great Transformation. But how? You are not old enough to have lived through that time."

Alayna didn't answer. Neither did her companions, at first. Finally, though, Philip responded, "Our business is our own. How we came to be what we are is not your concern." He felt no desire to recount the tale of his Guild mentor and betrayer, Martin Astori, how the Guild magician had attempted to reignite a new Great Transformation and set the world on fire with chaos not that long ago in New York.

"Very well," The Alchemist ceded with disappointment.

"Is it sufficient?" Philip asked brusquely.

"It is."

"So, how will you fix my blood?"

Surprisingly, it was Beathan who answered, "He's goin' t' transform it. Completely."

CHAPTER NINE

"CLEVER, CLEVER," THE ALCHEMIST DIRECTED HIS COMMENT toward the fairy. Philip and Alayna stared at Beathan in astonishment as he continued, "Your half-breed friend is quite right. I'll have to completely change your blood into something else, then change it right back."

"That's madness!" Alayna interjected. "He'll die without any blood."

"He may very well do just that." The Alchemist did nothing to try and alleviate her fears. "But it is the only way. The trace in his blood is not easily disposed of." He turned his gaze to the fairy to see if Beathan wanted to prove again that he knew where the scientist's line of thought was heading.

Beathan opened his mouth and said grimly, "The trace is magic, but that sorta magic is particular. It requires a livin' host to attach itself to. If Mr. Alchemical Man over here transforms your blood completely into somethin' else and then transfigures it right back, the trace will've disappeared because its livin' host will be gone. That should break it."

"How very right you are, Fairy." The Alchemist looked as though he was anticipating the challenge of such a procedure.

"Do you truly think I can survive without blood for a period of time, even as short as it might be?" Philip asked.

The Alchemist smiled thinly. "I do not know. We shall have to find out during this experiment."

"This isn't an experiment, this is his *life* we are talking about." Philip could hear the worry in Alayna's voice.

"Oh, but it is both, my dear, and isn't the prospect so very exciting? Part of me thinks that I should be paying *you* just for the chance to conduct it."

Philip watched Beathan and Alayna shoot dark looks at The Alchemist. He pondered the idea. It was a risky procedure—too risky, maybe. But could he afford to go the rest of his life with the trace still in his blood, still lighting a beacon for the Guild to follow and use to harass him wherever he went until ultimately, they had him killed—or worse—captured? An even scarier thought crossed his mind at the idea of Alayna being hurt or captured because of the curse he bore in his blood. He leaned toward the idea of the experiment, feeling inclined to say yes. He saw the glint of anticipation in the Alchemist's eyes as he watched the desired answer register on Philip's face.

He was just about to acquiesce when Alayna practically shouted, "Absolutely not. I forbid it!"

"Forbid it?" Philip turned a quizzical eye toward her and saw a smile playing at her lips despite the seriousness of her statement. She could find humor even in the midst of a dire situation.

"Yes. I forbid it. You will not do this. It is far too dangerous, and I don't trust him." The look she shot The Alchemist was filled with contempt. "He is much too excited for you to risk your life."

"But Alayna, love, you were the one who thought we should come here in the first place."

"And I never would have agreed with Beathan if I'd known he had this in mind all along!" She sent a look of pure venom the fairy's way.

Beathan held up his hands in apology. "'tis the reason I was deliberately vague. I knew ya'd not be keen on such a plan."

"It's not a plan, it's suicide."

"Not for certain," Philip contradicted her. "The Alchemist says there's a chance of success."

"I swear to you, Philip, if you do this, even if it works I will not forgive you for it. We can keep on as we have been. We can continue to fight the Guild like we've done for months. We're still here, aren't we? And who knows, maybe another idea will come to us." Her voice lost some of its anger and had taken on a pleading note.

Philip looked at Beathan. The fairy shrugged. "I knew it was a long shot, mate, comin' here. It's up to you."

He turned to The Alchemist. "What are my odds if I do this?"

"Less than half, I'd guess. But if you don't do it, I am quite certain that your odds of evading continual and concentrated pursuit by the Guild are even worse." The Alchemist stared at him with a coldly dispassionate description of their plight.

"Don't do this, Philip," Alayna begged.

The terror in her eyes eventually won him over. He could not refuse her when she looked at him like that. He turned back to The Alchemist. "I think we'll be going now, and not without our blood. No services rendered, no payment required."

Beathan flitted over to the table with the three vials and gathered them up. Then he scampered back to Philip with a smirk on his face.

The Alchemist's faced contorted in rage, an emotion which he quickly tried to smooth over. "This is a mistake. You will not long survive with the full weight of the Guild pressing down on you."

Philip looked at his companions. "I guess we'll take our chances."

The older man stared hungrily at the vials of blood as Philip took them from Beathan and tucked them away in his pack. "You do not want to cross me. Backing out on our deal will not end well for you." The menace in his voice was palpable.

Philip stared at him coldly. "There was no deal agreed upon; we are reneging on nothing. We came here for help, and we are leaving having decided that we no longer want it."

The Alchemist practically gnashed his teeth with frustration as he watched the vials of their blood slip out of his reach.

The three of them backed slowly out of the workshop. Philip kept his eyes on the scientist's hateful gaze until they were out the door and had shut it behind them.

"Let's be gone from this place," he said firmly.

His companions agreed, and they set off into the night. Philip couldn't help but feel a gnawing concern that perhaps, just perhaps, The Alchemist was right and he should have risked the procedure. After all, who more than Philip knew what they faced when it came to the Collectors Guild? He shrugged the thought away. Now was not the time for what-ifs. They had ground to cover.

CHAPTER TEN

SHE WAS NEVER SHORT OF BREATH. HER BLOOD—HER NATURE—
ensured it. They covered ground quickly coming down out of the
mountains, each of them eager to be away from that place. Alayna
enjoyed the motion, the swift movements along narrow mountain
trails. As a fairy, Beathan kept up with her pretty well. Philip was
slower than both of them, but he had reserves of endurance, enough
so that although she could hear that he was winded, he nonetheless
did not fall far behind. The ground gradually leveled out, and a snow-
carpeted forest replaced the steep mountain terrain.

"Enough. We've been at it for hours. You may not need a rest, but
I do," Philip gasped as he slowed her down with a hand upon her
shoulder.

The three of them stumbled to a halt. Alayna didn't exactly feel
springy, but neither did she feel the leaden limbs she remembered
from exerting herself as a human. Philip seated himself on a rock and
was joined by Beathan. Even the fairy looked a little the worse
for wear.

"Tired, boys?" she asked with a twinkle in her eye.

Philip just looked up at her and shook his head, still catching his
breath. Beathan's eyes narrowed.

"Not all of us are Elfas, Alayna, m'dear."

"Surely fairy-kind is comparable, no?"

Beathan shrugged. "Well, in truth, I'm only a half, ya know. The rest o' me is human. Mostly."

"Don't you have a charm or spell from your jangles that can help you run faster?"

Philip looked with interest at the fairy following Alayna's line of questioning. He rubbed his leg muscles, massaging out soreness and any kinks that had arisen from the swift and forceful downward passage out of the mountains.

"I do, indeed," Beathan responded, "but speed is not the same as endurance."

"No?"

"No. I have a few amplifiers relatin' t' me quickness an' agility, but none o' me charms possesses the gift o' durability or fortitude. I simply do me best t' keep up when the occasion arises."

Alayna put a friendly hand on his shoulder. "Well, you both did just fine."

"Nothing like you, though. You don't even look tired." Philip sounded almost jealous.

Alayna smiled. They were both better fighters than her, Philip could heal more quickly, and Beathan had his charms and spells, so this was one area where she was superior. And she enjoyed it.

"That's because I'm *not* tired, love."

Philip just stared at her, and Alayna enjoyed the few moments when she could see envy in his eyes before that envy turned to a look of pride. He shook his head. "Well then, I'm glad you're with us. I'd hate to have one of your kind running me down."

"What's good is that no one is running us down," she responded. "For once it doesn't seem like we're being chased. We'd certainly have seen the vampires by now if they had stayed around the cabin to follow us, wouldn't we?"

"Aye, they'd have showed themselves by now," the fairy chimed in.

Philip nodded slowly in reluctant agreement. "True, but that doesn't mean we're safe."

As if to punctuate his statement, a crossbow bolt buried itself in the trunk of the tree next to Alayna. Another whizzed past and missed Philip by a hair's breadth.

"Collectors!" he shouted.

The three of them were up in a flash and sprinting again. If Alayna hadn't known that their adrenaline was pumping, she might have felt sorry for Philip and Beathan for having to take off again so quickly after hours of running. They hurried along the narrow forest trail while the occasional bolt screamed past them to vanish into the dim woods. Dawn was approaching, yet somehow the idea of their pursuers catching up to them in the light felt more ominous than the dark. At least with the shadows of night they stood a chance of shaking their pursuers. One bolt nicked Philip's shoulder, leaving a streak of blood. Alayna might have worried if it wasn't Philip; she knew that he could ignore pain and heal like no one she'd ever seen.

The headlong rush through the forest felt wild and out of control. After their hunters had alerted them to their presence, they'd made no further effort to conceal themselves. Alayna could hear their shouts, and she looked back over her shoulder to see their shadowed forms running in their dark clothes and darker cloaks. For a moment, it was almost easy to forget that they were human, so sinister did they seem in pursuit.

Out of nowhere, the trail forked ahead of them. Alayna made to follow the left fork before a cry called her to a halt.

"You go left. I'll try and draw them away to the right—I'm the one they want!" Philip's desperate shout sent an arrow of fear through her heart. She made to resist, turned to tell him no, that in absolutely no uncertain terms should they split up and leave each other, but he cut her off. "Alayna, go! I'll catch up with you." Then he sprinted right.

Somehow Alayna found herself being herded left by the fairy. Somehow, she was allowing it to happen and, before she knew it, she was alone with Beathan, racing through the night with her prayers for Philip pounding as loud in her head as the sound of her heartbeat.

An owl screeched in the dark, and the night was awake with other noises. It seemed as though their plan had failed because bolts still shot through the gloom around them. Their followers must have divided their forces to pursue both forks in the trail. There must have been quite a few Collectors for them to be able to split like that.

Alayna ran. Another crossbow bolt missed her head by an inch. She heard Beathan's panting breaths by her side. Suddenly, a form tackled her out of the brush on the side of the trail. The man sent her to the ground with crushing force, but she had already turned the fall into a roll and was throwing him off of her before leaping into an attack. She put a fist into his face with all her might, and in one smooth, fast motion, she drew her belt knife and slit his throat. Beathan had turned around and was coming back for her, unnecessary as it was. Her training with Philip had made Alayna more than enough of a match for one lone Collector.

She started toward Beathan and began to run again. More bolts whizzed through the night. Idly, and in a strangely faraway thought, she marveled at their poor aim. Could they not hit anything? Perhaps a moving target in the dark was not the easiest of prey, though, especially one so lithe and quick as an Elfas.

And then it happened.

The bolt took Alayna through the shoulder and sent her spinning to the ground. The pain was shattering, and as she fell it only hurt more as the shaft jarred from the impact. She struggled for air, struggled to stay conscious despite the dizzying agony. It felt like lightning had struck her in the back. Maybe it had, maybe this was some new kind of weapon, some magical projectile. It had to be. Simple battle wounds didn't hurt this badly, did they? How did Philip manage to shrug away the pain like he always did?

She fought to regain her feet. She made it all the way to her knees, even with the pain, before she realized that she was facing the wrong way. She glanced over her shoulder to see Beathan down the path ahead of her, saw the look of fear in his eyes. She turned her head back to see a form advancing on her out of the dark.

The next crossbow bolt struck her in the chest, and blackness consumed everything.

CHAPTER ELEVEN

RAGE. BLINDING, INSENSIBLE RAGE. THAT WAS ALL BEATHAN COULD feel as he watched the bolt bury itself in Alayna's chest, watched as she crumpled to the dirt with a feeble moan, saw her brilliant hair splayed across the ground, around her head, illuminated by a few shards of moonlight streaking through the canopy.

Followed by anguish.

Beathan knew a mortal wound when he saw one. He should run. He should stick to the plan. He and Philip could meet up later down the road, but first they had to ditch this cohort of Collectors on their trail. And while, by the sound of it, many had followed Philip just as the former Collector had intended, not all of them had. Clearly, since Alayna was in a heap upon the earth.

He should run. But he just couldn't. Alayna was one of the few people in the entire world that he counted as a true friend. Beathan couldn't leave her lying there undefended for her attackers. So he did something he rarely did: Beathan prepared himself to fight a fight where the odds were not in his favor. He was a gypsy and a fairy—he took risks, he was flighty and chanced death—but he rarely knowingly put himself in a losing position. There were times to make an exception, though.

He flicked a few of his jewels, a couple rings, and a bracelet all at the same time. He muttered spells to activate the charms and then charged back toward his foes.

A few bolts fired from the darkness flew toward him, and at the last moment they glanced away with a strange ringing sound as they were deflected by the defensive charm from his stone ring. The charms would hold the worst of the dangers at bay *if* he could maintain them while fighting. He'd never tried to do that before—he had only activated the defensive charm as a last ditch effort when all other hope was lost. Beathan wasn't sure if he had the focus necessary to maintain such a rigorous and exhausting spell while fighting and keeping his speed and agility charms active, as well. There was only one way to find out.

He charged onward, back up the trail, until he reached Alayna's fallen body. He stood a defiant vigil over her. Three more bolts ricocheted off his charm before the Collectors had enough and decided to engage him at close range. Four bodies appeared out of the darkness, their stoic faces illuminated by the pale moonlight. The utter lack of rancor on their faces, the matter-of-fact way they advanced made Beathan hate them more than some of the most sinister creatures he'd faced in his lifetime. Collectors possessed an implacable resolve, an icy disregard for any other way of life, and that ruffled his feathers more than any hungry vampire or terrifying werewolf ever could. They made him feel utterly sick.

Beathan screamed his challenge as his four opponents neared and raised their weapons, preparing to fight. Two fought with short blades, one with a vicious-looking club, while the fourth was armed with the traditional stakes that were so common and versatile among a Collector's arsenal.

"Come on ya' bastards!" he spat with particular venom. He sneered as they slowed their advance to cautiously proceed the final few feet toward him.

Beathan took the fight to them. He lunged forward, pulling a knife free from his belt and flinging it all in one motion with practiced aim. It struck the nearest target's shoulder, causing him to fall back and let the other three advance first. Beathan closed the gap. He engaged them all at once, the speed charm giving him an advantage, but there were four of them, and they were all highly trained.

It was a short, brutal fight. Beathan felt a knife gash his chest as he wove in and out of their weapons and blows. So much for his defensive charm. He kept his speed and agility charms active instead.

He broke a few arms, shattered a knee with a hard, swift kick. One Collector got his throat slit. Beathan suffered another wound, this time to his left arm, followed quickly by another to his thigh. Still, before a full minute had passed, he'd somehow dispatched the four Collectors much more easily than he had expected. He'd thought he was standing a death vigil over his friend's body. Apparently, though, anger and anguish were more powerful motivators than he had realized.

A few groans emitted form the last surviving man. Beathan knelt down and put a knife in his throat. It was done. Hurriedly, he limped back to Alayna. He looked at her sadly, his heart clenching. He ground his teeth in fury at the senselessness of it all. He liked a good fight as much as the next fairy, but the Collectors went too far.

Crouching, Beathan put a finger to her neck and felt for a pulse. It was there—faint—but it was fading. He kept his finger on her pulse, watching her sightless gaze until the weak pulse finally flickered and then died. He threw back his head and howled. It was a primal sound. The cry reverberated through the forest. He poured all of his pain into it, imagining what it would be like to tell Philip. The tears came unbidden. They fell, and Beathan didn't stop them. She was gone. One of his only friends in the world was gone. He smoothed her hair. He closed her eyes.

In the not-so-far distance, he heard the sound of approaching feet and a few hoarse cries—quite a few cries, actually. More Collectors. Beathan considered staying. He considered lying in wait for the bastards, waiting to kill them all for what they'd done. Fairies were flighty, but they could also be vengeful. And what deserved vengeance if not this?

His sense won out as he heard the approach. There were more coming than he wanted to fight. Wounded—shallow wounds, but enough to slow him down—and tired, he wouldn't last through another round. It was time to say good-bye. He kissed Alayna's eyelids and then her forehead, saying farewell the way an Elfas would to their own dead, and then he stepped off the trail. He'd have less chance of pursuit if he ghosted through the darkness of the woods and left the trail behind him.

Beathan heard a twig snap, then another. His head whipped

around. Who was there? Was there someone near, nearer than the oncoming Collectors? Or was he hearing things? *Perhaps the noise was made by an on looking animal*, he thought. Either way, it was time to go. Beathan ran.

He ran swiftly and silently. He navigated his way through the woods until he crossed the distance to the right fork in the trail. He followed its path, paralleling it from the underbrush and trees along-side it, keeping pace for a few miles. Every so often, he'd pass the body of a dead Collector. Occasionally, he would pass a couple. Philip hadn't been entirely wrong: they had sent the bulk of their company after him, leaving only a few to follow Beathan and Alayna. Those few had been enough.

Beathan ran in a crouched squat, but he did not pass any more Collectors. Likely the sounds of approach he had heard nearing Alayna's body had been that of the Collectors who had turned around from following Philip. He began to worry. Had they overwhelmed Philip, as well? Fear gave his legs life and made him discard his caution. He stepped back onto the path and ran, ran as fast as he could. Philip could be bleeding out somewhere, just like Alayna had done.

Time seemed interminable until, finally, he reached a clearing. Philip sat on a rock, shrouded in an icy resolve, surrounded by the bodies of at least six or seven dead Collectors. He must have proved too much for them, forcing them to retreat and regroup with the rest of their cohort.

Blood streaked Philip's face and covered his brawling knuckles. It was other people's blood on his hands, no doubt. The knuckles were too callused to split any longer—they were more like hardened wood than flesh. Beathan remembered how it had felt to be on the receiving end of one of those fists on the night they had met in New York, the night this journey had begun.

Philip could hear his approach, since the fairy was making no effort to muffle the sound of his passage.

"Beathan." A grin flashed across the previously somber face. "I was worried about the two of you."

Beathan didn't respond, and he could only imagine what his face looked like. He felt tears forming in his eyes again. Philip's grin faded as he searched for Alayna. His eyes clouded in grief as he read the look of pain on his friend's face.

"No." Philip shook his head in denial. "No." This time the word was tinged with a desperate need to refute what he knew to be true.

Beathan swallowed. He didn't know what to say. Didn't really need to say anything. Philip knew.

"No," he said again, like it was the only word he could think of. Beathan nodded gently and stepped closer.

"Philip—," he began, trying to find words.

"*No!*" Philip roared, flinging away the extended hand of comfort. "*No!*" he roared again, clenching his fists and storing up enough rage to shake the mountains.

And then Philip lost control.

Beathan had seen his friend resolute. Beathan had witnessed Philip committed. He had seen him dangerous, angry, even furious. But nothing prepared him for the bestial grieving, the utter anguish that he was now exhibiting. If Philip had not still looked like a man— long hair just above his shoulders, plain yet somehow wild features, slender and deceptively strong frame—if Beathan had only been able to hear Philip from beyond the range of sight, he might have thought it was a troll. The roar that ushered forth from his mouth shook the very forest.

Beathan backed away. Something told him that right now was not the time for comfort. No, right now was the time to maintain a safe distance. He wasn't sure how trolls grieved, and right now Philip appeared to be more beast than man.

Philip ripped up a tree by the roots and smashed it into another. He cracked a boulder with his bare fists. Beathan turned and sprinted away, watching from a distance as Philip in all of his terrible, sorrowful fury laid waste to the clearing. Beathan might have worried that all the noise would attract the Collectors and alert them to their location. He might have worried about attracting the vampires or other creatures of the dark that roved the Transylvanian night. He might have, if it weren't for the fact that, right now, Philip was probably the most terrifying thing he'd ever scene. Anyone and everyone within a few miles of this place would avoid the sound of his fury the way forest animals avoided wildfire.

When Philip was finally done, kneeling in an exhausted heap in the middle of the clearing, it looked like a funnel cloud had ripped through that section of the woods. Stumps lay splintered, trees had been felled, roots were torn out. Philip stared ahead in a glassy-eyed stupor, gazing at Beathan picking his way carefully across the wreckage toward him.

When the fairy was finally close enough, he put a tentative hand on his friend's shoulder. Still not knowing what to say, he stood there in silence until finally Philip spoke.

"You're sure?" The pitiful lack of hope in his voice tore at Beathan's soul.

This time, his tears fell again. "I'm certain, mate. An' I'm so sorry, but there's no gettin' 'round the fact that Alayna's dead."

CHAPTER TWELVE

BEATHAN KEPT HIS HAND ON PHILIP'S SHOULDER. HE WASN'T entirely certain how calm his friend was. He looked exhausted, but the fairy knew all too well what had just caused the scene of mayhem in the clearing. Philip continued to kneel, so Beathan squatted down and rested near him, trying to allow his presence to communicate his support. Besides, what did one say at a time like this?

What must have been an hour passed. Still Philip sat slumped on the ground.

"Come on, mate, we've got t' get up now. Ya've been quiet for some time, and the Collectors are still out there. They might just feel a wee bit braver now that ya've calmed down some."

Philip's eyes flashed dangerously. "Let them come."

Perhaps he wasn't anywhere near as exhausted as he appeared. Beathan edged away surreptitiously. Philip's grief was making him unstable, and an unstable troll was beyond dangerous. He might not be fully troll, but he had enough of their attributes to give anyone pause.

As if on cue, a few bolts fired from the tree line, barely missing them. In fact, one grazed Philip's shoulder. Beathan swore.

Philip stood up, an uncaring look of wrath on his face, and stared at the darkened edge of the clearing. He roared again like he had before, an inhuman sound.

Beathan tried to tug him down behind the split boulder. "Get down, ya' fool. Ya' won't get a chance to avenge her if ya' take a bolt to the throat."

His friend shrugged off his warnings and his cautions. He roared again. This time, the sound was an unmistakable challenge. It rang out into the night, echoing off the trees. Philip stood there, unafraid, grieving, and altogether terrible to behold, framed by the moonlight. He roared his defiance again. It was too much.

Even the rational, methodical, precise tactics of the Collectors Guild could be goaded by such supernatural contempt. The remaining Collectors flooded out of the trees and sprinted the remaining distance toward Philip and Beathan, their dark cloaks and grim faces nearly as frightening as his friend's. Philip charged as well, and he met the group of attackers—no more than eight after the carnage of this night—a few yards away from the rock behind which Beathan had for some reason remained crouched.

Every instinct in him cried out for the fight. The fairy in him wanted revenge, the gypsy wanted fierce justice, and the friend in him wanted to fight back to back with Philip if this was to be their final stand.

But it wasn't necessary.

Beathan watched, mesmerized, as Philip dismantled the completely unprepared Collectors. Perhaps fueled by desire to pay back their own losses from this night, they had taken the bait and been goaded into an open field with a half-troll in a full rage. They had bitten off far more than they could chew.

Philip fought with a viciousness Beathan had never before witnessed. The fight was grisly. He decapitated one man with a blow of his fist. He ripped limbs from bodies and buried his teeth in the neck of another. They stabbed their weapons into him once or twice, but he ignored the wounds and fought on with an incredible strength that could only have been surpassed by the grief Beathan could see etched in every line of his contorted face. He howled and bellowed and smashed men to the ground with his hardened fists, never to rise again.

Finally, the two remaining Collectors cut their losses and broke. They ran, and Philip gave chase. Beathan watched as his friend disappeared into the trees following the two terrified men. The fairy was no longer even remotely concerned for his friend's safety. If anything, he just hoped that the two Collector's met with swift deaths. On second thought, he didn't care, as the memory of Alayna's vacant eyes returned to him. They deserved what they got. They had started this fight, they and the twisted organization they answered to. If there was one thing Beathan had learned from his time in captivity in the dungeons of St. Thomas Prison, it was that the Guild had become warped. The men following them this night and for the last few months might not be entirely aware of it—or maybe they were, there was no way to know— but it was nevertheless true. The Guild had changed; even a biased opponent such as Beathan could see that. Since when had the Guild decided to attack first and attempt capture second, if at all? That was not the protocol Philip had once described to him.

Beathan's mind wandered through these dark thoughts as he waited for his friend to return. Occasionally, he'd hear a roar from afar. At least one of the men must have run faster in his fear than Beathan had expected. Eventually, when Philip didn't return and the sky began to lighten incrementally, he decided that he had better go and follow his friend.

He entered the trees and followed an obvious path of smashed branches and twisted trunks. Philip was not a large man, but he was strong, and his rage-fueled might had allowed him to destroy what-ever was in his path rather than go around it. It was like the clearing behind, only in a line that stretched ever onwards into the woods. Beathan saw one of the men lying dead, a look of frozen horror upon the corpse's face, but the second body was nowhere to be found, and the path of destruction continued on. A few rays of grey light began to sift down through the dense branches. The path and the land around the fairy began to lighten, but the longer he went without finding Philip and the final Collector the more his sense of unease and apprehension began to grow. Some extra sense, something distinctly fairy, made him increasingly wary of what he was heading toward.

Finally, a sound pierced the early morning stillness that always precedes full light. It was the muffled sound of an animal. But it couldn't be an animal—Beathan hadn't seen or heard the slightest hint of any animal near Philip's ragged trail of broken branches and trees. Animals knew danger. They fled fire, they avoided predators, and clearly they knew to avoid an inhuman half-troll in a rage. No, the noise up ahead had to be Philip.

Beathan approached cautiously, picking his way forward on light feet. Something told him to activate his speed charm just in case; it never hurt to be prepared. As his ma had always said, "The bold are fearless, but the quick stay alive." Something told him that, right now, being quick wouldn't hurt one bit.

He picked his way through the woods along the damaged pathway until eventually he saw him. Philip was hunched over, his back to Beathan, making noises. At first the fairy wasn't sure what he was seeing, but as he continued to approach, the hairs on the back of his neck prickled. Blood was everywhere. Clearly, Philip had caught the final Collector, and there wasn't much left of him. The legs and arms had been torn free of the body. The head had rolled some few feet away from the torso, likely where it had landed after being swatted from its shoulders. Philip was crouched and holding something up to his face.

Beathan's heart raced. His skin prickled. Deliberately, he stepped on a twig. He trusted his instincts—they had kept him alive this long, and right now they were screaming at him that sneaking up on and startling Philip would be the worst possible idea.

The twig snapped crisply in the cold morning air. Philip's head swiveled around like a predator and, for a moment, Beathan wished he hadn't found his friend. His face was covered in blood. Whether he'd eaten some of the body or simply covered himself in blood by biting into the man's neck, Beathan wasn't sure. All he knew was that the eyes staring back at him—the angry, bestial eyes looking at him like he was a meal, not a friend—were not Philip's. They couldn't be, could they? Not even grief could change a person's nature that drastically, could it? Then again, Philip was part troll, and trolls were omnivores, opportunists that ate anything and everything they could get their hands on. Fairies included. Perhaps the maddening grief had triggered some latent instinct buried deep within Philip's psyche.

Beathan instinctively took a step back.

Philip flung the Collector's carcass away and took a step forward in Beathan's direction.

The fairy took another small step back. He held up his hands, not sure what the cautionary gesture would do. "Philip..."

Philip stepped forward menacingly. He bared his teeth as he advanced.

"Philip, mate. Come on. Snap out o' it!"

Beathan continued backing up while the now more trollish than ever Philip continued to advance.

All Beathan could think was that he was glad he'd trusted his instincts and activated the speed charm. It looked like he was going to need it. One more try first, though.

"Philip. It's me. Beathan. We know each other. Ya' have t' remember, mate. Try. Please, try. For me. For Alayna. She wouldn't want t' see ya' like this."

For a moment, just the tiniest of moments, something flickered behind the troll-induced madness clouding Philip's mind. Just as instantaneously it was gone, the insanity of overwhelming grief taking over again. He took another step forward and made an unintelligible noise. It was a guttural sound, a tone from some primordial language.

Beathan knew that it was time to run. He was a thief and a con artist: chicanery, mischief, and danger were second nature to him. As such, he knew exactly when it was time to flee and, through no fault of his own, that time was now!

He tapped into his speed charm, turned, and sprinted back down the path from which he had come. With an enraged roar, Philip leapt to the chase. As Beathan ran, he cast a glance over his shoulder. His companion was not a large man, yet somehow Beathan was more than certain that right about now Philip was the last thing he'd ever want to be caught by. Luckily for him, there was little chance of that. Philip might have the strength, endurance, and healing characteristics of his trollish heritage. He might plow his way through tree trunks, but he was not fast. Dogged, perhaps, but not quick. Trolls were relentless in their pursuit of a quarry, and Beathan fully expected that from his friend, but he also knew that his charms should allow him to stay ahead of Philip until he could figure out a way to free him from the madness that had changed him into whatever it was that was chasing him now.

So Beathan ran and, as he ran, he formulated a plan.

CHAPTER THIRTEEN

WHEN SHE OPENED HER EYES, SHE WAS INVERTED AND THE WORLD was spinning. She must have been draped over something. Alayna shook her head to try and clear it, but the slight motion sent a dizzying wave of pain streaking through her head. The more awake she became the more the ache grew. The pounding in her head accompanied the bumping ride of being draped over the back of a horse. No, she was lower to the ground. A mule, maybe?

Alayna turned her head again, forcing herself to push through the pain. Her surroundings were the same as they had been before she'd lost consciousness. The forest stretched endlessly all around the narrow path they were following. A figure walked ahead of her. A slender figure that had black hair with patches of grey. A figure carrying a cane that seemed less required for actual use and more of an affectation.

She tried to speak. Alayna wanted water right now more than anything she'd ever wanted. Her dry throat felt like she could pour a river down it and still not have it be enough. Finally, she managed to get a word out.

"Water." Parched and weary, the word came out weaker than she would have expected of herself.

The figure stopped, and the mule stopped also. Around turned The Alchemist.

"Ah, so you're awake, my dear. How very lovely." A light breeze ruffled his black and grey hair which stood on its end in some places but not others. His piercing gaze was unsettling as it came to rest fully upon her.

She gathered her voice. "Can I have a drink?"

"Why, of course you can." He grabbed a flask from his pack and tilted her head slightly upward so that she could drink without spilling too much. A few drops dribbled across her cheek, but the rest of the liquid made it into her gullet. It was lukewarm and had a faintly acrid taste for some reason, but it was probably the most delicious thing she'd ever tasted. She drank as much as The Alchemist would allow.

"Now then, that's enough." The man pulled away the flask. "My, you certainly were thirsty. But, then again, I suppose that's to be expected after a few days without a proper drink."

"A few days?" Alayna tried to put one hand to her head to soothe the aching, pounding feeling that was only increasing, but her wrists were tied. She kicked her feet and found that she was bound tightly there, also. Helplessly, she lay draped over the mule as The Alchemist bent down and spoke with her face-to-face.

His grin was not at all soothing. "Yes, days. You've been unconscious since that ruckus in the woods with those nasty Collectors. I say, they are quite determined to catch you and your friends. I suppose they don't take kindly to escapees."

Alayna tried to think coherently. Something was missing. She was forgetting something. And then it clicked. "How am I alive? I should be dead. I took a bolt to the chest."

"Ah, that. Well, let's just say that I dabble with more concoctions than just what is relevant to transfiguration and alchemy. Needless to say, I was able to pull you back from the brink. After all, I have a few elixirs up my sleeve. And I do mean literally." The Alchemist winked and flicked his wrist so that a small vial popped out of his sleeve and into his hand. He unstoppered the tiny bottle and poured a few drops into the flask from which Alayna had just been drinking.

"What is that?" Her voice was coming more smoothly now that her throat was coated with liquid.

"Just a concoction I've added to your water supply to ensure that you stay—how shall we put it—docile."

Alayna closed her eyes in frustration. That explained the water's acrid taste. Whatever it was, it was spreading a lassitude through her limbs. She felt ready to sleep.

Alayna fought to maintain consciousness. "Philip?"

"I have no doubt he survived. He threw quite a tantrum that night. Wicked fellow when he's angry, isn't he?"

She wanted to tell the man that he had no idea, that Philip would be coming for him next. She wanted to threaten him and see the fear form in his eyes, but the effort was too much. Whatever she had drunk was taking effect more swiftly as the minutes passed.

"Where are we going?" she managed to force the words out through thick lips and a wide tongue.

The Alchemist tilted his head. "We are going to a place where creatures like you are amassed."

"The Guild?"

"Not exactly, my dear. Not all those who gather are bound strictly by the code of the Collectors Guild. In fact, many are not, and they are quite a different sort. The kind who pay well for my services, although not usually *this* sort of service. I'm not in the habit of capture and sale, but you were too good an opportunity to pass up. I was following you and your friends, hoping to sneak in and steal back the vials of your blood when you were unsuspecting, but this is even better. A fresh creature like yourself, not bred but, rather, created. Oh, you'll fetch a magnificent price."

The Alchemist put an intimate hand on her head and stroked her hair, lulling Alayna to sleep.

"Where we are going is not a prison. No, it is more like a menagerie. You know the kind of thing I speak of, do you not?" His voice was practically crooning now, and her eyelids were too heavy to keep open. Then his voice changed and the crooning grew darker, "Only this menagerie isn't for animals. It's far less humane, and it operates from the shadows."

———

THE NEXT DAYS were a blur of consciousness and delirium. Whatever brew The Alchemist was putting in Alayna's water was potent enough to keep her in a constant state of unbalance. Not that she had many opportunities to stand up and try; he kept her draped across his mule like a slab of meat. Which, she supposed, was only necessary considering that she continually fell in and out of consciousness.

He fed her sparingly, enough to keep her healthy and help her body heal but not enough to allow her to gain the strength to fight back. Alayna had never felt quite so weak in her entire life, trussed up as she was like a captured animal. She hated it more than she'd ever known she could hate anything. She'd struggled at first, but the rope bonds had rubbed abrasions into her flesh and she'd quickly lost the energy. Whatever he was using to drug her was simply too powerful to overcome. It hurt to admit it, but until the concoction was completely out of her system, there was little she could do.

Alayna took up a different tactic. She spent every lucid moment she had trying to strike fear into her captor. Or, at the very least, a few ounces of worry. Unfortunately, her words didn't often seem to have the desired effect.

"You won't get away with this, you know," she murmured bitterly.

"Quite the contrary, my dear. I think I will. I've gotten away with far worse in my day."

"Philip will come for me."

"Yes, you would think so, wouldn't you? But then, where is he?" The Alchemist raised his shoulders in a mocking shrug. "He's had days to catch us, yet he is nowhere to be seen."

Alayna stayed silent. She had no ready retort.

"You know what I think? I think your hybrid lover got tired of you. Decided that rescuing you was too much work, too much risk. I'm betting that he figured this was just the easiest way out for him. I won't be surprised if he shows up at my door one day to offer his thanks." He winked in her direction.

Alayna spat at him and thrashed in her bonds. He chuckled evilly. "Tut, tut. How very unladylike of you. Although, where I'm taking you, that fire will raise your price somewhat. So, by all means, hold onto it. Stoke it, get angry. Philip abandoned you. That fairy saw me take you and yet he did nothing. I am going to sell you. Yes, that's it! Get angry!" The Alchemist spoke with a particular glee that drove Alayna wild. If only she had hold of one of her crossbows right now. What she wouldn't give to put a bolt through him.

She forced her anger down to a simmer. It wasted energy and gave him what he wanted. She calmed her face, put on a stoic mask of contempt, and stayed silent.

The Alchemist pouted. "Oh, don't stop on my account. You're as fiery as your hair. You shouldn't squash it." He poked her a few times with the tip of his cane, but still she stayed silent. She wouldn't give him the satisfaction of a response.

He sighed. "Very well. Just make sure you bring that gumption back out when it's time to sell you."

The rest of the day passed in silence. Well, silence on her part, at least. The Alchemist kept up a steady chatter about all kinds of things: what he would buy with the money he earned from selling her, what his favorite foods were, which concoctions he enjoyed making and which he did not, how much he loved her strawberry blonde hair, how her pointed ears made him feel things he hadn't felt in quite some time, and on, and on, and on, until she almost wished he would just feed her more of the drugged water. But when the time finally came, she felt only trepidation as the poison trickled down her throat. What use was it to offer resistance, though? She was bound and weak, alone without Philip who had, for some reason, left her to deal with this on her own. Her only hope was to go along with the man for now and wait for the right moment. She might only get one opportunity to escape, and this was not it. So she drank. Blackness spun in silkily and shut off her senses one by one, slowly but surely, until she slumped against the plodding animal's side and drifted off to The Alchemist's chattering even as she fell asleep.

When she awoke again, it was morning. He must have given her a heavy draught of the concoction this time, enough to knock her out for an entire night.

"Ah, awake, are we?"

Alayna groaned in assent. She had aches and pains she never imagined she'd have from having spent days slumped in an awkward position.

"Where are you taking me?" she asked, not for the first time.

"I told you. I'm taking you to the menagerie—the menagerie of shadows. Where folk such as yourself are...observed...in one capacity or another."

She made a sound of frustration. "Yes, but where is that?"

"Fret not your little head over it. We are still in the Carpathians. Not anywhere near my home, where I saved you, but in same mountain range nonetheless. Only much further north."

Alayna ignored his definition of the word 'saved'.

"How much farther?" she asked.

"A few days."

"You don't have to keep feeding me that drug, you know. It's not like I'll be able to untie myself. I'm sure you don't want to keep having to waste it on me. It must be expensive to find and secure all the ingredients."

"Clever girl, clever, clever girl. But not crafty enough!" The Alchemist giggled a bit, almost to himself. She couldn't help but think that he sounded a little bit mad, more mad than he had that night in his cabin.

"Well?" she prompted again for a response.

"No, no. Absolutely out of the question, my dear. I'll not be tricked by you. Besides, the induced sleep helps you heal more quickly. That wound of yours will be gone soon enough, much sooner than if I hadn't found you."

Again she ignored his self-indulgent thinking. She declined to point out that even if he had saved her, he'd only done so to turn a profit.

"Enough chitchat," he said, clapping his hands together briskly. The Alchemist picked her up with a strength that belied his apparent age and affectatious use of that cane before draping her over the saddle once more. "Off we go. The sooner we get going, the sooner we'll reach the manor."

He strutted out ahead of the mule and once again they began drudging north. Manor. It was the first clue that he'd dropped in all the days they'd been together. A rich person owned this menagerie, then. She supposed that was to be expected. Who else but the rich could afford to pay exorbitant prices for a pound of supernatural flesh? But still, it was something, and Alayna clung to it. She clung to anything, really, that even hinted at knowledge of what lay ahead, anything she could pour her mind over to try and see a way out of this predicament.

All of a sudden, she saw a flicker of motion, a darkness, out of the corner of her eye. She turned her head as best she could to see what it was, but nothing was there—only an empty trail right where the flicker had been. Alayna decided that the drugs must have been addling more than just her ability to remain conscious. Perhaps they were affecting her wits, as well.

But the flicker of shadow appeared and disappeared all day long.

It felt like someone she knew was standing just over her shoulder. She never saw it for more than a brief instant before it was gone again. Sometimes she even felt a prickle, like a presence, other times there was a familiarity to it that pricked her memory. But the sensations quickly faded, leaving her more puzzled each time it happened than the time before. Often, due to the delirium of the drug, she wasn't sure if it was even a physical shadow at all. Perhaps it was something mental instead, something only in her mind. It was maddening, especially because she couldn't shake it no matter what she tried. Alayna tried ignoring it without success, and then she paid particular attention to it. She tried to anticipate when and where she would see it and turn her head quickly to look where it might be next, jerking awkwardly in this direction and that, but to no avail. By the end of the day, she felt wearier than she had in a long time. She almost welcomed the blissfully terrifying oblivion of concoction-induced unconsciousness.

Tomorrow, she promised herself as The Alchemist forced the nightly dose of acrid water into her mouth. Tomorrow she would figure out what it was. And then it hit her, right before she fell asleep. It was so clear even in her fuddled state that she prayed she wouldn't forget.

It wasn't a flicker of motion. It was all in her head, but she wasn't crazy. She'd felt something similar to it before, that strange familiarity. It wasn't a dark flicker on the edge of her vision. That was only the physical manifestation of what she was experiencing internally, in her mind.

It was a shadowy residue on her consciousness, the residue of a familiar presence she had felt before.

CHAPTER FOURTEEN

DURING HER NEXT BOUT OF CONSCIOUSNESS, ALAYNA TRIED TO recall whatever crucial piece of information—that familiar memory—she had managed to remember the night before, but it was slow in coming. The drug that The Alchemist forced her to drink was difficult to shake, and even when she was awake her mind felt fuzzy and muddled. Nevertheless, Alayna set it as her objective for the day to make sure that she recalled whatever it was she had briefly remembered before passing out.

They set off at the same steady, plodding pace at which they had traveled for days now. However, her captor appeared in good spirits, better than he had been for almost the entire journey. That boded ill, and Alayna couldn't help but feel worried and continually vexed by her helplessness. It had been a long time since she had felt this way, certainly not since before her transition to join the ranks of the Elfas. Her human self might have felt like this occasionally, even frequently, but that version of herself was a slowly fading memory—not gone, never gone completely, yet receding away like a powerfully vivid dream which, over time, drifts away but is never fully forgotten.

At one point during the day, The Alchemist turned back and prodded her with his cane. "Today's the day." He seemed particularly eager, filled with anticipation.

Her spirits dropped. "So, we finally reach the menagerie today, I assume," she responded dutifully. She had learned that it was better to indulge The Alchemist and engage him in conversation than to ignore him. He didn't take kindly to being ignored. She had any number of welts and bruises on her body, inflicted by that wretched cane of his, to attest to that.

"Indeed, my dear. I get my pay day and secure the continued good favor of a powerful person. Not quite an ally, no, I wouldn't go that far, but someone I do not care to cross. Then I can return home to my workshop." He sighed with contentment at the thought.

"A good day for you. Not so much for me," she replied, trying to control the bitterness that infected her voice. It was hard not to let it show, though. Days draped over the saddle of a mule had worn sores on parts of her body.

"Don't sound so glum, girl. Perhaps there will be hope for you yet. After all, not every prisoner remains so indefinitely." He didn't sound particularly convincing.

She swallowed back a needlessly vicious retort and answered with as flat and uncaring a tone as possible, "Whatever you say, scientist. Besides, Philip will come for me."

As she said it, she couldn't help but feel like she had almost replaced Philip's name with another's. Now that was strange. Was that the key to the crucial bit of information that had been at the edge of her mind last night?

The Alchemist chuckled a short, wicked little laugh. "I think not. If he were coming, he'd already be here. No, he's abandoned you, my dear."

That was enough. Her composure broke and she spat curses at him, things she reserved for only the vilest of creatures, names she'd never called anyone before. A tiny part of her couldn't help but think that a portion of her vitriolic rage was due to the fact that, on some level, she agreed with what he had said. And it hurt. It hurt more than being captured and trussed up for sale. Philip couldn't have deserted her, could he?

The Alchemist laughed again. "There it is, there it is! That's the spirit I want you to demonstrate when it comes time for the sale. I'll get double if you carry on like that." The man's glee sickened her. She closed her mouth grudgingly.

She had to accept it: Philip wasn't coming for her. If he was, he'd have been there by now. Wouldn't he? She alternated back and forth between those conflicting thoughts.

And then it was there again, that shape hulking over her shoulder. This time her head felt clear enough, this time she recognized the truth. It wasn't actually over her shoulder, it was simply the sensation of proximity. Proximity to something, or someone, with whom she was familiar. Someone who'd left a mark on her. Someone with whom she was inextricably, vexingly, connected. And she knew exactly who that was. He was near. Perhaps not yet within a day's journey of her—if he were closer, there would have been no question in her mind of what it was she was sensing. But now the realization settled firmly in her more lucid state of mind. She was certain.

Azir! The hybrid vampire-Elfas was nearby. Alayna, surprisingly even to herself, couldn't help but feel relieved.

———

THE REST of the day passed in a daze. The Alchemist fed her another small sip of drugged water, just enough to put her under. He claimed that it was to make sure she was as rested and healed for their arrival as possible. Maybe that was true, but Alayna felt quite certain that it was also an insurance policy. He obviously wouldn't want her to escape the menagerie after he handed her over. If she did, he knew she'd likely head straight for his cabin to claim revenge. Therefore, the less she knew of her surroundings the better. Any advantage he could give those with whom he would be negotiating would surely be in his favor. So, even though he didn't say it, Alayna knew that this final drugging had more to do with his own safety than her health.

She stared augers into his coldly curious eyes as he forced the potion down her throat. When she awoke, it was nearing sunset. Azir was still a distant distraction in her mind. Close enough to sense—just barely—but far enough that he could be hours or days away. She wasn't sure.

They crested a hill and, as they did, Alayna looked down on what The Alchemist had referred to as a 'manor' the other day. It was a large estate, larger than anything she had seen during her previous life in the Americas. It was old and heavily fortified. It was just a large house, not a castle by any means, but it was surrounded with a tall, thick wall—likely the remnants of a feudal, more lawless past—a wall which the builders of the newer manor house had decided to keep intact.

It didn't look particularly grim. No moat, no sharpened stakes or high, crenellated turrets. Yet, there was a distinctly sinister feel to it. Perhaps it was the wail she heard piercing the twilight sky from far below. Or maybe it was the steadily burning bonfire that emitted a thick, black smoke from one corner of the grounds. Whatever the reason, Alayna was absolutely certain that, with the exception of perhaps her brief sojourn into the bowels of St. Thomas, there was nowhere else on earth that she'd been before and would be less likely to return.

"Good, you're awake. I wouldn't have wanted to cart in a bedraggled looking Elfas for sale. Need to prepare you for show, I do." The Alchemist pinched her cheeks until he was satisfied with what must have been a rosy hue. "Act lively, now."

She sneered at him and remained silent. She'd not go out of her way to help him in any way. The man sighed in frustration and led the mule down the hill. When they reached the gate in the outer wall, they were halted by a pair of sentries holding muskets.

"Who are you and what is your business?" a voice called down from atop the wall.

"Who I am is of no importance," The Alchemist answered cagily, "but our business is exactly that—business. With the Lady Helmsted, to be precise." The name jogged something in Alayna's memory, but it was hard to grasp hold of through the slowly receding fog caused by the drugs.

"She is occupied at the moment, and even if she weren't, I doubt she would associate with the likes of you." The guard jeered down at them. Alayna laughed, drawing a sharp look of spite from her captor. He couldn't deny that days on the road had only contributed to his normal disarray, though. He resembled nothing quite so much as a vagabond, hair sticking every which way and clothes soiled from the journey.

"She *will* see me," The Alchemist snapped back.

"No. Be on your way before we make you leave."

He let out a sigh of exasperation. "Fine, fine. I will give you my name. Title, really. Tell Helmsted that The Alchemist is here. Tell her that he has something particularly noteworthy to sell her. She'll want this." He put a possessive hand on Alayna's shoulder, and she cringed away in disgust at the momentary touch.

There was a whispered conference between the two guards before they reached some sort of conclusion. "Wait here. Word will be sent to her quarters."

"Where else would I go?" The Alchemist snapped in annoyance.

Only a few minutes passed before the guard came puffing back up to the top of the wall and again whispered something in his comrade's ear. Then the gates creaked open, and The Alchemist led the mule laden with Alayna into the compound. She could see the self-satisfied smirk on his face as he walked past the guards. The two men looked at him with expressions of increased caution. Apparently, his reputation had been recognized and was feared here. The Alchemist wore his title as a badge and strutted his way toward the manor with his head held high. Alayna, conversely, had never felt so ashamed.

It was a surreal sensation to be tied up and ogled by every guard they passed. If the menagerie was indeed here, then this couldn't be the first time they'd seen such a sight, yet she couldn't help but feel the color rise to her cheeks, no pinching necessary.

She swallowed her pride and forced herself to think of what Philip would do in this situation. Regardless of where he was or why he hadn't come for her, he had taught her well. He would appraise his situation, gather intelligence on where he was and who his captors were. So Alayna kept sharp eyes peeled around the compound as they moved slowly toward the manor.

There were more guards than she would have expected at a house of this size, even as big as it was. They amassed a small army, and many of the guards had a distinctly familiar feel to them. A set of the shoulders, a specific type of gait, the way they held their weapons. She couldn't quite put her finger on what that familiarity was. She hadn't spent much time around military men before, but that was what they appeared to be.

And then she saw it.

One man's cloak billowed in the breeze, revealing a belt laden with an assortment of weapons, including stakes. Two, to be exact. He was a Collector. They all were, or at least most of them. That was why they were so familiar to her; she had seen their ilk before. She'd traveled beside one for many months now. They resembled Philip—more the Philip she had known before her transition than who he was now, but the resemblance was still clear. It sent a shiver down her spine.

Why would The Alchemist be dealing with the Guild? Or the opposite: why would the Guild deal with *him*? For some reason, she couldn't help but feel that his interaction with the Collectors was an extremely ominous sign. Leaving the mule, they were led into the house and directed by a guard—another Collector, from the way he carried himself—toward the reception room in which Lady Helmsted waited. Upon entry into the main hall, Alayna's feet were untied and the bond was replaced by a looser set of manacles that made walking possible, albeit difficult.

They reached the room and another guard opened the door; Lady Helmsted was nothing if not well attended and protected. The door opened soundlessly—not a creak. It swung open to reveal a woman waiting for them in what looked to be a study. She was leaning against a desk, dark of hair and possessing sharp, hawkish features. There was a power to her demeanor, to her stance. She commanded people and they obeyed. Lady Helmsted was not old. Late thirties, perhaps, with only a few wrinkles and no grey in her hair. She wore divided skirts for riding, and a belt at her hip held a sheath filled with a slender dueling sword, the type one would find at court. On the other hip hung a firearm—a revolver. Not common among the Guild normally, although Alayna had certainly seen more here than she would have expected from a Guild compound. The Collectors did not favor firearms. They were too loud and, when fired, would draw attention. Collectors fought in cities and towns, and they needed to capture or kill their prey without the general populace becoming aware of their presence or the existence of the supernatural, lest mass hysteria break out—the type of hysteria that had only narrowly been averted when The Great Transformation had taken place some decades ago. Firearms were also slower to reload, and speed was often crucial when dealing with a variety of deadly creatures. So, the weapon at Lady Helmsted's hip and those present in the manor's compound spoke of Guild members who were not afraid to break from tradition. Again, Alayna felt that such a fact boded ill.

She looked into Lady Helmsted's eyes and saw cunning, ambition, and an utter disregard for anything opposing her wishes. Alayna hadn't often felt fear, not after receiving so much training from Philip, yet something about the woman sent a chill down her spine.

The lady's sharp gaze bore down on her, and Alayna did her best not to wilt. She swallowed her fear and focused. *Observe*, she told herself. *Do what Philip would do*. She quashed the bitterness she couldn't help but feel at the fact that he wasn't there beside her. So much for 'through thick and thin'. A small warning flickered in the back of her mind, some distant thought that this wasn't like her. That normally she'd be glad he was safe and away from this danger. That she would never jump to such conclusions without giving Philip the benefit of the doubt. He'd earned that consideration, hadn't he? Why was she thinking this way? Just as quickly, though, the thoughts were gone and she shoved them aside with an uncommon ruthlessness.

No, he had left her. She was alone in this. Nobody was going to save her but herself.

CHAPTER FIFTEEN

"How very brave of you to come here. You're not exactly welcome, you know." Lady Helmsted spoke with a clipped but very proper accent denoting her British heritage. A foreigner operating in the east. She peered—not unhappily, but also not kindly—at The Alchemist.

The man in question spread his hands with a slight grin on his face. "I have something you want."

Her eyes narrowed. "And what is to prevent me from taking it from you and sending you away with nothing—if I let you leave at all?" Alayna hated the way they spoke of her as if she were a thing rather than person.

The lady's eyes were blades as they pierced into The Alchemist. To the old man's credit, he stood up under the gaze much better than Alayna figured she herself would have.

"We both know I'm under the protection of someone that you don't want to cross—not with your beautiful home this close to Transylvania." He paused with that same self-satisfied smirk on his face that he'd had at the gates when his title had granted them entrance. "Besides, it would be bad precedent. Word would spread. No one else would sell to you."

Lady Helmsted continued to stare, but Alayna noted just the slightest lessening of that raptor-like gaze. Regardless, she wasn't ready to relinquish her stance yet. "We tend to procure our own samples, Alchemist." Her eyes flicked to Alayna briefly, indicating just what she meant by 'samples'.

Alayna's gut twisted. Both of these people sickened her. Suddenly, she was overwhelmingly glad that she was no longer human. Humans, by and large, were the most nasty, duplicitous creatures around. At least a monster was upfront about its desire to eat you.

"Not always. You don't procure every one of your samples, and I have something you want. Trust me." The Alchemist spoke with all the self-assurance he possessed.

It seemed his confidence was enough to win the argument, at least for now. "Very well. We shall deal. But first, tell me: I've always been curious about why exactly He grants you protection." Lady Helmsted had lost her side of the argument but was pressing to retain whatever advantage she possessed—in this case it was a search for information. Even information that appeared trivial could aid one's cause. Another lesson from Philip.

The Alchemist responded with no reluctance to hide the details of his arrangement with his protector. "I do a few things for Him. *Vital* things. People find their way to me who would otherwise avoid His kind. I sometimes procure samples of their blood as payment—a tribute you might say—and funnel delicacies His way to taste. I also make a number of elixirs, among which is a particularly difficult and time-consuming concoction that allows one to walk in the sun. It's not long lasting, but our friendly Dracula has a yearning to strut about during the day. More than most of his kind, at least. In other words, I find a need or a desire and then make myself indispensible."

Lady Helmsted turned up her nose. "I find vampires repellent. I don't favor any creatures that are so consumed by such a base emotion as the desire to feed. That, and they are far too messy for my taste. Better to kill them and be done with it than have to deal with them." Her casual discussion of killing vampires indicated that she had likely served as a Collector herself in the past. Alayna made a mental note of that little fact. The lady wore her weapons well enough to support such a detail.

Lady Helmsted stepped forward and brushed the hair back from one of Alayna's ears. Alayna leaned away slightly as she did so, but the look in Helmsted's eyes froze her in the act. She had to pick her battles. A light touch and a gaze at one of her ears was not reason enough to incense her soon-to-be captor. Alayna refused to think of either of the two humans as an owner.

The lady clucked her tongue in disappointment. "Please, Alchemist, an Elfas? Even if I wanted one of her kind, I could easily get one myself. Don't think you can play me for a fool!"

"Easy, Lady Helmsted, there's more to her than meets the eye."

She raised one eyebrow skeptically. "Really?"

The Alchemist grinned like the fox he was. "Indeed. You are of course privy to the details of the debacle that occurred in your organization last winter in New York?" *Confirmation*, Alayna thought: so she *was* a Collector herself. It stood to reason. Why else would she be able to command Collectors?

The lady turned to look at him sharply, a dangerous look on her face—a wary look. The Alchemist paid no heed to the expression.

"Well, a certain wayward Guild member—not entirely unlike yourself who is operating somewhat outside of normal Guild proceedings—took it upon himself to try and recreate The Great Transformation."

"Martin Astori," Helmsted murmured guardedly.

He inclined his head. "Indeed."

"How do you know this?" she asked.

"I have ways of gathering information. I take many different forms of payment for my services, and sometimes that payment comes in the form of whispers. At any rate, Astori attempted to ignite another Great Transformation."

"But he failed!" she interjected sharply.

"He did," The Alchemist conceded. "His attempt was thwarted by another of your own."

"Not one of ours," Helmsted responded. "He deserted."

Alayna decided to stay silent and not point out the hypocrisy of that statement coming from another Guild member who was clearly working outside of Guild protocol.

"Yes, Astori failed," The Alchemist continued, ignoring her statement. "Well, mostly. He failed in his attempt, except for a solitary success." Recognition of what he was saying broke on Lady Helmsted's face.

"You don't mean—," she said, almost breathless with excitement. It was a strange look on her: a thin, excited crack in her regal façade.

"I do, indeed. This one," The Alchemist petted a hand down

Alayna's hair, "this one is fresh. Freshly made, created by magic rather than born. Magic that can only be likened to The Great Transformation."

"I don't know when the last time was that I heard of a creature being created in such a fashion—outside of the normal ways of turning. Especially a creature from a race that doesn't even turn humans into one of their own." Lady Helmsted took a step closer to Alayna until she was a few mere inches away from her face. Her breath smelled of chamomile.

The Alchemist had a satisfied grin on his face. "You want her, then?"

"Of course," Helmsted breathed. "She is...exquisite. Truly one of a kind. You will, of course, be well compensated."

"That is all I hope for," he said happily. "Oh, and by the way, make sure she doesn't escape. She's fiery, this one, and she'll come straight for me if she gets away, I know it."

Helmsted shot him a look of scorn. "We don't *have* escapees."

The Alchemist shrugged. "So you say, but don't underestimate this one. She was with your deserter when they broke out of St. Thomas. The Elfas will be a handful, believe me."

She looked at Alayna again, as if seeing her for the first time. "Really? She was with him? Interesting. She does not look particularly adept at combat, but perhaps that will be of use at some point." The way she mentioned combat sent a chill through Alayna's body. There was an unspoken agenda here. There was something about her captivity, some crucial piece of information that she was still missing.

"I thought so myself. She will make a great addition to your menagerie in a variety of ways," The Alchemist agreed.

"You can go now, Alchemist. Name your price on the way out and my people will pay it." The dismissal in her tone was clear. She had a new toy to play with now and was tired of the man's presence. He nodded his head to her in the slightest of bows, the only deferential move he'd made since arriving, then turned and walked out of the room, leaving Alayna alone with Lady Helmsted.

"I have amassed quite the assortment of inhuman creatures here. You will be a nice addition."

"And what, exactly, will be my purpose here?" Alayna asked, finally speaking.

Helmsted leaned toward her, all subtle yet haughty menace. "My pets do many things. Some are simply observed, others perform in a variety of different ways. Some are punished. And some...interact with one another." She left unspoken the particular ways in which those creatures who were held captive here 'interacted'. Alayna swallowed back her fear, not for the first time since meeting the domineering Lady Helmsted.

"I see. You will find that I am not easily cowed. When the day comes that I make my escape, you should be worried." She put as much venom as she could into the calm, quiet statement.

Lady Helmsted didn't grow angry or strike her. Instead, she looked at Alayna with an expression of near pity. "The life you had is over. This is your new life. It would be best for you to embrace it sooner than later. It will go easier for you if you do—well, that is, for as long as this new existence of yours lasts."

The words sounded like nothing so much as a pronouncement of doom to Alayna's delicately pointed ears.

CHAPTER SIXTEEN

ON THE FIRST DAY, WITHIN THE FIRST FEW MINUTES OF CAPTIVITY at the manor, Alayna tried to escape. It was a bad idea. They walked out the back of the building and stopped just outside of what could only be described as a holding pen. Two guards opened her cage's door and stepped inside with her. The second her shackles were off, and before the cage door could swing shut, she slammed her forehead into the first guard's nose and sent the second sprawling with a vicious kick to the knee. Then she was off, racing for the wall and a glimpse of freedom. She did not get very far. In hindsight, she probably should have waited, been patient for her first chance to escape. As it was, the poorly executed attempt earned her a beating.

Worse than the bruises, however, was the fact that her actions had tipped her hand. The guards now knew what she was capable of doing. They didn't see her golden-red locks or exotic features, they ignored her tipped ears and slim frame—all things that, as a female, she might have been able to exploit with mostly men guarding her. No, they now saw her as the threat she was rather than a pretty little Elfas girl. Philip had trained her well. They might not know how she had come by her training, but they now knew that she was not a normal Elfas. Her kind were not the most warlike of species, but these Collectors had found out that she was dangerous and treated her as such. It would make her next attempt more difficult. She swore as they dragged her back to her pen, bruised and a little bloody.

Lady Helmsted was waiting. Apparently, she had been notified of the situation with her newly acquired prize.

"Do you feel better now?" Helmsted asked coolly, looking at her the way a hawk looks at prey.

Alayna was tossed unceremoniously onto the dirty floor, and the door grated shut and locked with a *click*. She pulled herself up off the ground and wiped some blood from her mouth. She stood near the bars and stared out at Helmsted, not answering.

The lady waited a few more moments until she realized that she would get no response. Finally, she spoke. When she did, it was with a terse, succinct voice, listing rules she had no doubt given many of her new captives: "You are surrounded by armed men, more than you can count. Your old life is over, your life here begins now. It is best if you accept that. One mistake is all you get. You have made that mistake already, and are now without any mistakes left to your credit. The beating you just received is no more than you deserved and far less than you will get for the next escape attempt—or any other form of disobedience, for that matter. The next time you will be made to seriously regret your actions. Are we clear?" Her piercing gaze burned into Alayna's eyes. Her look, her tone, demanded an answer. It was time to play the role of a good, little, subdued captive.

"Yes," Alayna muttered.

"Good," Helmsted continued in her clipped tone. "You will do what I say when I say it. That goes for any of the other guards, as well. The Alchemist asked a hefty fee for you, and I paid it. You are mine now," she emphasized each word of the last sentence with a steely finality.

Alayna swallowed, allowing the fear to leak in just a little. Still, she remained quiet.

"You learn your place already." There was a hint of satisfaction in Lady Helmsted's voice and expression. "You are here for my pleasure. If I want to simply observe you, like an animal in a normal menagerie, I will. If I wish you to fight with another of my possessions, then you will. Without question."

At that last statement, Alayna glanced around, really seeing her surroundings for the first time. She was in the midst of a sea of cages, filled with all sorts of supernatural creatures. It was like an above-ground version of St. Thomas, only somehow even more sinister, if that were possible, due to the fact that it was clearly a rogue operation. Helmsted's discussion with The Alchemist had certainly alluded to the fact that she was not necessarily adhering to the Guild's policies.

Alayna nodded. "Yes, I understand. I can rot away in this cage for your pleasure, or I can fight when you tell me too."

"No." Lady Helmsted's voice cracked like a whip. "You will do *whatever* I say, not only those two things. Do you hear me? If I want you to fight, you'll fight. If I want you to sit here and pose for me, then you will. If I decide to breed you, then you'll couple with whomever I please. You will do as I say. Is that clear?"

Alayna fought to keep the revulsion she felt from her voice. "Yes." She imbued as much of her own steel into the statement as possible before realizing that was counterproductive to having her captors lower their guard. She subsequently dropped her gaze and stared at the ground as dejectedly as she could manage without seeming overly false.

Lady Helmsted kept her hard gaze on Alayna, lingering for a few long moments before she appeared satisfied that her words had struck home. She nodded in satisfaction and then turned to stride away forcefully. Alayna believed that the woman must do just about anything and everything with force. She hated Helmsted after only a few minutes of knowing her, hated her more than she'd ever hated anyone. But the lady had also managed to acquire Alayna's grudging respect, the type of respect a person has for an enemy whom they cannot wait to kill with their bare hands.

She watched the woman depart, stepping purposefully along the path between cages, walking past a captive werewolf here, a vampire there, and any other supernatural creature she'd kept for the menagerie rather than sending them to an officially sanctioned Guild prison. Then she was gone, and Alayna was left staring out of her rusty, barred cage at the newest pair of guards set to patrol this corner of the menagerie.

She couldn't help it. She dropped the subdued act and stared them straight in the eyes. "I'm going to escape, and when I do, you had better hope you're not the ones who get in my way." She poured all the menace, all the confidence she had left into her words. She said it more for herself, to help her believe that this nightmare would end one day, than out of any need to intimidate her captors.

The Collectors just stared at her stoically before turning away, each in a different direction, to march their patrol of whatever portion of the grounds they had been assigned.

The next time had to be the right time. Her free pass was already used up, according to Helmsted. Her next attempt at fleeing would have dire consequences should she fail. If nothing else, Alayna believed Helmsted about that threat. No, the attempt had to be well-thought-out, planned. Once again, she found herself reverting back to Philip's training from over the past few months. She began to scan her surroundings. Observe, watch, and note the details. She could almost hear him speaking those words, a whisper in the back of her mind. She had to be patient and prepare. The next escape attempt had to be her last.

———

ALAYNA DID NOT TAKE her own advice. She tried to escape again on the third day of her captivity. For all her thoughts of patience and planning, all the promises she'd made to herself that she would plan and then execute an informed getaway, she couldn't help but snap. One of the guards made an obscene comment and gestured toward her when he stepped into her cage as he brought her morning meal.

She promptly broke his arm and then choked the second guard to death, bursting forward like quicksilver and lithely wrapping herself around him like a constrictor, holding his throat in the death grip that Philip had showed her, the kill hold Collectors used sometimes to subdue a larger, stronger opponent. The man thrashed as he strug- gled for air, and Alayna could honestly say she'd never been gladder to take a life. She promptly felt sick at having such a thought, but she shoved it aside. There was no time for self-recrimination. She sprinted through the paths between cages, but Lady Helmsted had apparently doubled the guard in her area of the menagerie—it seemed as though Alayna's charade of being subdued had not fooled her at all. There were many more Collectors than there had been during her first attempt, and she couldn't get far with only her bare hands as weapons. She badly injured another guard by putting a finger through his eye but, all in all, the fight was short, messy, and mostly in her captor's favor. She was trussed up with rope and carried back to her pen, struggling all the way.

As a whole, the escape attempt was even less successful than the first, and it put Helmsted in a fury. Alayna was promptly punished by receiving another beating, this one with canes and fists, and much more severe than the first. She also had three of her fingernails pulled off, one for each of the injured guards. Her screams did nothing to drown out the pain, and the resident torturer—she could think of no other, more clever, name for the Collector who administered her punishment—left her in a crumpled heap in her pen, ruing her foolish attempt at escaping, cursing Philip for not coming for her and Beathan for abandoning her in the fight. The bout of pain forced thoughts of despair that she'd struggled to keep at bay to come to the forefront. Alayna fought to push them away again but couldn't stop her anguished thoughts.

The only thing that gave her any sense of hope was the small, dark, presence of Azir in the corner of her mind. He was still growing closer. Today he felt especially close. Alayna wondered if he was coming for her. But no, she didn't know how this residue between their minds worked, if it functioned the same way on both ends. She had to assume that it didn't. It could be nothing more than coincidence that he was in this territory. It was not far from the vampire strongholds of Transylvania, after all. And he was a vampire—a hybrid vampire-Elfas, to be sure, but still a vampire. No, she was alone in this. She had to operate on that assumption until she learned otherwise.

Still, she couldn't help but feel a small sense of comfort in his familiar presence, someone she knew did not want her tortured, would never want her captured. Azir may be many things—most of them less than what would traditionally be called 'good'—yet somehow, she was certain that he would never wish this suffering upon her. Perhaps her certainty regarding the issue was influenced by the growing awareness of his presence both nearby and in her mind. It even felt like Azir's residue was beginning to affect the way she thought; how she viewed him, herself, and others. At least, she might have thought that if it didn't seem impossible. Even a stain on her mind couldn't actually make her think and see the world differently, could it?

Alayna forced herself to regroup after her first ever bout of torture. She pulled herself together, or at least tried to. She started by wiping away her tears, but that just smeared blood from her hands onto her face, so she quit trying. She simply sat up and leaned against the back wall of the enclosure. *Time to think*, she told herself. What would Philip do in this situation? He would observe. She forced herself to go back to his methodical training.

Start with my immediate surroundings, she thought. So she began with her pen for what seemed like the hundredth time in the last few days of her captivity. It was a square, ten-foot by ten-foot cage, spacious by some standards but not clean. Refuse and remnants of the former occupant remained, scents that most people would pay to avoid assailing their nostrils. The pen consisted of one solid wall at the back and three rusty, barred walls on all other sides. A pathway stretched out like a small road in front of her cage across which another line of cages stretched like rickety houses on a nightmare block. Those in her own line, on the left and the right, were only a few feet away, hardly separated at all, really. The left enclosure was empty, but on the right huddled another form. It was a creature that Alayna wasn't familiar with—at least, it didn't seem so—but, truthfully, it was hard to tell given that it was curled in upon itself. She might have tried to speak to it, to find out what it was and learn more of her surroundings if it hadn't looked more dead than alive. Besides, there was no guarantee that it could speak her language. Not all creatures communicated the way some species did, humans included. Again, she was on her own. The cages across the narrow road were too far away to reach without yelling and attracting the guards' attention.

Screams and moans rang out occasionally. The sounds of struggle and fighting came from somewhere in the distance. Pain coursed through Alayna's body as she stood and wandered the length of her cage, craning her neck to see as far down the path as she could in either direction. Her body ached from the beating; it was a good thing her training with Philip had included a lot of physical contact. He had never held back—well, not much—she had made him promise not to. Because of that, she had gone to sleep bruised and sore many a night. Her fingers, however, burned with a fire that was much harder to ignore. Just thinking about it made it worse, like simply looking at her fingers made her feel like the nails were being torn off all over again, one by one. She stifled a moan. They would not break her!

Even as that determined thought steeled her soul, a tear leaked out. She shook it away. There was no time for weakness. She spent the remainder of the day observing guard patterns and actions, watching how they patrolled, how they interacted. Any piece of information could help. All the while, she felt Azir's presence grow in her mind. It grew so much that she even began to hope. He was heading for her like a bloodhound on a scent. He *had* to sense her the way she sensed him. Alayna even allowed herself to hope that perhaps he'd figure out a way to get her out of here. After all, she had been party to the endeavor that had freed him from St. Thomas. She and Philip had broken in looking for Beathan and had ended up freeing the hybrid vampire as well due to a promise the fairy had made to Azir. It could be said that he owed Alayna, couldn't it? Perhaps he was coming to pay that debt. Whatever the reason, it was more than she could say for some people.

When twilight fell, her earlier hope deserted her completely. She heard a sound and looked up to see two guards dragging a limp form between them. The unconscious body was dumped into the empty cage on Alayna's left. She watched them kick his body once or twice and spit on it for good measure. Collectors particularly disliked vampires. To be fair, there were not many races outside of their own that really enjoyed interactions with the blood-hungry beings, but with Collectors it was an especially sore spot. Vampires were one of the more dangerous foes that the Guild faced on a regular basis, owing to the fact that it was easier for a vampire to inhabit areas of civilization than other supernatural creatures. Or, at least that was how Philip had explained it.

Azir groaned as the guards kicked him, but he did not regain consciousness. His face was bloody, like Alayna's. She waited until the guards had locked him up and strode away before she moved over to the side of her cage nearest his pen.

"Azir!" she whisper-shouted once, then twice. She raised her voice and tried again, but still the vampire did not wake.

Alayna settled down on the left-hand edge of her enclosure. It appeared as though she would have to wait to learn his reason for capture.

CHAPTER SEVENTEEN

"Captured by cursed Collectors again."

Alayna, having slipped into a doze, was startled awake by the vampire's disgusted voice.

She wiped sleep from her eyes. How long had she been napping? She didn't realize she had voiced the question until Azir answered.

"How should I know, Alayna? I only just regained consciousness, and there you were slumped against the bars next to me." His normally refined voice carried a slight harshness, a rasp that was likely due to exhaustion. The eastern accent was still thick. They were in his region of the world now.

She shook her head once to clear it. "Are you all right?" The question seemed silly as soon as she asked it aloud, but it did have to be asked. How could he be all right, though? They were both prisoners, captives to a heartless Guild leader. Neither of them would be all right until they were free again.

Azir rubbed his hands along the sides of his head, combing back the dark, silken strands of his shoulder-length hair. It held the appearance of a habitual act. "Well enough, I suppose, Elfas. Are you?" His piercing, predatory eyes carried a hint of concern.

How must she look right now? Likely as bad as or worse than he did. "Fine," she answered.

Azir just nodded back to her. "How were you taken?" he changed the subject, probing for information.

"Collectors have been chasing us since we took our leave of you in England. They finally caught up with us. We were separated—Philip thought to lead them away from me, but it didn't quite work out that way." She left the rest vague. She had no desire to relive the moment of black oblivion that had followed the two bolts striking her body. It seemed too similar to how she imagined death felt. A shiver trickled down her spine unbidden. Besides, the tale carried a certain bitterness with it. Having Azir right there in front of her made it easier than ever to ask what might previously have been hard to imagine— why Philip hadn't come for her, as well.

"You mean, when you abandoned me in enemy territory, left me unconscious and unaware, easy pickings for the Guild to snatch up again?" Azir's tone carried a bitterness that she was not expecting. He seemed the type to understand pragmatic decisions. It wasn't like they could have lugged his unconscious form with them as they fought the Haunts—the supernatural guards of St. Thomas—or when they left to find a ship.

"You attacked Philip. What did you expect?"

"Technically, he attacked *me*."

"You goaded him and you know it. In my opinion, you got what you deserved." She almost made it sound like she believed it. Almost. It wasn't quite enough to fool the vampire, however.

Azir smirked slightly. "You nearly sound as if you truly believe that statement. Nearly. What, do you regret leaving me to die?"

"We didn't leave you to die!" Alayna's guilt surged. "Beathan spelled you invisible so that the unsuspecting eye would pass right over you. You're here, aren't you? So it must have worked."

He relented. "Fair enough. What the hell was Philip thinking, leaving you like he did? I never would have left your side."

Alayna didn't like his tone or what he was implying. "It wasn't like that. He was trying to draw them away." She couldn't quite make herself jump as vociferously to Philip's defense as she usually did. Something in her mind just didn't seem to want to fight for him as fiercely as she once had. She felt she should know why that was, but she couldn't quite put her finger on it.

Azir smiled condescendingly. "I'm sure he did."

"He *did*." Once again, she couldn't muster the desire to speak on

Philip's behalf. What did it matter, anyway? He wasn't here. *They* were. Maybe Azir was right; maybe if Philip had stayed with her she wouldn't be in this predicament.

She looked at Azir. There was dried blood on his face from a cut on his cheek and another on his scalp. He looked tired but healthy enough overall. There was a hollow elegance to his features, and his skin was like many of the vampires she'd seen—pale as any creature of the night. Yet, there was an unmistakable attractive quality about him. He smiled, noticing her gaze.

Alayna blushed and looked away, then grew angry with herself for blushing. She decided to broach a new subject: "So, how did you get captured?"

"Why, by trying to rescue you, of course." He smiled charmingly.

"Great rescue attempt."

Azir's face darkened slightly, but he kept his composure despite her needling. "It is the thought that counts, correct?" The vampire slowly got to his feet, and if he had been a piece of furniture, Alayna was sure that he would have creaked.

"Are you very sore?" she asked.

He winced as he limbered himself. "I have had worse."

"So, you were trying to rescue me..." she prompted.

He nodded curtly and then proceeded to tell his story in that overly proper eastern accent of his, accentuating every single syllable to make sure he pronounced each word perfectly and correctly.

"Yes, I have been sensing your presence for days now." He looked her way to see if she understood what he meant by 'sensing', and after seeing that she did, he continued, "As soon as I started sensing you, I noticed that something was different. It did not feel like before, when we were in England. You felt wrong, somehow. I sensed... extreme discontent. When I reached the manor and you felt so close, I knew that you must be inside. After some observation, I saw Collectors everywhere, heard the screams from within the walls of this forsaken place, and knew that you were likely not here of your own accord."

"So you decided to rescue me?"

He nodded, his straight, black hair falling forward to obscure part of his face as he did so until he shook it back out of the way.

"You only decided to rescue me after you got here?" she pressed again.

"That is what I said," he responded, a hint of annoyance in his voice now.

"Well then, why were you following me before that? What did you plan on doing before you realized I was being held prisoner?"

Her question caught the vampire off guard, and it was his turn to look uncomfortable. Azir cleared his throat. "The answer to that question is of no importance now. We are here, we are prisoners, and that is what matters."

She wanted to argue with him but couldn't disagree in good faith. More pressing matters were at hand. "How did you end up captured?"

"I conducted my reconnaissance, and afterwards scaled a back wall of the grounds for entry. Once inside, I was seen relatively quickly and, well, the rest is history. I did manage to put a few in the ground before they caught me," he said with vicious satisfaction.

"That was a foolish plan." Alayna shook her head in disbelief. "You should have waited for night to cover your venture. You would have had a better chance of getting in and getting me out undetected."

Azir gritted his teeth in frustration. "You think I do not know that? What, am I a child?"

"Well, why didn't you wait for nightfall?"

"Your...presence in my mind...changed. It felt like you were in extreme pain, like you were being tortured. I did not think that I could afford to wait. I did not *want* to wait." He spoke slowly, as if the words had to be dragged out of him.

Alayna softened her tone. "Well, we are here now. There's no changing the situation. Besides, I was caught and then sold—an even worse way to arrive."

Azir nodded curtly. "Coming in daylight did give me one advantage: I was able to see much of what they do here."

"And?" she asked. Alayna had come in trussed and bound for sale before being taken directly to her pen. She hadn't had a chance to see anything of her own accord.

The vampire-Elfas hybrid grimaced. "Nothing good, I am afraid."

"That bad?"

He nodded. "In some ways, this den of flesh is nearly as bad as St. Thomas. Nearly. And yet in others, it is worse. In the English prison, conditions were terrible, and the guards did what they wanted— broke bones, cut you, bled you. It was a vile hell. But here, I fear our kind are not only captives. We are also here for exhibition, something which can often be an indignity far worse than pain or death."

"What do you mean by 'exhibition'?" she asked nervously. That sounded ominous.

"I saw fighting pits, viewing cages, torture pens, and even what appeared to be a breeding kennel before I was overtaken," Azir answered, spitting to show his disgust. "These Collectors are different than most with whom I have crossed paths. Regular Collectors, bastards though they may be, have at least one thing in their favor. As much as I find it annoying, their self-righteous attitudes at least ensure some sort of reasoning behind their actions. Our current captors possess no such protective sensibilities toward their own kind. They are Collecting for profit or perhaps entertainment, not to protect humans. They are bending their own rules, and that makes them very dangerous," he finished with an ominous look.

Alayna swallowed. Everything in her screamed to be free of this place. She wanted to thrash at the bars of her cage, she wanted to put every ounce of her strength into fighting to gain her freedom, but she had to be smart. After two failed attempts at escape, she needed to make sure that the next succeeded. She couldn't afford another failure. Lady Helmsted had made that abundantly clear.

"What do we do?" she finally asked.

"I will tell you what I cannot wait to do—eat some of those damn Collectors!" Azir growled. Alayna almost flinched. She sometimes forgot just who and what Azir was: a vampire. The connection between their minds—the leftover residue from when Azir had contacted her from afar while transitioning from Elfas into vampire during his first captivity—masked that understanding at times until he said or did something to remind her. To remind her that he literally *ate* people. Drank them would perhaps be a better way of putting it.

His fangs gleamed as he spoke, and Alayna could see the anticipation in his eyes. She forced herself to look at him, at the being whose mind occupied a tiny portion of her own.

"Planning vengeance won't help us escape," she told him.

Azir's lip curled into a sneer. "It may not help you, but it helps me focus on why I want to escape."

She ignored the statement and was about to push onward with planning some sort of escape when he quickly motioned for her to be silent. She looked over her shoulder, following the Azir's eyes, and saw a group of guards approaching. Five of them. When they arrived at the two cages, they stopped and stared.

"Friends, are we?" a tall guard asked in a monotone voice, glancing back and forth between Azir and Alayna. He appeared to be the leader and spoke again when neither of them answered. "Lady Helmsted wants you," he directed his comment toward Azir.

"She is more than welcome to come in here and Collect me if she likes," the vampire said sinuously, "or you can. You want to come in right now, don't you?" His voice took on a silken quality that carried with it a compulsion, caressing the guards' minds. One of the Collectors in the back took an involuntary step forward before another put a hand on his chest and snapped him out of the mesmerizing trance.

It might have worked on the single guard, but the lead guard stared at Azir uncaringly. "We are Collectors. Do you think we would have been cleared for active duty if we hadn't proven ourselves able to withstand a vampire's voice?"

Azir's mouth twisted sourly. "So, mighty guardsman, what might your name be?" Alayna could hear him infuse as much mockery as he could into the query. The Collector retained his impassive expression.

Blank-faced as he might have been, he still answered the question. "I am Ashford. Now, you will be coming with us, and you will not resist."

"Won't I?" Azir asked with a tilt of his head.

"No, you won't." Ashford lifted a crossbow and swung it to point at Alayna. "You will obey me, or I will put a bolt in your friend."

Azir's eyes narrowed. "Your master just purchased her. I doubt she'd want the Elfas dead so soon."

"I'll put one in her thigh. It'll be painful, but it will heal."

"Of course, my dear Ashford, I'll be coming with you directly," Azir relented, although there was still a flash of anger about his eyes.

One of the guards stepped forward at Ashford's command and unlocked the cage. The vampire stepped close and loomed as intimidatingly as possible, but the Collectors managed to appear unaffected by him. Azir allowed himself to be bound at the wrists and led away from the pen.

Alayna watched him go, worried but without any recourse of action but to wait. Again. She hated waiting. Alayna enjoyed action, and this enclosure was maddening. She paced the ten feet of her cage, light footsteps barely leaving a mark on the dirty floor. A few wails from far away and the sound of crying could be heard. When she looked through the bars of her cell toward the eastern side of the compound, she could see the steady plume of dark, greasy smoke wafting up like it had on the day she'd arrived and every day since.

Hours drifted by, and the longer Azir was gone the more worried she grew. He hadn't been bought as she had. Would Lady Helmsted wish him dead for attempting to break in? If so, she had only to order it done. Alayna began to fear that she was alone in this again. For a short, fleeting moment in time, she had not felt alone. Azir might be a lot of things—and most of them could not be called 'good'—yet their mental connection, while unwanted, still provided a sense of closeness, of solidarity. With Azir around, she had begun to think that escape might be forthcoming. Now, though, that might all be gone again. Her hope had been dashed away just as soon as it had appeared.

Alayna forced herself to ignore her thoughts of gloom and doom. She had no way of knowing if Azir was dead, no reason to think that he was. As she made herself think positively, she was rewarded by the sight of a band of guards marching up the pathway between kennels. They dragged a lifeless form between them.

He can't be dead, she thought desperately. There would be no reason to bring him back if he was. Likely, he'd just become fodder to feed that plume of smoke if he were actually dead.

They opened Azir's cage and tossed him inside. He tumbled roughly to the floor and then dragged himself up against the back wall. Alayna hastened to the corner of her cage nearest his. He was only a few feet away with just two sets of bars between them.

He looked terrible. His face was a beaten mess, there were knife wounds all along his body and one gaping wound in his side. But he was a vampire, and they were Collectors. If they had wanted to kill him, a stake to the heart would have been their method. This had the look of an interrogation, maybe.

"Are you all right?" she asked for the second time that day, again hearing the ridiculous nature of the question.

"Do I detect worry in your voice?" Azir asked, opening one swollen eye to peer at her. She would have said he was smirking if it were possible to see through his injuries.

"Shut up. Are you?"

"Nothing like a good bout of torture every now and then to remind a person that they are alive," Azir said with as much nonchalance as he could muster. Only the grimace of pain as he spoke ruined the effect. That, and the fear behind his eyes. He masked his emotions well, but Alayna could see that he was hurting.

"What did they want? Did they ask you questions?" she inquired.

He grimaced again and shifted his weight, presumably to find a more comfortable position in which to slump. "Not really. They called it 'preemptive punishment'. No questions asked, no quarter given."

"What?" she exclaimed. "They did this to you for no reason?"

"Who did you think captured us? The Pope? These are Collectors —they are the bad guys. You should know that by now. Besides, I did not say it was for no reason. Preemptive punishment has a purpose."

"Which is?" Alayna prompted.

Azir turned a keen eye on her and spat some blood out of his mouth. "If they did this to me after I did not break any of their rules, imagine what they will do to one of us if we *do*." His head lolled back against the wall in weary exhaustion.

"Are you—" she nearly asked if he was all right again.

"I will be fine, Alayna. Just give me a moment to collect myself." He almost managed to imbue his words with the suave sophistication with which he normally spoke.

Alayna stayed silent and watched him take shallow, painful breaths with his eyes closed. He was all she had to count on in here. Philip wasn't coming, that much was clear. If he were, he would have been here already. Azir was all she had to count on now, and he looked practically broken. She could vaguely sense his excruciating pain through the link between their minds. It made her fingers ache again; the realization of his pain was a reminder of her own.

Whenever she and Philip had spoken of the vampire, Alayna had always thought of him as some sort of smear, a stain, a taint upon her mind. But now, gazing at him bleeding and exhausted in the corner, she couldn't help but feel sorry for him. He was here because of her. Alayna also couldn't help but feel that Azir's 'dark residue' on her consciousness simply wasn't all that dark.

CHAPTER EIGHTEEN

With Philip gone berserk from grief, events were balanced on a knife's edge, and tension along with fatigue were building in Beathan. Their packs were slowing him down, tiring him just enough so that he didn't even have to try and keep Philip close behind him any longer. It was all he could do to stay ahead of his friend. Fairies were speedy and clever, and with his charms and his amplifier bracelet Beathan was exceptional. He could magnify his speed to inordinate measures. Still, the wildcat might be lightning quick, but it would tire sooner than the horse. So it was with him and Philip. Trolls were not fast, but they had notoriously strong endurance both for fighting and traveling. Their bodies could take a beating and their minds could retain focus on one single objective, allowing them to push on where other beasts might not. Philip wasn't fully a troll, but then Beathan wasn't fully a fairy; it balanced out. He needed a new plan. Maybe if he were like Alayna—fast, lithe, and resilient like her Elfas kind—but no, he wasn't her. *She's gone*, he thought with a pang that cut like a blade, cut sharper than he'd ever expected anyone's loss to do outside of immediate family.

He needed to get rid of their travel packs, or stash them somewhere, and soon. He'd taken them from the clearing, because his friend didn't need them any longer. In his current state of mind, Philip would sleep rough, eat raw, and generally do just about anything a troll would do. But Beathan had thought that this would be over sooner, had thought that Philip would snap out of it and require his belongings once again. He had spent weeks zigzagging across the countryside, keeping Philip occupied so that he didn't hurt anyone—his friend would bury himself in guilt if Beathan allowed him to harm an innocent, he knew that much—and trying to concoct a plan of action to return Philip's mind back to normal. Beathan hadn't expected it to take this long.

At first, he'd tried sneaking in close to his friend and wafting a few items of clothing that had belonged to Alayna in front of his sleeping face, thinking that perhaps the memory of her would restore sanity. Philip had awoken with rage in his eyes, an inhumanly ferocious light, the fury of a troll on the hunt. But the scent had caught, a tiny breeze bringing the smell of her tunneling down his nostrils to connect to his subconscious. And for a moment, just for a snap second, Philip had been normal again. Beathan had seen it in his eyes for an instant before it disappeared again and his friend had leapt up with a hungry look on his face. He had abandoned that approach in favor of running and staying alive. Even with his charms and capabilities, Beathan had seen what Philip had done to the cohort of Collectors in his current state, and he didn't want to chance an encounter like that. The way things stood, Beathan would have to fight to kill to survive, and he didn't want to do that. Not yet. Not ever, hopefully.

However, he had not given up on the tactic of using Alayna's clothes—her scent—to elicit a change. He'd carried the packs, and every few days he'd tried again to no avail. Nothing even resembling that first momentary light of recognition in Philip's eyes had reoccurred, yet Beathan couldn't quite bring himself to give up on the method—at least not until he had a new plan, and as yet he did not.

Beathan ran tiredly but quickly through the forests of Transylvania. The setting was beginning to grow familiar to him—he'd run in so many circles for the last few weeks. He kept to the foothills, not too low so as to bring Philip in contact with many people, not too high into the mountains to jar loose yet more of his trollish heritage. Beathan was afraid of what might happen if Philip climbed into the jagged, snow-covered peaks of the Carpathians. In the rugged heights, so familiar and comforting to a troll, would his friend ever return? He didn't know, so he couldn't take the chance.

He could hear Philip grunting in the underbrush, smashing

through a small tree, kicking loose a tiny boulder in his pursuit. He was a few hundred yards behind, close enough to make the sweat on Beathan's face bead into droplets. A fight had to be avoided. *What to do? Think!* he told himself. He'd worked his way out of worse messes before, hadn't he?

And then an idea came. His charms had to have some use here. Thus far he'd mostly been using his amplifier bracelet—the one Astori had so coveted—to magnify his speed. Perhaps some of his other charms might be of equal use. Beathan conducted an abrupt mental inventory of his charms, ticking off a few in his mind, a few on his fingers, all the while stepping assuredly through the sparse forest. There was as much underbrush as trees in this region, unlike the densely wooded path of the pass leading up to The Alchemist's cabin.

What of the memory charm? The thought came and immediately his inventory stopped. That had to be his best bet. He should have thought of it weeks ago. Beathan cursed his inability to think beyond the chase. It would be backward though, inverted. The fairy's memory charms—well, most memory charms in general—were used to erase memory, to wipe away an encounter with a particularly worrisome foe or opponent, or perhaps to blot away the mind of someone dear to a person, someone whom a person wanted to keep safe and ignorant. Beathan had never actually tried a reverse charm, a charm to make someone else recall a memory they wanted to forget. He had no idea if it would work, but he had to try.

All of a sudden, he stopped, feet skidding in the snow. No more running. At least, not for now. He needed to be close, had to see Philip in order to have any hope of the memory charm working. The sounds of his friend's approach were menacing, and Beathan stilled his nerves. He wasn't usually this nervous, even in times of dire peril. What was going on? Then it dawned on him: this was about so much more than just surviving a difficult or dangerous encounter. This was about recovering his friend—one of his few true friends in the world —because there was no doubt that the individual chasing Beathan was *not* his friend. Not at all.

Philip crashed into sight and, as if to punctuate the fairy's immediately preceding thoughts, the half-troll wore the most ravenous look on his face that Beathan had witnessed yet. The contorted mask of Philip's visage sent a chill through the fairy. He shook it off and steeled his nerves. *Just a little closer.* He waited as Philip barreled toward him, angrily smashing a fist through a sapling as he bared his teeth in the rictus of a snarl.

Now.

Beathan flicked one of his jangles—a necklace, the one housing his memory charm—and then sent the spell careening toward Philip. Right when it left his mouth, right when his nimble fingers did their spell work, he knew something was off. He had known that reversing a memory charm on another person would be risky, but he hadn't expected it to feel so awkward, so *clunky* coming off his lips! In confirmation, Philip recoiled slightly from the charm as it hit his consciousness, but he recovered quickly, pushing onwards with a renewed vigor and force. He was only twenty yards away now. There was no time to evade and run.

Beathan casually flicked his defensive charm housed in the odd stone ring he wore, plucked from the finger of a stranger right before Beathan had been taken captive by the Guild and shipped to St. Thomas. This was what he was used to—combat and challenge. His nervousness evaporated as quickly as it had come when he recognized that a skirmish was at hand. The defensive charm bubbled upward, invisible to the naked eye, but he could sense it. Philip charged directly into it, and the impact would have flattened the fairy if the charm had not been in place. As it was, the former Collector rebounded with terrific force, snapping the low-hanging branches off a tree as he flew through the air.

Beathan shook his head. The charm had won him the bout, but trolls were resistant to magic in unknown ways. He could feel the reverberations of that contact traveling through the defensive charm. He doubted it would work a second time in this fight so soon after using it once, at least not with the same efficacy. But it *had* worked. It had bought him the time he needed. Philip was shaking his head groggily, the way a beast would, no cognition in his eyes beyond that of a stunned predator. Beathan took advantage of the moment and darted in to land a decisive punch on his friend's face. It didn't quite knock Philip out, but it did stun him quite badly, enough so that Beathan could regroup and plan a secondary—or was it tertiary now? —course of action.

He only had a few minutes. *Think!* He forced himself to focus. In a couple minutes, he would either have to run, fight, or enact a new plan. He didn't want to run. He was tired, and he'd been running for what seemed like forever, sleeping in trees for safety with hardly any breaks for rest.

Philip's eyes were gaining focus, his face twitching with desired action.

Beathan certainly didn't want to fight. For the moment, he had used up as much of his defensive charm as was likely to work against troll blood. A fight would only go downhill from there.

Philip was struggling to rise, shaking his head to clear his thoughts. Anger etched his face.

Think, Beathan cajoled himself. The time to run was almost past. It was either fight or come up with a better plan. At long last, he thought of another idea, a *new* idea. He didn't know if it would work. It was risky. Beathan would have stared at himself incredulously if he'd told himself the plan in any other circumstances, but desperate times called for desperate measures, and there was no more time.

The fairy rubbed a couple fingers along the earring in his right ear, one of his oldest, most precious—if little used—jangles. The small, gold hoop housed a finding charm. He'd only ever used it to find something twice. First, when he was a child, to find the pot of gold at the end of a rainbow on the Emerald Isle. The small amount of leprechaun blood he possessed had probably helped make that happen with more ease than it should have. Beathan hadn't kept but a few coins from the pot he had found. Even then, stealing wasn't as fun when there was no risk involved. The second use had been to find a woman—well, a sprite, to be exact. She was a particularly alluring and bewitching water sprite who he'd caught a rare glimpse of while traveling through back country before she had disappeared. He had found her again, and it had been quite the encounter, delightful for both of them, until it had ended in utter disaster, as was often the case when dealing with water sprites, romantically or not.

Philip was on his feet now and roaring with wordless, trollish rage.

Now or never. Beathan closed his eyes.

It was risky to close his eyes with a half-troll en route to rip his head from his shoulders, but Beathan had no other recourse. It was a last resort, but he owed Philip. He had to try.

"Besides," he muttered to himself, "it's like Ma always used t' say —'If y'aren't on a last resort at least once a fortnight, ya' must be doin' somethin' other'n livin'.'"

Another second passed, and Beathan murmured the finding

charm, sent it coursing out through the ether to meet Philip. It was risky, it had no guarantee of success, and his life hung in the balance.

All of the other times he'd used the charm it had been to find something firm, concrete. A being and even a mythic horde of wee folk treasure could be touched. This time it was different. He sent the charm into Philip, questing not for a thing to be touched and felt but for an abstract thought, an idea. It was Philip's identity—his true self—that needed finding, and Beathan had no idea if it could be found. He closed his eyes for focus and whispered the follow-up spell to partner with the finding charm. Cutting off his vision to enable concentration, though a peculiarity necessary for this charm, left Beathan feeling especially exposed.

And yet, nothing happened. No mammoth beast of a man tackled him, no teeth bit into his neck. Nothing—even Philip's trollish roaring had ceased. Beathan cracked open an eye and realized that he'd been cringing slightly, bracing for an impact that hadn't come. What he saw before him was Philip—the actual Philip. Finally, the former Collector was back. His friend was squatting on the snow-dusted earth, hands on his head, whether in shock or returned grief at the memory of Alayna's death Beathan did not know. But it was him, which meant that, somehow, the finding charm had worked.

Beathan waited, giving his friend the moment he needed. Eventually, Philip raised sad eyes to confront the half-fairy.

"How many?"

"How many what?" he asked cautiously.

Philip swallowed. "How many people? I mean, did I hurt anyone? I was about to kill you, my only friend. What must I have done to those I didn't know?" There was bitter dread in his voice.

"Almost," Beathan answered, and a ray of hope filled the pitiful man's eyes. "Ya' headed for a farmstead a few days back, but I got in close and distracted ya' again, then stayed close enough t' keep ya' on me trail henceforth."

The relief on Philip's face was palpable. "Thank you. You've been keeping me busy on your trail for what, weeks?"

Beathan nodded.

Philip continued morosely, "It's strange. I can't really remember doing anything before just now, but somehow, I can recall the passage of time. Does that make sense?"

Beathan shrugged. "Trolls often note the passin' of the seasons without retainin' any real memory of the day before. They focus forward on the future. It's actually one aspect of their nature that ya' should cling to in this moment. Ya' need t' look forward, mate."

"I don't know if I can. I don't know what I am right now. Am I a beast, a man, or both?"

Suddenly, despite all his affection for Philip, Beathan felt a little fed up. He'd just crisscrossed the Transylvanian countryside keeping his friend from wreaking the kind of havoc that would have crippled him emotionally with guilt. He just wanted a little bit of resolve. Was that too much to ask?

"What is it ya' want, Philip?" Beathan snapped. "Do ya' want t' wallow? Do ya' want to run 'round more beast than man? Or do ya' want t' pull yourself together? What is it that ya' *want?*" he uttered the last words emphatically.

His curt tone had the desired effect. Philip recoiled slightly, like he'd been slapped in the face, but then his expression firmed and Beathan recognized the determination that so characterized his friend.

"What I want is vengeance," Philip said with a gaze like iron.

CHAPTER NINETEEN

"You are a rarity," Helmsted said with a purr of satisfaction in her voice. "I can actually say that I am pleased you attempted to rescue your—what, friend, lover?—over here before your inevitable capture."

To his credit, Azir kept his composure better than Alayna would have. She was watching the interaction from the few feet of distance that separated her cell from his, and she wished more than anything that she could get her hands around Lady Helmsted's throat.

The hybrid vampire-Elfas just cocked his head and smirked before speaking in his elegant, eastern accent, "Are you now? Pleased, really? You may not be quite so optimistic in the not too distant future." He licked his tongue over one bared fang.

Lady Helmsted threw back her head and laughed. "You are in there, and I am out here. Besides, the Guild has had centuries to learn how to deal with your kind."

That darkened Azir's face slightly. "And are you still part of the Guild?" he questioned sharply.

It was Helmsted's turn for her face to tighten, but she ignored the question. "Why did you seek to rescue her?" She directed a look toward Alayna.

"Tsk, tsk, tsk. Answer for an answer. It is awfully naughty of you to believe that I will answer your questions without receiving answers to my own," he said with a disappointed look while waggling a finger in front of her face.

Lady Helmsted swallowed back a sharp retort and changed the subject. "No answers for you. You should dwell on other things, like how to stay alive. You know you'll be fighting today—your first bout in front of a live audience," she practically crowed with delight. Alayna felt a surge of disgust.

"Who, me? Fight in front of an audience full of such grand, important people?" Azir put his hands to his cheeks in mock shock. "I do not think I am worthy of the task. Perhaps another should go in my stead."

Alayna couldn't help but admire the vampire's composure. Most of her own interactions with Helmsted or the guards resulted in insults and curses, bitter and angry outbursts, rather than calculated slights.

She could see that the vampire's needling was working, but Helmsted shook her head with a sour look on her face. "You'll not get out of the fights so easily. High noon. Should be interesting. We've never had a vampire—well, half of one—who could fight during daylight. You are a rarity, indeed."

She turned to Alayna. "Pay close attention. You may or may not fight today, also. I haven't decided yet. But, eventually, you will." And with that, she swirled away in her sleek, divided skirts, her slender sword hanging at one hip like it was a part of her body, one hand hovering just near her pistol as if it were second nature to keep it within striking distance.

Alayna resisted the urge to spit. Well, it was less resistance and more a lack of ability, as her mouth ran dry at the thought of a caged fighting match. Something about being in front of an audience felt different than open combat. Was it really, though, or was she just worrying herself needlessly? She had no time to ponder the question, because Azir interrupted her thoughts.

"You will be all right, Alayna. If there is one thing that useless sack of a half-man did well, it was train you to fight."

She didn't even feel the desire to retort. *It's strange*, she thought. Once she would have risen to any bait with the intent to impugn Philip's name. She couldn't seem to muster enough care for that now. He wasn't there. He was gone somewhere, free somewhere, and she had to focus on staying alive.

She faced Azir through the bars. "Why *did* you come?" she asked.

"I beg your pardon?"

"Don't play coy with me, Azir. I want to know why you're here."

"You know me, the thrill of breaking in to take a drink from a ruby-gold haired prisoner was too much to pass up."

"You're lying," she stated flatly.

His mouth twisted sourly, and a lock of his straight, dark hair fell in front of his face, obscuring his features from vision. Azir shook the strands away. "What, you want me to say something profound? Or perhaps you want me to tell you what you already know, Alayna." He sounded almost angry now.

"And what is that?"

"That we are connected! I do not know why I came!" he burst out in frustration. "But I know that you can sense it as well as I. We are connected in some way, since the moment I contacted you with my mind." He ran his hands back through his silky, shoulder-length hair. "I speak to humans and they obey, they do exactly as I say. It was like that; as soon as I felt your presence, it was like a compulsion to find you. Tell me, if you hadn't been hogtied across the back of a mule, would it have been any different for you?" A pleading note almost entered into his voice, begging her to confirm the existence of something he couldn't explain and did not want to be alone in thinking.

Alayna didn't answer, only nodded slowly. It was chilling to hear him speak of the residue on each other's minds in the same breath as the dark powers of persuasion that he possessed as a vampire—that silken voice, crooning and bewitching people to do what he said and allow him to feed. She swallowed, unsure of how she felt.

"I can speak mind to mind with some of my kind, experience a gestalt sort of consciousness. But then, you know that: you were an Elfas once."

He stared at her silently, waiting for her to continue. She obliged.

Alayna stared off into the distance, not making eye contact. "I can sense some of them when they are near. I can hear them from far away. Even you contacted me from a thousand miles distant."

"Your point?" Azir asked with a grimace.

"My point is that just because there is a connection between us doesn't make that connection special. I have a link with lots of people." The lie tasted bitter on her tongue. She couldn't afford to alienate her only ally, but neither was she prepared to venture down the line of questioning as to what the residue between their minds meant or what effect it might already be having on her.

Azir shook his head in annoyance and did not respond. They remained in silence until the morning sun rose to near its zenith. The guards came then, opening both cages and leading them in manacles through the menagerie. Alayna passed fauns, werewolves, and even some creatures she had never seen before. She heard pleading and cursing, promises and threats made to the guards, as well as spiritual beggars hoping for a quick release whether it be through death or other means. It made her shudder. She was beginning to think that this place of shadow might be as bad as St. Thomas. It was a microcosm of filth.

They reached the first fighting ring, and Alayna was surprised to see a small set of stands erected in an amphitheater around the dirt ring. Blood from old fights stained the ground. A small crowd had already gathered to watch. Guards on break, but what also looked to be rich patrons—locals and nobles from afar—were there to watch a gladiatorial match not between mortal men but between supernatural creatures.

A werewolf in human form was waiting on the other side of the ring. He looked battered and dejected, and right away Alayna knew that he stood no chance against his opponent, Azir. The hybrid vampire was fresher, had been in captivity for only a few short days, and there was an air of supreme confidence about him that made everyone in the ring and in the stands draw the same conclusion.

Shouted bets on the fight began to take place between guards and patrons. Money changed hands. Suddenly, the menagerie made sense. It was for exhibition, for the sake of power over another's kind, but fundamentally it was for money. Helmsted had set herself up a nice business here, charging entrance to fights and to view the menagerie she had created. It was even further afield from traditional Guild philosophy than Alayna had initially thought. Historically, the Guild only captured to keep humankind safe, not for profit or personal gain, at least according to Philip.

Alayna was so lost in staring at the burst of commotion that occurred upon their entry into the ring that she didn't notice Lady Helmsted's approach.

"It should be an easy victory for your friend. *Should* be. Baturak is worn and weary from, but he was once one of our better fighters.

After all, he's killed many before today. Perhaps fortune will bless him once again and turn its face from the hybrid."

Alayna disagreed. Baturak, the werewolf, looked more battered than ready, unhealed wounds still apparent all over his body. Yet Helmsted's comment sent a flurry of doubt worming its way into the back of her mind.

She turned to Azir and put a manacled hand on his shoulder. "Be careful."

He tilted his head. "So you do care." With that, he stepped down the stairs leading to the sunken level of the fighting ring, accompanied by two guards. On-duty Collectors encircled the top of the ring where the stands began and the spectators sat. They provided defense in case any of the participants tried to turn their aggression on their captors.

Azir walked regally into the ring, of his own accord, and waited for his manacles to be unlocked, like royalty waiting for a servant to do his bidding. Alayna shook her head. He somehow managed to maintain his bearing in the midst of his captivity, and she realized that his haughty demeanor was like a cloak, or even armor, in which he wrapped himself for protection.

The werewolf was unchained, too, and before the guards had even exited the fighting ring, Baturak charged Azir. A roar went up from the crowd. Alayna couldn't help but think that the maneuver reeked of desperation. The vampire had the advantage here, and the werewolf knew it.

The fight wasn't exactly short, but it wasn't a close contest, either. Azir toyed with Baturak who was unable to change form due to the sun overhead and the lack of a full moon. Oh, he was faster and stronger than a human man, but he was not a match for the vampire. Azir was lightning-quick, and his kind had a predatory instinct that allowed them to intuitively pinpoint an opponent's weakness—an old wound, a subconscious fear, whatever. Azir preyed upon a particularly nasty, unhealed wound on the werewolf's thigh and attacked it repeatedly until it was all Baturak could do to stand. The crowd loved the viciousness of it all. A new favorite fighter was born.

"This is horrible," Alayna said with disgust to no one in particular.

A guard named Elgin answered with a grunt, "Careful with that tone missy, or it'll be the Night Pits for you." He jerked his head in the direction of a large but low and squat building that Alayna could see in the distance through a gap in the stands. "Houses our worst offenders, most of which can't be touched by sunlight. A pretty little piece of flesh like you wouldn't last long in there. You go inside, and you won't come out again. Leastwise, you won't come out whole. They'll take pieces of you—bits of your soul." He bared his teeth in a grin.

"And how much of *your* soul still remains?" she retorted.

He snarled and raised his baton, but Ashford, the head guard overseeing her captivity, caught Elgin's forearm in a vice-like grip. "Not today, Elgin. Maybe you can beat her tomorrow—if the lady says so." His words carried the implicit threat that if Elgin disobeyed them, he would be made to regret it. Elgin swallowed and turned his gaze back toward the ring. Alayna did so, as well.

Azir played with his opponent from start to finish, until eventually he grew tired of the game and came in with a brutal slashing attack using his nails—not quite claws, but still dangerous—as weapons. When his opponent was staggering and barely conscious, Azir went in for the kill. He lunged with snakelike speed and fastened his teeth into the werewolf's neck. Blood spurted and ran down his face as he fed. Alayna grew sick. She had never actually watched a vampire feed long enough to completely drain the life from its victim. She had now. Even from afar she could see the light drain from Baturak's eyes, watched as his feeble struggling weakened until the life was gone from his body, and still Azir fed. The ground rumbled with the shaking and stomping of the spectators' enthusiastic feet. Yet, as Alayna chanced a glance at the Lady Helmsted beside her, by far the most disturbing aspect of the entire spectacle was the idle amusement with which the woman watched the scene unfold.

Finally, the vampire had drunk his fill. He pulled himself to his feet from the bloodstained dirt. Blood covered his face, yet he daintily licked his fingertips clean—whether from any real need or simply out of affectation Alayna didn't know. He walked calmly back to the guards and held out his wrists for the manacles. One of the Collectors sneered as he did so, that is, until Azir gave him a toothy grin. Then the guard slammed the manacles closed with unusual haste, and the vampire laughed at his discomfort. The Collector looked down for a moment with a red face of shame. They climbed the stairs and returned to where Alayna stood next to Helmsted.

"So? How did I do?" he asked their captor.

She shrugged dispassionately. "Considering you fought pig-feed, I'll reserve judgment for a more difficult match." Her hawkish eyes pierced his, waiting for a reaction. Instead of taking the bait, he threw back his head and laughed. Alayna couldn't help but think that, in the midst of captivity, while being forced to fight as a slave warrior, Azir was somehow in his violent element. It was not a comforting realization.

Helmsted smiled slightly and nodded for the guards to take them away. It appeared that there would be no fight for Alayna today. She turned to go, but was restrained by a hand on her arm.

"I wanted you to see what you'll be up against before I match you. I paid handsomely for you, and I didn't want to throw you in the ring unprepared."

"If you paid so much for me, then why have me fight at all?" Alayna asked with genuine curiosity.

"It's what we do," Lady Helmsted answered simply yet severely.

Then Alayna was led back to her pen alongside Azir. They shuffled in manacled silence until they were thrust into their separate enclosures. The wind whipped brutally through the open bars, making this by far one of the coldest days Alayna had experienced in the menagerie. The open-air pens made her long for a room and a bed—even more for a sheltered camp in the forest somewhere. Or, at the very least, it made her wish for a cloak. None of those things were forthcoming. The nights were the worst; she anticipated a particularly cold one tonight.

She huddled up in a corner of her cage without looking at her neighbor. Finally, he spoke after a few minutes of silence.

"He was going to die either way. It was him or me, and I preferred it to be him."

Alayna turned to answer and saw that his face was still a bloody mask. "But did you have to eat him?"

"I am a vampire, Alayna. It is what we do." He shook his head in frustration. "Besides, the stronger I am, the better our odds of escape. You do want to escape, do you not?"

She sighed and didn't answer. Alayna wasn't exactly sure what to say. Her only ally was a semi-psychotic killer who ate people.

"You know, you could always join me," he left unsaid exactly what he meant, but Alayna could hear the sly tone in his voice.

"You asked me once, and I said no then. I still say no now. I do not want to be a vampire, nor will I ever want to."

"Easy, I meant no offense."

"None taken," she responded tiredly, suddenly feeling as if the weight of all creation was pressing down on her.

"Alayna, are you really angry with me for surviving?" Azir's tone was different, but she couldn't put a finger on exactly how it had changed.

She turned back to look at him. "Did you have to revel in it, enjoy it so much?"

"Enjoy it?" he retorted indignantly. "I hated it. I was playing the crowd. The more people who are in our favor here the more likely we will somehow be able to engineer an escape. But no, I did not enjoy that foul werewolf."

"They don't taste good? Werewolves, I mean," Alayna asked with a sort of sick fascination.

Azir looked at her as if she were insane. "Of course not. I mean, my kind will eat just about anything, but there is something infinitely more tasty about mortal, human blood."

Alayna's disgust returned. "So, you'll eat anyone," she restated the harsh truth.

He seemed to take it as a further, probing question. "Well, just about. Pretty much anything with a physical form, other than fellow vampires, that is."

"Why not vampires?"

Again, Azir looked at her in disbelief. "Why not?" he quoted incredulously. "Come now, Alayna, nobody appreciates a cannibal. That is positively barbarous."

For some reason, his insistence that cannibalism was repulsive but eating other people was not struck Alayna as incredibly humorous. Perhaps it was exhaustion, or maybe delirium. Perhaps she was simply losing her mind due to weeks spent in captivity. Whatever the reason, she laughed and laughed. She laughed until Azir stopped being affronted by her laughter and decided to join in her mirth. She laughed until she couldn't laugh any more.

Something told her that finding a reason to laugh in the midst of this ordeal might be more important than escaping it altogether. Someone would have told her that once. Philip—that's who. Immediately, the fact that he felt so distant after such a short time of separation caused her laughter to cease.

After some time, she sensed Azir. He was napping. She could see that and somehow sense it with her mind, through the residue connecting them. Suddenly, she couldn't help but wonder if the proximity of the vampire and his dark residue were somehow affecting the way she thought. Wondering about that unpleasant possibility kept her awake long into the night.

CHAPTER TWENTY

"Where're we goin'?" the fairy asked with a note of caution in his voice as Philip strode purposefully forward. He walked as if his life depended on it. Each step felt like it cleared a little more of the fog that had enshrouded his mind for the majority of the past month.

"You know where we are going. It's why you're asking me with that tone." Directness had always been his preferred manner of interaction, so why stop now?

With his peripheral vision, Philip could see the fairy shake his head. "Do I, now? Humor me anyway."

Philip sighed but didn't slow down as he answered, "We are going back up into the passes, into the mountains. I need to see The Alchemist and get rid of the trace."

"An' why might that be?"

"You asked me what I wanted, Beathan, and I told you. I want revenge." He tried to speak calmly yet purposefully, but even he could hear the sound of cold-hearted malice and menace in his voice. It sent a shiver down his own spine, although how or why that was even possible, he wasn't sure.

The half-fairy sensed it too and tensed. Beathan had been on edge around him for the last day or so, and Philip couldn't blame him. After all, he had hunted his friend for nearly a month in hopes of catching and killing him. But it hurt. Now that he was back to himself—or as much himself as possible at this point—it was difficult to see the wary look in Beathan's eyes, to notice him tense up, ready to flee at a moment's notice, to see him fondle the hilt of a dagger just in case. The fairy never said anything, but he was careful around Philip now.

"So, vengeance then. That's the course ya've settled on, is it?" Beathan murmured.

"Is there something wrong with that? Would you feel any differently in my circumstances?"

The fairy shook his head as they continued to stride forward. "No, mate. If the love o' me life was ripped from me, I'd be goin' through somethin' akin to what ya' must be feelin' right now. I'm just wonderin'...why The Alchemist?"

"I told you, revenge. I'm going to make the Guild pay for what they've done. But I can't do that if they can see me coming. With the trace still in my blood, I don't stand a chance of succeeding. I want this damn thing gone once and for all!" he practically yelled the last sentence in an explosive breath. He had to vent somehow, and if yelling was the method, so be it. He had too much pent up anger, energy, and aggression to be able to expend it all simply by walking, even at the clip at which they were moving.

"I just have one question. I thought you decided this procedure was too dangerous?"

"That was when I had something to live for," Philip responded, voiding his voice of all emotion.

"Fair enough, fair enough. I see the point," a troubled Beathan mused. "Well then, I'm with ya'."

"Are you?"

The fairy put a restraining hand on his friend's lean, muscled arm and pulled him to a halt. "What exactly d'ya' mean by that, now?"

"I see the way you've been looking at me. You're worried. You're scared of me. Frightened that I'll revert back to the troll version of myself again."

"Frightened? Me?" Beathan scoffed. "Please, mate. I've been half dead in a cave full o' Redcaps an' didn't take fright then. It'll take a wee bit more'n a troll-man t' make me squeamish."

Philip heard the lie on his tongue but was grateful for it anyways. Worried or not, Beathan was with him and, for some reason, that made all the difference. Philip would go through with anything to avenge Alayna's death, and something told him that Beathan felt similarly.

As if to punctuate his thoughts, the fairy said, "Seriously, Philip, I want this revenge also. No question that I'm goin' t' help ya'."

Philip nodded, at a loss for words, and cleared his throat. Without saying anything, he started back along the trail heading deeper into Transylvania and the heart of the range in which The Alchemist resided.

———

THE DAYS BLURRED TOGETHER, but not in the same way they had for the past month. No, during his mental break, his trollish blood had overcome him and Philip had lived, thought, and acted like a beast. He hadn't acted beyond his immediate aim which, at the time, had been catching up with Beathan. That had caused his days to fog, caused a sense of nothingness beyond his foremost thought. This current blur was different, the continuity of repetition, the haze of doing the same thing over and over again. They walked and ran in turns deeper into the forest and then higher into the mountains, day after day. It was not exactly monotonous, but Philip was impatient. He wanted to get on with his revenge, so he found it hard at times with the slow pace of his plans. And he was cautious. That feeling of blurring days made him nervous. He fought to retain his hold on reality; he didn't want to lose his mind again. If he did, he would never make the Guild pay for what they had done to Alayna. So he struggled to formulate his thoughts like the hybrid he was, even though many of his impulses still reflected the wild north that flowed through his veins. He was a man! Or, at least, enough of one to be able to think coherently. Yet, at times, he still struggled to do so. Sometimes he would look over at Beathan and, just for a moment, think of how good he would be to eat. It would only last a fraction of an instant, but the thought was still there. It sickened him.

They traveled without speaking much. Philip was in no mood for chatter, and Beathan, showing more interpersonal perception than he normally did, seemed to recognize Philip's need for solitude and let him be. They passed pines and firs still dusted with snow, although late winter was beginning to give way to early spring. Philip could taste springtime in the air, and a part of him—the northerner within —mourned the passing of the cold season.

Their passage was quiet, almost uncannily so, and Philip began to wonder if word of the half-man monster had spread before them. He wondered if his behavior during the past month and his new reputation had warned off even the most volatile of vampires from crossing their path. Whatever the reason, their journey through the passes and high trails was uneventful, something for which Philip was grateful. It was not that he wasn't itching for a fight—he was, perhaps more than he'd ever been in his life. But he wanted the *right* fight; he wanted to kill Collectors right *now*. That thought alone would have stunned him a month ago, but everything had changed with Alayna's passing. Death. Her death. He would not let himself sugarcoat what had happened as some sort of defensive maneuver of his mind. She had been killed, murdered for no reason other than keeping his company. That thought alone was enough to set his blood boiling.

They climbed higher and higher along the trails until the trees thinned and the forest became sparse and interspersed with patches of boulders and rocky mountainside. When they finally reached the clearing, The Alchemist's cabin was puffing smoke in a cheery fashion. The normalcy of it angered Philip. Irrationally, it felt like an affront that anything in the world could continue as normal without Alayna in it. She had been his heart, and in many ways, it had felt like she was the heart of the world, too. It stung to be reminded that she was not.

Beathan approached the door and knocked, Philip close behind him. The door cracked open and then opened a bit wider when The Alchemist recognized them.

"Back again? What do you want?" He was nowhere near as forthcoming and welcoming as he had been the last time.

"We—I—want your help," Philip said. "Can we come in?"

He extended his hand to push the door open, but the man inside blocked his efforts. The Alchemist had an odd look. Why didn't he want them to enter?

"What is it, mate? Don't want us t' find somethin' ya' got tucked away inside?" Beathan asked in his typically inquisitive and irreverent fashion.

"Nothing of the sort, not at all," The Alchemist blustered. "But must I remind you that we parted on less than cordial terms. I've half a mind to turn you away." The threat did not feel idle, and Philip could feel all his plans unraveling around him.

About to break down the door, he resisted his wild instincts—crushed them—and opted for a different tactic: Flattery. Perhaps even a little bit of begging.

"Nobody but you can help me. I need you, Alchemist. Please." It hurt to say those words after the way the man had coveted Alayna's blood the last time, but it wasn't entirely untrue. Philip did need him.

Beathan caught on to his tactic. "Please?" the fairy's wheedling tone was so syrupy that it was almost too much, and Philip thought he might have ruined the effort.

He had to counter the negative emotions playing across the scientist's face. "Same deal as before," Philip declared.

The Alchemist's eyes narrowed. Philip had hooked him, he could tell. Still, the old man looked unsure.

"Double," Philip said. "Two vials from the both of us.

"Triple."

"Fine," Philip grated out in frustration. He glanced at Beathan who didn't seem preoccupied whatsoever with the fact that Philip had just sold three vials of his blood. For a moment, he was reminded of why he liked the fairy so much. Loyalty. Beathan was a thief and a scoundrel, but damn it if he was not loyal to his friends, willing to sacrifice just about anything for them. He smiled. With a friend like that he could do just about anything, even exact revenge upon the Guild. Any price was worth making them pay.

"Done," he said to reiterate his agreement.

"Well then," the scientist muttered, his hair sticking up as if the wind had ruffled it, "to my workshop we go." He motioned to them to lead the way toward the larger building.

"You want to do it now?" Philip asked as he walked through the path of slushy snow between the cabin and the workshop.

"No time like the present," The Alchemist responded briefly and then chuckled. He had a nasty laugh, Philip reflected. Unsettling. It did not inspire confidence.

They entered the workshop's darkened interior, dim for lack of lamplight. The Alchemist lit one lamp, but only the one. It was just enough to dispel the gloom around the three of them and cast what seemed like infinitely more shadows. He grunted something unintelligible and motioned Philip over to a table with firm legs that would support added weight. There were straps attached—restraints, no doubt. Philip swallowed. A part of him hated that he was subjecting himself to the mad ministrations of this disreputable scientist, but another part of his will firmed at that thought, shoving the disgust away to a far corner of his mind. He'd not quail now, not when this was what he needed in order to avenge Alayna's death.

He got onto the table and reclined against the hard surface. The Alchemist leered at him in the darkness. "Good, you don't even have to be told. I like it when my subjects are pliable." He began strapping Philip down with the restraints even as he spoke.

"Do ya' really think those'll hold him, science man?" Beathan asked with a snort.

The Alchemist turned his gaze on the fairy. "I do."

Philip tugged a bit and knew that he could break free anytime he chose. He was about to voice his agreement with Beathan on the matter when the man continued, "I'll be doing a number of things to you—feeding you things, putting things in and on your body. It'll weaken you. Trust me. These straps will hold." The Alchemist patted the old table and restraints lovingly.

Philip shook his head and decided not to disagree. Besides, he wouldn't move. He would be as still as necessary no matter what happened. He needed The Alchemist's assistance to move forward with his plans, and he wasn't going to ruin it because he couldn't handle a bit of pain. No, he'd endured many terrible things in his years as a Collector and had endured others since leaving. He could handle this.

The Alchemist stared at him for a moment. "Ready?"

Philip nodded brusquely but suddenly Beathan interjected, "Wait, how do we know ya' won't just kill him?" The question came almost unbidden, although it was not an unfair one.

The Alchemist smiled one of his discomfiting smiles and addressed his response to Philip instead of the fairy. Clearly, he still hadn't gotten over their last encounter. "You don't. I may kill you, but if I do, it will not be by intent. After all, I cannot very well boast of accomplishing this feat if I don't manage to keep you alive. And believe me, it will be something to boast about."

He raised one bushy eyebrow in unspoken question. Philip nodded his agreement. "Get on with it, then."

"With pleasure."

The Alchemist bustled away for a moment, leaving him strapped to the table. Philip turned his head to look at the fairy, and Beathan nodded solemnly yet encouragingly. The scientist came back with his hands full, his cane having been discarded to lean against the next table. The wood was cool against Philip's back, and somehow, he found that sensation reassuring. Cold things usually were.

"Silence Elixir to keep you quiet—I can't have your screams interrupting my process—a few injections of the transfigurative agent into one of the major arteries should start the process and act as a catalyst. Two drops of Pyranxia on the tongue to slow down your heart enough to—hopefully—survive the procedure..." he muttered on and on, listing a number of different actions and agents to be used in various ways, but Philip was beginning to grow too nervous to listen to them all. The casual way the man had simply assumed he'd be screaming, and screaming loudly, had shaken him.

Again, Philip firmed his resolve and, much to his surprise, he felt Beathan's hand on his shoulder. This time it was the warmth of that hand, not a chill, that comforted him.

"We must begin. Step back, Fairy."

Philip felt Beathan release his shoulder and step away. He kept his eyes locked on the ceiling lost in the dimness above.

First came an elixir that the scientist poured down his throat. It must have been the Silence Elixir, because as soon as it touched his tongue Philip couldn't utter a sound. It was unsettling, to say the least. He stopped trying to speak or make a noise so as to avoid the sensation altogether. Better to pretend he did not want to speak at all.

Next, The Alchemist began with a few injections, but Philip didn't even try to keep track of them all. There were too many. Lastly, as the process began to take place and Philip felt a strange sensation building in his veins, after having been injected with the transfigurative agent and catalyst, The Alchemist tugged open Philip's jaw once more.

"Now for the Pyranxia, to be administered last so as not to slow the heart down for any longer than absolutely necessary..." he muttered almost to himself as if reciting a recipe. All of a sudden, Philip's body felt heavy. He was lying down, restrained, and yet it still felt as though that was too much effort.

Then the pain came.

Whatever the man had injected began to take effect. First there was fire burning all the way down his arms and legs, coursing through his core and radiating up into his head and face. He wanted to cry, he wanted to scream, but the elixir kept him quiet. He blinked back tears but only succeeded in creating them. They trickled down the sides of his face.

Next came the ice. Philip never thought that the cold would bother him, but this unnatural sensation piercing his organs felt somehow wrong. It should not be in his body, and yet he had allowed it in. The sensation lasted and lasted. The cold continued for so long that he felt as if it burned more than the fire had.

The Alchemist put his head over Philip's face and looked down at him. "I told you you'd be screaming. Didn't I? I can tell by your eyes. Silence Elixir can silence the tongue, but it's impossible to quiet someone's eyes, and yours are positively shrieking." The man sounded pleased. Philip couldn't disagree, though. He would be screaming right now if he could, screaming as loudly as possible. The scientist puttered around and did more things, but Philip couldn't focus on anything beyond the pain.

It went on and on. It went on for so long. Had it been hours or seconds? Minutes or days? He didn't know. All Philip was sure of was that he must be dying. The Alchemist was, in fact, trying to kill him despite all his earlier protestations. But just when the pain felt like it could go on no longer, when Philip was certain he could endure no more without his body giving way, it stopped. He was left quivering, trying to gather his wits as best he could. He worked his mouth, but no sound came out.

The Alchemist began unhooking the straps. "You'll be able to speak again soon." He sounded so pleased with himself, and no doubt he was, because he'd managed to keep his subject alive through a procedure that should have killed him.

When the restraints were removed from his body, Philip sat up. He worked his jaw and a groan came out. He stood up unsteadily, and Beathan put a hand on his arm to help him balance.

"Ya' all right, mate?"

Philip blinked his eyes blearily and shook his head to clear it. He opened his mouth to try and speak again, and finally some words came: "I have no idea." He turned to the scientist with a questioning look.

"Yes," The Alchemist nodded, "it worked. The trace is gone."

"How do ya' know?" Beathan asked.

"It is like you said when you first came here—the trace needs a host of living blood. I removed your blood, transfigured it into something else completely and then changed it back, so for that brief period of time the trace didn't have a living host of blood, therefore I know that it cannot exist now," The Alchemist stated matter-of-factly, but to Philip it all sounded garbled and confusing. Perhaps his head was still too foggy from the agony he'd just put himself through. Still shaky, he sat down on a stool. He looked at Beathan who seemed to have accepted the statement as if it made sense. Philip trusted the fairy. He had charms and spells at his disposal, and magic was not too different from alchemy, at least in Philip's mind. If Beathan thought that the statement made sense, then it probably did. The trace was gone.

Immediately, Philip felt a keen sense of bitter grief. If only he'd done the procedure the last time and ignored Alayna's wishes, she might not now be dead.

"Well, I guess I should thank you," he began, looking keenly at The Alchemist. The man ducked his head in a nod of appreciation. "Although, I am pretty sure you let the procedure continue longer than necessary. Didn't you?" The man was just sadistic enough to push Philip's body to its absolute threshold.

"Aah, well, I may have tested your limits. It was an experiment, after all." He made no apology.

"So, what did ya' turn his blood into?" Beathan chimed in.

"Ice water. Or, I should say, more of a combination of ice and water. A bit of both. I figured that, with your heritage, the cold might give you the best chance for survival.

Philip nodded. It was the first thing The Alchemist had said that made sense to him. "But what about the initial fiery feeling?"

The Alchemist shrugged. "I don't know. There's always a factor of unpredictability to these sorts of procedures, and the body reacts in different ways. But you did feel the cold?" he asked curiously.

Philip nodded. "Mostly. It was mostly the cold...piercing, burning cold."

The Alchemist had pulled out a notepad as Philip spoke and was began jotting down notes about the experiment. Philip was about to offer that they settle the payment so that he and Beathan could get out of there—it was a testament to the scientist's preoccupation with his research that he hadn't yet remembered to ask for the payment himself—when something caught his eye.

It was almost lost in the dark recesses of one of the shelves that lined the near wall. It was almost too dim to see, yet it was not a thing that Philip could miss. It was gold and red, a lock of hair tied around a vial of dark, red liquid. Then his eyes locked on yet another and another tiny vial encircled by ruby-blonde locks. His jaw clenched in recognition.

"How did you get that?" The menace in his voice surprised even himself.

The Alchemist looked up from his notes. "Hmm?" He took one look at Philip's face and blanched. Philip had never seen the scientist so unnerved.

"I said, how did you get this?" He walked over, his legs steadied by anger, and grabbed a vial off the shelf. He held it under the lamplight for Beathan to see. The fairy tensed, and Philip could see hard lines of anger etched into his face, as well.

"Now, I don't know what you are implying," The Alchemist spluttered. All bravado and sinister tones had gone from his voice. He was a man arguing a losing cause, a foregone conclusion, and his disquiet was obvious.

"What he's inferrin' is that those wee locks o' hair resemble a certain fair lass we both cared for deeply." The fairy's voice carried just as many hard edges as his face did as he continued, "I cannot help but notice that ya' never once asked about her lack o' presence in our company. Could ya' possibly have already known her fate? Is that why?"

"Did you follow us? Did you mutilate her corpse?" Philip's rage was gaining force. He crushed the vial in his hand, not even feeling the tiny bits of glass that cut into his rough palm. He stepped closer to The Alchemist and crowded the man back into a corner. His prey's eyes took on a wild look.

"No, no, that's not how it happened! Well, partially. I did follow you, but there was no mutilating, I swear. I promise I didn't kill her!" The frenetic look about him only grew as Beathan stepped into place just behind Philip. The Alchemist might have his skills with alchemy, his agreements with the vampires, and hold the respect—if concerned disapproval—of the Guild for his talents with elixirs, potions, and poisons, but he stood no chance when cornered by an angry fairy and a furious hybrid man with troll blood. And he knew it.

"Kill her? Of course you didn't. The Collectors saw to that," Philip spat bitterly.

This time, The Alchemist displayed his first reaction to their comments that wasn't fear. Philip saw confusion on his face. "Dead? No, no, she's not dead. I saved her."

"Liar. I felt her pulse go, Alchemist. She died, an' ya' came along an' harvested her while her body was still fresh." Beathan's voice carried a quiet threat.

The Alchemist held up his hands. "True. Sort of. She was dead, but just barely—or not quite, depending on how you view it. I *did* follow you, and I *did* come across her body. But I used one of my most expensive elixirs to bring her back." The coldness that had been so evident in the scientist's eyes during their previous encounter was now replaced by a frantic desperation. He knew that his life was on the line.

"So, you saved her and harvested her. Then what?" Philip's anger was still at a low simmer, yet the flicker of hope building in his chest threatened to explode into full flame at just one statement—the fact that Alayna's existence in this world could be verified in a believable manner.

"I...well, I..."

"Spit it out, Alchemist. Where is she?" Philip growled and clutched the man's collar in both hands.

"I sold her!" he burst out and then practically cowered in fear of the rage that he expected to burst forth, that almost *did* burst forth from Philip who was only barely able to restrain it. Only barely, because the one thing more important than paying the scientist back for what he had done was the realization that he was speaking the truth. Alayna was, indeed, alive, or at least had been, and he needed to know everything there was to know about where she might be now.

"You sold her," he stated flatly.

"Yes, I sold her. To one of your kind."

"His kind?" Beathan queried, disbelief in his voice.

The Alchemist nodded. "Yes, his kind, or near enough—although I don't rightly know if they're still Guild or not with the operation they're running. I can tell you where they are," he offered eagerly, almost greedily, at once seeing a way to free himself from the worst of the blame by directing their attentions toward a goal, as well as the fact that it would get them out of his cabin.

"You'll do one better," Philip responded grimly, staring at The Alchemist with a cold fire in his eyes. "You'll show us."

CHAPTER TWENTY-ONE

Despite what Helmsted had said, Alayna had not yet been made to fight. Azir had three more bouts, one every day, and each one against an increasingly dangerous opponent. It was clear that although his matches increased in difficulty and danger, he was still facing the dregs of the menagerie—opponents he could dispatch with relative ease. Alayna, however, did not fight. The Lady Helmsted had implied that she would be entering the ring soon, though, so she mentally prepared herself. She had even talked through various strategies with Azir based on what type of adversary she might face. He had been surprisingly serious about preparing her, lacking his usual quips and haughty demeanor. It almost seemed as if he cared about Alayna's well-being. Yet, for all her mental preparation, no fight came. Only Azir was thrust into the ring, over and over again. Lady Helmsted forced her to observe the bouts, no doubt as a way of torturing her with the knowledge of what she herself would soon be facing when her time to enter the arena finally came. Each time Alayna watched, horrified yet filled with a sick fascination as Azir tore one opponent limb from limb and drained another of its lifeblood.

Worse than watching him fight, Alayna was forced to endure the indignity of being ogled by a steady stream of rich patrons. Helmsted spread the word about fights, but she also allowed patrons to take a guided tour through the narrow streets of the menagerie between the various cells holding all manner of supernatural creatures. Alayna could see the enthralled look on each patron's face as they were paraded along from one cage to the next in small groups until they finally reached hers. She had never wanted blood so much as she did when under the fascinated scrutiny of their gazes. Sometimes men would come and look at her with the kind of lust they usually reserved for the whores she was certain they frequented. Other times, the patrons brought their wives and the women would gaze at her exotic Elfas features with jealousy. But the one common theme was that every single person who frequented the menagerie looked at her as if she was some *thing*, not a person. They gazed at her the way a person would look at a rare animal, and it set her blood to boiling. For the first time in her life as an Elfas, Alayna began to understand and accept the divide that existed between human and inhuman kind. She wanted nothing more than to teach them a lesson, but she could not, trapped as she was behind the bars of her cage.

Lady Helmsted herself strode up with one group of patrons, sword on her hip as always and wearing her usual riding skirts, this time in a dark forest-green color. Her firm, angular features gave her a harsh, if not completely unbeautiful, appearance.

"This, ladies and gentleman, is one of my prized possessions." She indicated Alayna within the enclosure. At being named a possession, Alayna spat through the bars of her cage, barely missing a patron's feet.

Lady Helmsted's face darkened. It wouldn't do for her guests to have a bad experience while visiting. Yet, the nobleman grinned as he leered at Alayna. "Feisty. What is she?"

"She is an Elfas, hailing from the forested regions in the north of Europe. But she is no *normal* Elfas," Lady Helmsted lowered her voice the way a storyteller did to garner the crowd's rapt attention. Duly, her audience quieted.

"Why not?" one woman tittered as she fanned the ugly scents of the menagerie away from her cultured nostrils.

Helmsted grinned slightly as one of her customers took the bait. She looked at the one who had spoken—a soft, stout noblewoman who was likely on the first excursion that she'd taken outside of her own manor in weeks. "I'll tell you why not," she said, drawing out her syllables theatrically. Alayna never would have guessed it, but Helmsted was quite the performer, quite the storyteller. She supposed that she had to be in order to cultivate continued interest in her establishment.

Lady Helmsted addressed the small crowd of eager onlookers, "*This* Elfas here is no normal Elfas. You may have heard tell of creatures that can transform the very genetics of their prey—a vampire or a werewolf, perhaps." There were a few uneasy murmurs of confirmation.

Alayna heard Azir snort in disdain at the performance. Alayna's nostrils flared as she listened to Helmsted make her a selling point. "Those who transform into vampires and werewolves, as strange and otherworldly as that might sound, do so through supernatural yet largely understood functions. Their genetics are changed by a bite. But not so with Alayna, here." She flourished a hand in her direction.

"What's so different about this Elfas?" A young, pimply-faced patron shouted from the back, squeezing his way through the small crowd of people. Yes, they were definitely eating up Helmsted's story.

"I'm glad you ask. This Elfas was indeed once a human, but her kind do not have the ability to transform the nature of another race the way that a vampire can. She is an anomaly. She was transformed by...magic." Again, Helmsted paused melodramatically before saying the last word.

There were gasps of awe at the confession. Alayna understood Azir's snort now. This was a farce, little more than a means for Lady Helmsted to make a few bucks off of the ignorance and petty interest of the region's nobles. It was utterly demeaning. She spat again, this time toward Helmsted's feet. There was only so much she could endure. The lady frowned a warning at her. Alayna wasn't feeling particularly inclined to obey, though. She sneered back.

The same man who had spoken first repeated himself, "Feisty, isn't she? Are her kind dangerous?"

"Elgin." Helmsted motioned for the guard to open Alayna's cage. "No, my good sir, not the way other creatures are. Elfas are more peaceful in nature. They can be taught to fight, but they do not have natural inclinations toward violence—not like her neighbor, here." She indicated Azir with a lazy wave of her hand. All the while, her hawk eyes stared a warning at Alayna as Elgin cautiously opened the gated cage and she made her way inside. "In fact, I can stand here without fear for my safety. Alayna has yet to even fight a bout. She is virtually tame."

That was it. Alayna felt the blood rush to her head. She could only endure so much. Being used as a source of amusement and entertainment, even a spectacle, was one thing. But humiliation in order to boost Helmsted's stock in the eyes of her patrons was quite something else. In a flash of motion, Alayna crossed the distance and put her forehead through the bridge of Helmsted's nose.

Caught by surprise, Helmsted crumpled to the ground in a spray of blood as Elgin and the other two guards leapt forward, throwing fists and beating her back with clubs. Helmsted climbed to her feet, one hand angrily grasping at her sword hilt. Her eyes flashed, and there was not an ounce of fear to be seen in them, only rage and flickers of embarrassment at her humiliation. Blood streaked down her face from the blow, but she stood erect and forceful. The guards followed her back out of the cage as soon as Alayna was beaten back, and they slammed the cell shut.

Helmsted leaned her bloody mask of a face through the bars. "You will pay for this," she hissed quietly. Then she declared more loudly, "It's the Night Pits for you, Elfas!"

———

TRUE TO HER WORD, later that day the Lady Helmsted returned from guiding her guests through the menagerie to pay Alayna's cage a visit.

"You'll wish you hadn't done that," she said with satisfaction.

"I'm shaking," Alayna mocked.

Helmsted grinned viciously. "You haven't seen the Night Pits yet. You'll change your tune when you do. Tomorrow you fight. So rest up, sweetling." she added the pet name as she sometimes did when addressing Alayna and, as usual, it drove her mad. She slammed her fists against the cage.

"Why don't you and I just settle this?" Alayna burst out angrily. "Frightened?"

Lady Helmsted threw back her head and laughed. "Me, frightened of you?" And Alayna could see the truth in her incredulity. There was not even a tiny bit of fear in Helmsted's eyes. "I'm a senior Guild member, girl. I was trained for years, spent time in the field. I'm reigning dueling champion within the Guild, and I'm a dead shot with this." She tapped the pistol holstered at her hip. "The number and types of creatures I've captured and killed, all far more dangerous than a mere Elfas, would set the hairs on the back of your neck standing up. No, you don't frighten me one bit. I have nothing to prove to you. But I do have a score to settle."

Alayna swallowed, at once frustrated that Helmsted couldn't be baited while at the same time feeling a sense of fortune at having escaped a fight with the accomplished Guild member. Philip had always cautioned her against underestimating Collectors, especially high-ranking members—those high in the Guild did not rise by bureaucracy and financial station but rather on the strength of their arm, their prowess, and their experience in the field. One could bet that a high-ranking member was just about as dangerous as a human possibly could be.

"Why not throw me into the Night Pits, instead?" Azir volunteered nonchalantly from the next cage over, leaning against the bars of his cage.

"Oh, now that's adorable. The vampire is sweet on the Elfas. No, a hybrid like you is too valuable for the pits. I once reserved the same thought for her, but an affront like earlier cannot go unanswered. All my clients from today have been invited back to watch you fight tomorrow, Elfas."

Azir's face darkened at her response. She ignored him, turning on her heel and walking away.

"I don't need your protection, Azir," Alayna said heatedly.

He held up his hands in apology, but there were lines of worry around his eyes. "We should talk strategy."

She grimaced. "We've been talking strategy for days. What more is there to say?"

He grunted in disagreement. "We have been discussing a winning strategy, Alayna, but this will be different. I have heard the guards and other creatures mutter of the pits. We need to talk about a strategy just so that you can survive."

"Isn't it one and the same? I can't survive without winning."

"True, but all the same, your plans for operating in the Night Pits will need to be different, Alayna." As he looked at her, he was clutching the bars of his cage so tightly that his knuckles had grown white.

"Ah, you are sweet on me," Alayna teased impulsively before feeling a moment of guilt at the realization of what she had just said. What would Philip think if he had seen that? The thought was replaced by anger. He wasn't here. He'd abandoned her. A dark smudge on her thoughts seemed to relish in the understanding and acceptance of that thought.

Azir made a disgusted sound in his throat at her statement. "Joke all you want, Alayna, but you will be lucky if you manage to survive the morrow. The pits are where they throw the worst that are housed in this forsaken menagerie."

Alayna sobered up a bit at his comment and nodded resolutely, a determination to stay alive filling her mind. "All right, then. Let's talk about survival."

ALAYNA STOOD in in the pit, waiting for her opponent to be brought out. The smell of old blood mixed into the dirt floor assailed her nose. Shouts and screams along with catcalls from particularly lustful men in the stands filled the air. She flexed her hands and then tightened her fists anxiously, feeling her knuckles crack as she did. She swallowed but could hardly do so for the dryness of her throat.

She'd fought before. First in St. Thomas, then during months of being pursued by endless Collectors. Alayna had fought and killed and bled, but nothing had prepared her for this. The fact that her life and possibly her death would be a spectacle for paying customers added a certain bleakness to it. There was something different about fighting for oneself with a back against a wall when compared to combat in a fighting pit.

And then her opponent arrived. The pits were darkened, illuminated only by flickering torchlight because the creatures that inhabited this squat building dug into the ground were largely unable to survive in the light—or simply hated the light of the sun. Vampires and misshapen werewolves who had stayed in their beastly form for so long that they could not change back. Dark fauns from the black marshes to the north, manticores from the east, and death sprites. All of them inhabited the Night Pits and were thrown against one another in the most vicious of fashions.

She tried to quell her fear as the dark faun—its black skin covering ropey muscles—strutted out of the tunnel leading from the stands above down into the pits. Its cloven hooves bit deeply into the dirt. It was muzzled to prevent its lies, and the creature was shackled at the wrists. Fauns in general were dangerous; Philip had warned her that even the most benign of their kind could spin a web of deception that would leave innocents dead in their wake. He had only briefly mentioned the dark fauns—a subset that trained with weapons as well as with spells, that spun webs and wielded blades with equal ease. He had seemed uneasy speaking of them, and that alone was uncommon.

Alayna watched from across the pit, staring as the dark faun's lean but muscled form accepted an axe from the guards that unshackled it. It knew better than to attack them—it had been tortured into subservience—but Alayna could see the fury in its eyes, knew that its rage would find its release in the battle with her. She hefted her own weapon, a sword. She was more comfortable with knives, and certainly with crossbows, but it was a short sword, and perhaps she could make do. She had to.

The hulking form straightened, and suddenly it towered above the heads of the guards, almost like an uncoiling snake. Alayna swallowed back her fear. She had to kill this thing, this black, sinewy creature that hailed from some distant and foreign land. She glanced up to the stands and saw the light of vicious amusement in Helmsted's eyes. Immediately, she could tell that Helmsted wanted her death. She wanted it like she wanted water on a hot day, and she wouldn't have matched Alayna with this dark faun if it wasn't lethal. As if on cue, the faun swung a few wickedly casual strokes of the axe through the air to limber up. It moved with a lithe but hulking agility, like a giant spider that knew how best to tie up prey in a web.

Before Alayna had time to collect any more of her thoughts, Helmsted's voice rang out, issuing the fight to commence. Right away, the dark faun closed the distance with a loping stride that ate up the yards between them at a frightening pace. Alayna bounded away, keeping the tip of her sword up and ready. The crowd booed her defensive strategy.

Stay alive. Use your strengths—your speed, agility, and most of all your endurance. She heard Azir's voice from their planning the night before. *Keep out of range of your foe's weapons for as long as possible. Tire them out. You aren't there to please anyone—you are there to stay alive.*

And so Alayna did. She ignored the crowd, she tuned out Helmsted's derisive laughter at her tactics, and she kept as much distance as possible between herself and the dark faun. The beast was crafty and clever, and its mouth had been unmuzzled. It spat a few curse spells at her, but the faun's particular type of magic required a certain willingness of its target to believe the worst, to buy into the curse. Philip had trained her, had helped her to craft her mind against such strategies, much like a Collector. Alayna felt the curses flutter against her mind without gaining purchase as she brushed them away like cobwebs.

The dark faun, black of body and skin, pursued her about the pit. They clashed occasionally—she couldn't avoid it forever—and when they did, more often than not Alayna came away with shallow wounds to show for it. But she somehow managed to keep her distance, to wear down the faun and protect her mind from the web of deception that was constantly spilling forth from its lips which were peeled back in a rotten rictus of a snarl.

They clashed weapons and spun apart, clashed and swirled away, all in accordance with her strategy and all to the sound of a crowd howling for blood. The dark faun's beady, black eyes locked on Alayna's as it stalked her around the pit, its axe scarring her sword with blows, its hooves punching holes in the ground. As it followed, though, eventually Alayna began to see that it was tiring. The creature started to breathe in swift, panting breaths. It swung its axe more erratically and landed fewer blows, pressed her slightly less.

Dodge, keep your distance, wait for it to tire. She heard the litany of Azir's instructions in her head, and she followed them. She followed them until she saw spittle form on the faun's mouth, saw its tired eyes grow angry with desperation. Alayna waited and bided her time until the moment was right. Finally, her opponent rushed in, wielding its axe with just a little less accuracy than before. It swung hard, hoping for a killing strike, hoping to land a blow that would send her head flying into the stands, send her blood coursing onto the earth, already blackened with the blood of the previous fallen.

But it was weakened, tired from the pursuit, and she was an Elfas. She had a few nicks and shallow wounds, but she'd been trained by a Collector and advised by a vampire. She had the endurance to last. Alayna ducked under the swinging axe and came in close and fast to the faun's side. As she swept past, the beast tried to right itself, attempted to regain the balance it had lost, but to no avail. She lithely bounded past and, once inside its defenses, she neatly hamstrung her opponent with one casual sweep of her blade.

The dark faun bellowed in agony and crumpled to the floor as it could no longer support its weight. It rolled onto its back and swung another vicious but wild swing from the ground as Alayna closed in again, but she blocked and kicked the weapon from its grasp. It spat a flurry of spells and deceptions from its mouth, and while Alayna felt them tugging, tugging, pulling at her mind, begging to be believed in order to gain power, she fought them off and lunged in close, thrusting the notched sword through her rival's throat. The dark faun shuddered and gasped its last. She looked up to the stands to see a relieved Azir exhale a long, shuddering breath. She saw Helmsted's mouth pucker in annoyance. Only annoyance, though. Alayna knew that her previous affront had earned her a daily bout in the Night Pits for as long as it took until Helmsted's aim was accomplished—until Alayna eventually succumbed to a foe much more dangerous than the faun.

She ripped her sword back out of her opponent's dead body and held it aloft. Blood dripped off of the blade and the crowd shrieked with pleasure. Customers paid for blood, and she had finally given it to them after much delay. She felt sick, yet there was a strange exultation at having survived, at having vanquished her foe. She gazed up into the stands and saw an understanding in Azir's eyes and he grinned at her, liking what he saw. It took a moment before she realized that she was grinning, too.

CHAPTER TWENTY-TWO

"HELMSTED WON'T STOP UNTIL SHE'S MADE ME PAY WITH MY LIFE," Alayna said.

Azir stared at her through the bars of their cages as moonlight poured in. "Alphas do hate to be humiliated in front of those they deem their lesser, and the good lady most certainly views herself as an alpha."

Alayna wracked her brain, but no answers were forthcoming. "We've got to get out of here. We both know I'll find it difficult to survive another bout in the Night Pits. A faun—dark or not—is the least of what I will encounter there. She'll soon begin pitting you against tougher opponents, as well."

"I can handle my end," Azir said with a smile that embodied supreme confidence. For the life of her, Alayna could not understand how he managed to stay calm during their captivity. She was an Elfas and he a vampire; if either of them should be the angrier due to their natures, it was him, the predator, the killer. Yet it was Alayna who struggled for composure, hence her bloodying of Helmsted and recent trip to the pits.

"You won't be able to last forever, Azir. Eventually you'll take an injury that will slow you down for the next fight, and the same for the one after. You've seen some of the creatures you've faced. They're practically mincemeat by the time she feeds them to you as fodder. That's your fate if we don't get out of here."

"Come now, Elfas, I want out of here as much as you do. But if you are not careful, I may begin to think that you care about me."

"I feel responsible," Alayna muttered while jerking futilely at the iron bars of her cage.

"Tit for tat, same thing now, isn't it?"

"Not really, no." She avoided eye contact as the lie slipped from her lips. It wasn't so much the lie that bothered her as the fact that the lie needed to exist in the first place. She did feel a strange compulsion around the vampire, a connection. It was hard to admit, but she did care, at least enough to not want to see him dead. He smirked at her through the bars as if reading her thoughts.

"Tell me what you are thinking..." he purred in a crooning voice. She felt the soft tugging, the dangerous caress on her mind.

Tapping into her training, she forced his voice away from her mind. It was difficult, but still it was accomplished. "Stop that," she snapped.

Azir laughed and his voice changed back to normal. "Never fear, Alayna, I am saving my voice for when the time comes to make our move. I won't waste more than a sample on you."

"Well, we should quit waiting. I don't think I've got more than a day or two at most before Lady Helmsted finds a suitable way to ensure her revenge."

Azir nodded, sincerity in his voice as he agreed, "We may have to abandon our plan for patience and simply force another exit. Better to fall fighting for our freedom than slaughtered for the fans." He bared his teeth in a silent snarl. Alayna agreed with him.

Just then, a cohort of guards walked up. They stopped in front of her cell. "Oh, do we have some fun in store for you, little lady." Ashford, the lead guard, smirked. "Lady's orders."

They unlocked the cell. Alayna's heart pounded as five of them entered. She fought; she fought hard. She heard one guard's nose pop, a sick crunching sound as it met the heel of her palm, but in close quarters the five-on-one odds were too stacked against her. They swarmed her and clasped manacles on her wrists and ankles before dragging her from the cage. All the while, Azir screamed angrily, and though her head was spinning from a few too many blows in so short a span of time, Alayna couldn't help but think that she'd never seen the vampire so angry. He snarled and snapped through the bars, but the Collectors simply chuckled smugly and continued to drag her by her hair.

The dirt path was abrasive as it met her pale skin, and patches were rubbed raw. Finally, she fought through the daze just as they thrust her into a new cell, a cage littered with metal instruments and sickening with the stench of blood. The torturer's pen. Thrashing, she fought, and involuntary 'no's came to her lips in shrieks that embodied all at once the desperation and indignity of this place. Shame at her fear coursed through her, but that fear itself would not abate. Three fingernails and a beating had occurred the last time she was tortured, but now she had a feeling that it would be worse.

It was.

They strapped her thrashing body to the table, and the torturer smiled almost benignly as he began to describe in detail what he would do to her. He spoke for what seemed like hours, detailing the precise cuts he would make, the burns he would inflict, the blows he would strike. It was a wholly sinister experience, and Alayna was entirely certain that this man was the evilest being in the entire world —human or not.

"I am instructed to make certain you know why this is happening, hmm?" the torturer said in a strange sort of singsong voice. There was an inflection at the end of nearly every statement that made them seem like questions.

"I know why!" Alayna spat. "I'm here because I embarrassed Helmsted in front of her little pets." She wasn't a fool. She knew that torture eventually broke everyone, but she was determined to hold on to her fire for as long as possible.

The torturer nodded happily. "Yes. Exactly!" He spoke as if she had won a prize, as if she was a model student and he the teacher administering praise. "I will not kill you. The good lady has reserved that for the ring. But," he held up a finger dramatically, "I am instructed to make you regret your actions from the other day. Well then, shall we begin, hmm?"

And he began.

Alayna barely managed to last a minute before screams erupted from her throat. All shame left. All hopes to hold strong and maintain her pride evaporated and all that remained was surviving the moment, keeping hold of her sanity through the pain. And she did that—barely.

He set to work on her with small precision blades much like a surgeon would use, cutting into muscles that were not as important, muscles whose injury would not hamper her ability to fight in the pits quite so much. The torturer then moved on to hot pincers, and Alayna felt burn after burn against her stomach and her legs, the palms of her hands, the soles of her feet. At one point, she blacked out from the agony until a bucket of cold, rancid water was thrown onto her face to awaken her. She longed for the day when losing a few fingernails and a good beating had been the worst of her concerns. In the corners of the torture pen, halfway concealed by the shadows, were more implements of pain and machines of agony. Racks, flaying apparatuses, screws, and wheels. Somehow, even worse than the present was imagining what her fate would be the next time she visited this pen.

And then it was over. Blissfully over. She slumped into the bloody table, tears pouring down her face. The torturer peered down at her with a fatherly expression. "It hurts, hmm? Yes, yes of course. Well, we are done for now, isn't that wonderful?"

He bandaged her wounds and put salve on some of the worst burns. For a moment, she was confused as to why he was tending to her. Then the reality struck: she would fight again tomorrow, and Helmsted wanted her in pain but not brutally injured, wanted the torture to continue, to last as long as she could stay alive in the pits. It would not serve Helmsted's cause to field fighters who were unable to entertain her guests. She wanted Alayna to suffer, but she still wanted profit from her purchase, as well.

Night was full when the guards dragged her limp body back to her cage. Only two were needed this time. The stars twinkled overhead under a cloudless sky, and Alayna wondered if she could join them, just vanish from this hell. Each guard held her by an arm so that, thankfully, only her heels dragged on the abrasive dirt path. She almost wept with relief.

When they reached her cage, Azir's screams of fury roused her from her semiconscious stupor.

"What did you do to her? I'll kill you!" The vampire's threats were entirely unimaginative, and yet they carried with them the authenticity of genuine hatred, of fury unchecked. Alayna would not want to be on the other end of those threats. After all, she had seen the vampire fight in the pits.

One guard let her go, and the remaining Collector deposited her on her back in the cell. They unshackled her, as was often the case, while in her cage—Helmsted wanted fresh fighters to impress her patrons, not prisoners who looked worn and sore from being chained.

While the one stood outside, the guard above her—she thought that it was Elgin, but in the dark and in her haze, she couldn't tell for sure—leaned in close to whisper, "Rest up, sweetling. Tomorrow's more of the same." Then he pinched her.

Something snapped. She couldn't do that again. Not the pits, not the torture. She couldn't endure one more pinch, one more affront to her dignity. It ended now.

In a flash of anger, she regained some of the strength sapped during her recent ordeal. From her prone position, she wrapped her legs around Elgin's neck with Elfas speed. She swiveled her hips and twisted his body to the ground, enjoying the look of surprise and shock on his face right before his body twisted with hers and she heard his neck pop.

The other guard shouted something and lunged for the cage door, but he froze as Azir turned his predatory vampire's voice upon him in full force. Against his will and in a hypnotic state, the young guard marched woodenly to Azir's gate and unlocked it, staring briefly into his eyes before the vampire locked jaws on his neck and drained him of life. Drained him messily, quickly.

Alayna struggled to rise, managing to get to her knees before Azir was at her side offering a shoulder to throw her arm over. They stumbled out of her cage and into the darkness of the night. A full moon lit their way, making it easy for them to see yet also making it easy for them to *be* seen.

"I couldn't wait," she mumbled nearly incoherently. "I couldn't do that again."

"Shh," the vampire whispered back in a strangely gentle voice. He continued to lead her from shadow to shadow, ducking into alleys to avoid patrols.

A moment of clarity pierced the fog of pain that was slow to dissipate. "Your voice. If you could do that against a trained Collector, why didn't you do it before and get us out of here?" she asked in a slurred but slowly strengthening voice.

Azir shrugged. "I can use the croon and the seductive trance it induces to varying extents, but it takes more energy to utilize it with greater force. A suggestion is easy, but a direct command that must be obeyed—like I just did with that guard—is more difficult. It depletes my energy in a way that a suggestion will not. I had to make sure that I used it at the right moment because I now will not get a chance to use my voice like that for some time yet. It is best in one-on-one situations, not groups, and we are usually guarded by at least three if not by more. But they must have deemed you weakened enough that only one pair of Collectors was thought necessary. When you killed the first, it was time. I finally had the opportunity to make my move."

She exhaled, breathing hard as she struggled to not be a burden for him in their escape. "Oh. I guess that makes sense."

They fought their way—or rather, Azir did most of the fighting—past two pairs of guards before they reached the wall. The vampire disposed of them in brutal and efficient fashion, as if he'd saved up every ounce of energy he had for just this time. Alayna was glad of it, because she certainly wasn't much help at the moment. Her wounds were burning, causing excruciating agony, and she felt at the point of collapse. Somehow she made it, though.

They reached the rough, low wall of the manor estate, and Azir disengaged himself from her draped arm. "You must climb now. I cannot balance with you on my back."

"I can do it." Alayna nodded her assurance, summoning upon whatever reserves she possessed.

Her hands, raw from the pincers, threatened to lose their grasp at every handhold, but thankfully the wall was not high. She climbed alongside the vampire. They scaled one side of the wall—the height of three or four body-lengths stacked upon each other—and then down the other. Then they were free.

Alayna breathed deeply as grey dawn threatened to break night's firm grasp on the land. Free air, for however long it lasted, was worth just about anything that might happen after this should they be caught.

"You are lucky I am a hybrid and can walk in the light," Azir said with a hint of pride at his uniqueness within the supernatural world. "Others of my kind would be forced to take cover and hide right in the shadow of the menagerie."

Alayna swallowed to wet her throat and answered as they climbed through ravines and gullies that surrounded the estate to the south, "If you were not a hybrid, you might also still be one of my kind, depending on how you look at things."

The vampire simply glanced at her for a moment before asking, "And would that make you happy?"

She didn't respond. Instead, she lead the way now, clambering awkwardly, tiredly, but determinedly upward and over a ridge, then through a gully as they struggled to put some distance between themselves and the menagerie. Alayna stumbled with exhaustion and found it difficult to pay attention to her surroundings. She needed rest—she needed sleep. So, when Azir paused with a strange look on his face as he grasped her arm to stop, she did so with oblivious surprise.

The vampire motioned for silence and then whispered, "There are people on the other side of the ridge. We must be silent."

Again, she noticed a strange look in his eyes, but she ignored it out of fatigue. She nodded wearily, and they picked their way along as quietly as possible. Soon, dawn would arrive and their escape would become apparent. They needed to place as many miles as possible between themselves and the menagerie by the time the grey light of morning finally arrived.

CHAPTER TWENTY-THREE

"You can go now." Philip didn't look at The Alchemist, but all three of them knew who he was addressing.

"Just like that? You drag me across the length and breadth of Transylvania just to let me walk away?" The Alchemist's tone was suitably dubious.

Philip clenched his teeth at the comment as he looked down on the manor compound from the crest of a small ridgeline. It was almost morning, and they'd been traveling for days without many stops. He would normally feel exhausted, but being so close to his goal had invigorated him instead.

"I needed you. I had to make sure you were taking me to the right place. I can see that you have." He half nodded, half thrust his chin down toward the compound as he lay on his elbows and belly to keep from sight. "I know the look of Guild sentries. I trust that you haven't lied to me. Besides, it doesn't matter if I let you go or not. If Alayna doesn't come out of this mess alive and well, I am going to track you down and do things to you that you've only seen in your nightmares."

The Alchemist gulped but didn't immediately leave. It was as if he still didn't quite believe he was being set free. For now, at least. Philip had not been bluffing with his threat. There was a very real chance that Alayna was dead or worse in there and, if so, The Alchemist would be only one of his stops on the road to retribution.

Beathan had crawled up next to them. "I can sneak in shadowy-like and reconnoiter a wee bit. See what we're up against."

Philip shook his head. "No."

"What d'ya' mean, no? We both know ya' don't quite have the necessary skills for reconnaissance, Philip. I'm the obvious choice."

He shook his head again, reluctant to answer. The sun was coming up, and he wanted to start before it was fully risen. Shift change just before dawn was often a weak point with sentries, even ones so well trained as in the Guild. Those leaving their post were tired, and those arriving had just risen, both instances lending to foggy thinking and inattentiveness. Now was the time to strike. He just had to get rid of his friend.

"We don't even know if she's alive, Beathan."

"Exactly, mate. That's why I go in and find out before ya' do anythin' rash. I can see that look brewin' in your eyes."

"I didn't break you free of the Guild just so that you could fall back into their clutches. I can't risk you, not when we don't even know whether or not she's alive. Besides, I'm going in one way or another, be it for rescue or revenge." Philip's callused fists clenched as he spoke, then he flexed and clenched them again with anger. The compound had no idea the type of fury he was about to rain down. This anger wasn't just a flash, wasn't spontaneous. It had been building steadily. The thunder of the north country pulsed through his veins.

"'tis madness t' go alone, Philip. Ya' have t' let me come along. Ya' won't survive alone, not against those odds. An' believe you me, I'm familiar with long odds."

That settled it. Philip had to act now. He wouldn't risk Beathan, his one friend, not when it was just as likely that he was embarking upon a suicide mission of vengeance as it was an actual rescue attempt. For all he knew, Alayna could have been used up already for some vile purpose. No, at least he could keep Beathan safe. He could ask forgiveness later—*if* he survived.

Acting with the element of surprise, he lunged toward his fairy friend, and in one sudden motion he landed a blow strong enough to knock the gypsy unconscious.

"Well, that was certainly unexpected," The Alchemist said, still hanging around.

"I told you to go," Philip growled. "If you don't want me to do worse than this to you, you should take my advice."

The old man stared at him with a flicker of the pride and curiosity he'd shown during their first meeting, an emotion which had been absent over the past few days of being bullied by Philip and Beathan while leading them to the manor compound. Perhaps the glimpse of freedom was restoring his usual temperament.

"You should not make idle threats, Collector." There was menace in his voice.

"They aren't idle. You should know that."

They stared at one another for a moment longer before the scientist finally melted into the woods and disappeared, moving much more quickly and smoothly than one would expect of someone with a cane.

Philip waited a few minutes to make sure that he was truly gone before checking Beathan to make sure he was fine. He didn't think that he'd hit him too hard, but it never hurt to be certain. Satisfied that the fairy would have little more than a headache upon awakening, Philip began slithering down the small slope in the steadily lightening sky. It wasn't yet dawn, but it would be soon. He wanted to be within striking distance when the sun peeked over the horizon.

What he was doing was rash, perhaps even foolhardy. In many ways, Beathan was right: he should have scouted, planned more. But Philip felt as though he would burst for any more waiting, and after everything he'd put his friend through—spending over a month trying to catch and eat him—he just couldn't ask, could not let the fairy help him in this, on what was likely a suicidal endeavor. Either they would meet on the other side of this event and resume their companionship or Philip would fail, in which case Beathan would be free to continue his wayward ways. Philip found himself smiling at the thought of the half-fairy slipping his sticky fingers into people's pockets, a notion that would have offended him in the past.

He descended to the flats leading up to the gate and covered the ground at a steady, half-crouched lope. The still-present darkness covered much of his approach until he was close to the opening. He sprinted, closing the final distance to the gate amid shouts of alarm, calls for him to declare himself, and hastily raised weapons. Philip ignored it all. He had one focus. He approached the gate like a battering ram. With one swift kick of his heel, the oaken doors quivered, the metal supports warping with a stressed screech. A second kick and the wood splintered inward.

And then he was in. The guards descended from their posts on the wall and rushed him. Philip made short work of them. A bullet flew past his cheek, close enough for him to feel the wind and hear the whine. He didn't flinch. He put his fist through one man's face and his foot through the other's knee with a sickening *crunch*. He'd leave nothing to chance, take no quarter, not until he found Alayna. With that thought in mind, he stomped on a downed man's jaw. Unsure whether the blow had killed him or not, Philip was sure of one thing at least: it had incapacitated him. He was willing to do whatever it took to find Alayna.

Philip stalked into the compound with the deadly grace of a trained fighter and the brutish rage of a furious troll. The manor had no idea what was coming. As steel-grey light finally crested the far mountains, Philip smiled grimly at the prospect of a bloody morning.

———

ALAYNA DIDN'T MAKE it much past daybreak before she collapsed to her knees and then slumped all the way to the ground.

"I need to rest, Azir." Her breath came in painful, panting breaths.

The vampire was at her side immediately, crouching down to one knee as he almost tenderly checked her myriad wounds. His fingers roved her body in a way that at once made her uncomfortable and excited.

"They are all shallow. The cuts were clearly meant to be painful but not to seriously injure." His coldly elegant accent made every word, every syllable lyrical.

She nodded wearily. "I know. That man—the torturer—he said I was being punished but that Helmsted still wanted me able to fight tomorrow. Today, I guess." She winced as he prodded one of her burned palms.

"Sorry, Alayna, but there is nothing I can do for you now. Even if I had the necessary medical supplies, I am no physician. Besides, we don't have time. They are already rousing. You will have to push through." He cupped her cheek in a familiar fashion.

She felt her blood rise slightly. To direct her line of thinking elsewhere, she turned an ear to what he had pointed out. It was true— she could hear a far-off ruckus that must have been coming from the menagerie, since there was nothing else close enough that might be the source. If they were hearing it this far away, then Helmsted must be in a fury and rousing her men accordingly. Alayna said as much to Azir.

The hybrid vampire nodded sagely. "All the more reason to continue on our way. We are already slower than we normally would be." He cast a pointed glance at her wounds.

"Help me up?" Alayna asked with an uncharacteristically plaintive voice. Exhaustion was creeping in.

Azir grabbed her hand and easily pulled her to her feet. However, Alayna, weakened by fatigue and the loss of blood, stumbled slightly. He caught her in his arms and, for a moment—oh so briefly—she let herself stay there. He was deceptively strong for his frame. He still had the lithe, agile-looking body of an Elfas, only it was combined with the power and cunning of a nightwalker. She looked up at him, black eyes set against graceful features framed by silky hair. The cold light of morning painted him pale, as pale as the moonlight ever could. He was more attractive than she remembered. Or maybe she was just tired and not thinking straight.

Alayna made to push awkwardly away. What was she doing? How could she think this way? A tiny voice in the back of her mind whispered that at least Azir was present, at least he'd endured captivity for her, broken out with her. He had never left her.

"Stop." Azir firmly pulled her close again, and she stopped struggling to escape his embrace.

He kissed her then, leaning in slowly. He kissed her softly, tentatively, but with gaining force when she did not immediately pull away. Azir's lips were chilled, whether from the cold morning air or by his vampiric nature she wasn't sure. And in the moment, she didn't care. She kissed him back, losing herself in the war of guilt and pleasure that she felt. The world blurred.

When it seemed the kiss would never end, a voice broke the stillness.

"Alayna. Well, this is certainly interesting."

She broke free of the kiss, and this time Azir let her go as she turned to confront that smugly smirking voice she knew all too well. The Alchemist leaned on his cane, watching them warily but with great amusement on his face.

"What are you doing here?" she blurted out, caught off guard and unable to think of anything else to say.

"Your oaf of a lover dragged me all the way across the land so that I could guide him to where you were."

"Philip is here?" she repeated in shock.

"Came to rescue you, or avenge you. Whichever was necessary. He's at it right this moment, I expect, due to the clamor I can hear."

"Is he alone?" Again, Alayna couldn't ask but the most basic of questions. Worry began to seep in. It felt like she hadn't thought of Philip in much too long a time.

"He wasn't. The fairy was with him, but he knocked the lad unconscious and went down to the manor himself. Some nonsense about not wanting to risk his friend's life. Although, seeing you now, I'm not sure why you would care." The old man smirked again, and his face held an insufferable look that Alayna itched to wipe away—with violence, if need be. He'd *sold* her. This was *his* fault. The entire situation, her confusion, the conflicted emotions she harbored. She could trace it all back to him. She took a step forward, but Azir stopped her.

"Who is this, Alayna?" The suspicion in his voice was apparent. The vampire's lips curled into a snarl.

"This is The Alchemist," she answered simply.

"The one you told me about? The one who sold you?" His voice carried a dangerous edge.

"Now, don't forget that I also saved her life!" The Alchemist protested nervously. "Everyone seems to overlook that part."

"You sold her," Azir stated darkly, as if that was all that counted. Perhaps it was.

In a flash, the vampire closed the distance between them and ripped the man's throat to shreds before Alayna or, indeed, The Alchemist could react. The man collapsed to the ground in a pool of his own blood.

Alayna watched as he sputtered his last bloody breaths, watched dispassionately as the light faded from his eyes, watched the terror of death set in as his last concrete emotion. There had been a time when this sort of thing would have bothered her, when she would have done nearly anything to avoid killing. Not now. The thought strayed across the outskirts of her mind, but she brushed it away. That had been the Alayna who had never entered the menagerie, had never been tortured or beaten, had never been threatened, humiliated, or forced to fight for exhibition.

She turned to Azir in annoyance. "If anyone was going to kill him, it should have been me. Besides, won't this turn out poorly for you if word gets out to Dracula that one of his own defied his orders and killed The Alchemist?"

An uncommon look of fear flashed behind Azir's eyes. "Well then, we'll have to make sure that nobody else learns of it."

Alayna stared at him for a moment. She could tell that he cared for her; he'd just killed the man who had caused her so much pain without even blinking. But then another realization crossed her mind, crushing whatever warmth she might have been feeling toward him.

"You weren't surprised."

"What?"

"You already knew. You weren't surprised when he told us that Philip and Beathan were near. I saw the look on your face, and it wasn't the kind of look a person has when given new information. That was them, earlier, when you said there were people nearby and you told me to be silent. Wasn't it?"

His black eyes went flat and flashed angrily. "They abandoned you! They left you to rot in that cage. *I* was there. I *helped* you. Or have you forgotten?"

His rage and the hurt look on his face caught her off balance. "No, they didn't. I mean, I thought they did, but now...they wouldn't be here now if they had." She hated the way her last statement came out like a question, pleading for Azir to agree. Why did she feel so conflicted? She loved Philip. Or, at least, she had. Now all she felt was a foggy confusion when she tried to confront her emotions. That confusion had been precipitated by Azir's presence. She steeled herself. "We are going back. I am, anyway. You can do whatever you wish."

He sneered. "You will die if you go back now, given your injured condition."

Alayna shrugged and turned back the way they had come. "So be it. Philip came for me, and now I have to be there for him."

She tried to make herself feel as convinced as she sounded, but she was finding it difficult to understand her swirling tangle of emotions. She felt light and joy over the fact that Philip hadn't abandoned her and had finally come for her—albeit late. She also felt anger toward Azir, since he had tried to hide that knowledge from her. She knew guilt too, though, from being so angry at the one person who had been by her side and her comrade in suffering for the past month. She worried that none of this would ever be set right.

Alayna swallowed, gathered whatever strength she had left, and hardened her will. Whatever came next, it would require every ounce of what she had left to give. Of that much she was sure.

CHAPTER TWENTY-FOUR

Philip prowled through the compound, laying waste to everyone he encountered. He left broken bones, crushed skulls, and shattered lives in his wake. Still, he also sustained injuries. He was just one man—only one half-man—against an entire legion of his former Collector compatriots.

He barely noted the decadent manor with its marble columns and elegant architecture. Instead, he struck straight for the menagerie. It was exceedingly easy to find. All he had to do was follow the sound of the screams and the plume of putrid smoke that was clearly used to burn the offal and other remains of the dead. Guards confronted him at every turn as he entered the maze of narrow streets and alley paths that wove like a warren throughout the vast array of shadowy enclosures.

A grim guard approached. He carried a pistol at his hip, which was uncommon, but in typical Collector fashion he went for his stake instead. Silent modes of combat were preferred in Guild training for a variety of reasons, and their use was ingrained in their subjects, especially those of the more mature generation. This was a rare veteran Collector, still a field operative even at such an advanced age. He was either very good to have survived this long without moving out of direct combat or he was very lucky. Perhaps both.

Philip leapt into the attack at the sight of the Collector. A one-on-one clash was nothing to shy away from, and he had the obvious advantage. The older man met Philip's bold rush steadily, firmly. He blocked a blow and thrust in with his sharpened stake—sharpened to a point nearly as fine as worked steel. Philip avoided the strike and landed a staggering blow of his own to the Collector's chest, causing the man to stumble to one knee and struggle for breath. He stepped close as the Collector tried to rise and swiftly broke his neck.

So much for the hardened veteran. It seemed that some patterns still held true. The older a Guild member, the more likely he or she was to move away from the field of combat else they end up like this. Philip stared down at the man. Wrinkles at his eyes and a weathered look to his face and hands put him probably more than a decade past Philip's own age. Once he would have felt sorry for the man, would have been consumed by sorrow for the death of a former comrade. Not now, not after the past few months. St. Thomas Prison had been an eye-opening experience. The treatment of the prisoners, the torture for the sake of pain, and now this. Philip could have forgiven even the pursuit he'd experienced over the last few months—he had keenly felt the loss of each Collector he and his friends had been forced to kill. But not now, not after this menagerie. Not after he had witnessed so many of his former peers go rogue all at once, all together.

Philip had been stalking through this menagerie searching for Alayna, hunting for any sign of her, but he'd also seen what else it had to offer. Captives—not dangerous creatures alone, but all kinds. Torture pens, fighting pits, breeding cages. Philip knew that this was a Collector base gone rogue, devoted to profit and entertainment. Something about that set his blood on fire almost as much as the fact that Alayna was imprisoned here. Almost.

And so he hunted and he killed. With each step he took, his ire rose. With each Collector he killed, the troll within him threatened to erupt as if he had only barely managed to control that part of himself, that primal force, in the time since regaining his cognitive abilities. Against his common sense he let some of it loose, released a portion of that fury. It was costing him too much to try and contain it.

Almost from another place, it seemed, he heard the roar erupt form his lips. It sounded more troll, more thunderous blizzard, than man. He let it loose and merged it with his mind, added words to the rage.

"I want Alayna!" he roared. He screamed it over and over again as he stalked through that dark menagerie, following his senses, hunting for a whiff of her scent that would lead him to her.

His cries for Alayna might have sounded petulant were it not for the sheer power pulsating through his veins, were it not for the force exuding from him, more force than he'd ever felt before. Perhaps this was what happened when he surrendered to the north, when he let more of the troll loose and retained just enough of the man to hold on to his wild nature, like a horseman who could barely keep hold of the reins.

And then it came. A scent hit his nose, and that instinctual part of himself registered it. It was hers. There was no doubt. Philip followed the smell, stomping through a cage rather than going around it, laying waste to the metal bars in his rage and hurry to get through. He was a cannon ball of anger. He bulled through a group of three Collectors, finishing them in moments, hardly feeling the wounds they inflicted upon him.

And then he was there. He smelled it, *felt* it, knew that this cage, the one in front of which he now stood, was hers. Her scent was all over it. The smell of her blood was everywhere. Only, she wasn't there. He tore at the bars, warped them, thrashed them in his anger. Where was she? A pit of fear formed in his stomach. Was he too late? Was she dead? Over a month in a place like this could sometimes be weeks too long to survive. Philip felt fresh rage at the Guild as he tore her former pen apart. It was almost worse to have the shred of hope that she was still alive torn away from him—better he had lost her only once than twice like this.

But he had stayed in one place for too long. He'd stopped moving once he'd found her cage, and that had allowed the Guild members to track him. Collectors began filing up in twos and threes—four at a time, even, running toward the primal sounds of his fury. Philip turned to confront them. These were who he wished to face, these men, these former comrades of his were who he wanted to kill. He stared death at them, beckoned them to come with a feral challenge in his eyes. If she was not here, then likely she was dead. And he would avenge her.

The Collectors stared at Philip warily. Even with so many they were cautious; they'd seen what he'd done to the rest of their compound. *Why wait*, Philip thought as he decided to take the fight to them. With a roar, he charged. Three crossbow bolts took him at once, and a musket ball ripped through his shoulder. Pain exploded across his entire body, threatening to reduce his mind to a fiery agony of ashes. Philip stumbled forward into the mass of Collectors. He laid waste to the few around him, his fists granite war hammers from the northern mountains. He crushed one skull and felt another throat snap in his grasp before their swarming attack became too much. He felt a wooden stake drive into his leg, cold steel bite into his side.

So this was it.

He could feel his strength sapping, yet he fought on. He struggled to exact as much vengeance as possible on her behalf. To avenge her loss. Again. He fought, and the world grew blurry, shadows stretching around the outskirts of his vision. Still he fought, still he drew blood. And lost it, as well. Philip swung his fist and shattered a kneecap. Strangely, he was on his own knees now, fighting even though he had not the strength to stand. Then the weight and strength of their combined bodies forced him down. The end had finally come. One of his last thoughts in that moment was relief—gladness that he'd left the fairy behind, not doomed him to die in this pit.

But before a killing blow could arrive, a voice sounded from the near distance, a female voice, a voice that rang with power and authority. A voice that was all too familiar with its harsh edges and demanding tone.

"I want him alive."

———

A HAND SHOOK HIM AWAKE. It was a gentle, friendly hand. Beathan shook his head slightly and struggled to sit up, fought to regain his focus and clear his bleary vision. What had happened? Why was he unconscious? And then it came back to him.

"That bastard!" he muttered angrily as he tried to regain his wits.

"Who?" Alayna asked.

"Philip's a damn martyr, a bastard friend is what he is!" Beathan answered bitterly. How could he have gone in alone, and without someone scouting first? Did he want to get himself killed?

And then it hit him. Alayna. She was here, kneeling over him. His wits returned and he stared into her friendly face for the first time in over a month.

He reached up and cupped her cheek with a friendly smile, an expression filled with wonderment. "Alayna, ya' really are alive. I half didn't believe it," he breathed.

She returned the grin for a moment, but then her seriousness returned. "Where is Philip? What did that idiot go and do?"

"He went in. For you." Beathan noticed the dark shape lurking behind her, then. "Hello, Azir."

"Beathan," the former Elfas, now hybrid vampire nodded as he answered in his crisp and perfect accent.

"Alayna, what are ya' doin' out here? We thought ya'd been sold t' them." Beathan indicated the manor below the ridgeline.

"I escaped—or, rather, we did."

Something in her voice, in the way she said 'we' gave Beathan slight pause. But now wasn't the time to ponder. He took her in, really looked at her and saw that she was different. She was rougher, both in spirit and in body. Beathan cast a regretful smile up at her as he looked. He understood that captivity could harshen a person, create jagged edges of what had once been smooth. She'd been through hell, of that he was certain. Wounds—shallow but still painful-looking—crisscrossed her body. They were the type of wounds that were earned by fighting, but also the type that were caused by torture. The fairy could tell because he'd seen their like before, the precise way they ended just before reaching a vein that could bleed a person out, the way they covered surface area but didn't bite deeply enough to sap life. Alayna had been tortured for sure, and the missing fingernails only confirmed that assessment.

She felt his stare, looked at him as his eyes roved over her body, took in her injuries. Then the shame came—it was obvious. She looked away, and Beathan grabbed her firmly but gently by the cheeks and pulled her gaze back.

"No lass, it's not your fault. Ya' didn't do nothin' wrong t' deserve such treatment." She swallowed. She moved to turn her face away again, but he held her gaze. "Ya' hear me? I said it's not your fault. Ya' gotta let all that shame go now. Ya' hear?"

Alayna nodded and finally pulled away, but not before he saw a tear form in the corner of her eye. The tear didn't fall, though, it just stayed there, almost seeming to crystallize for a moment before receding back.

Alayna cleared her throat. "If you're out here and he's in there, we both know it's only a matter of time. There are too many of them." Back to business. She was tougher now. Brittle, as well, but stronger.

Beathan nodded. "He won't stop until he finds ya'. They'll kill him eventually."

"We have to save him," she said determinedly.

"Do we? Do we really? He left you in there to rot." Azir could always be counted on to run counter to popular opinion.

"Actually, he didn't. It's me fault, it is," Beathan volunteered with a heavy heart.

Alayna tilted her head. "What do you mean?"

Azir growled something unintelligible. He had his hooks into her, Beathan could see that, and it sent a shiver of concern down his spine. But that was a concern for another time.

"Do ya' remember the night in the woods? Ya' took the bolts from a Collector crossbow an' I saw ya' fall. I felt the life leave ya', saw the light fade from your eyes."

She nodded. "The Alchemist filled me in a little when I awoke and he was transporting me here. He said he'd revived me."

"He did more than that. I believe he quite literally brought ya' back from the dead—least as near t' dead as ya' can be without actually passin' over. He's a terrible sort, he is, but in a queer way ya' owe him your life." Beathan finally managed to stand as he spoke. He noticed a strange, almost guilty look pass between the vampire and Alayna as he spoke of The Alchemist, but he chose to ignore it. There would be time for questions later.

"We need to save Philip," she declared again, and this time Azir didn't dispute her decision; neither did he evaporate into the ether at the decision to help the former Collector.

There was no love lost between Philip and Azir after what had happened on the grassy cliff tops of England when they'd escaped from St. Thomas. They had left Azir alone—concealed by a spell, but alone and unconscious to find his own escape. It was Philip who had rendered him unconscious. No, the two had never liked one another, and if Azir was staying around to help rescue him, there was only one reason. Beathan was certain that the reason had red-gold hair and pointy ears. A vampire, a Collector, and an Elfas. It was a triangle that resembled the start of a bad joke.

"Feels like we're always rescuin' somebody," he muttered with a half-grin meant for Alayna. She returned it in kind, and it was good to see that she was still in there, that the joyful Alayna he remembered was still present.

"Wouldn't be us if we weren't," she responded with a wink, but then she allowed her grim mask to return.

"Well, if we must, then we must," Azir grumbled. "We should strike now. After the wreckage that Collector likely caused—I know his capabilities," Azir said grudgingly, "they will not be expecting another attack so soon."

For once, the vampire spoke sense. "I agree," Beathan said.

"I never planned on waiting, anyway. I'll not leave Philip in that menagerie of shadow a moment longer than necessary." As strong as Alayna's voice was, it held only a fraction of the determination her face showed. Yes, she was indeed harder.

"Then it's settled. We go in. But first I need a wee sip o' water for me parched throat. Gettin' knocked unconscious by your best mate tends t' increase your thirst quite a bit." Beathan rummaged through his pack until he found a drinking gourd with some water left inside.

Alayna's laughter at his quip seemed odd considering that they were about to set out on a suicide mission. Since when had Beathan started to accept foolhardy plans and last stands as normal or even practical decisions? It was simply not the way a thief was supposed to think!

Well, he mused to himself, *I suppose it must've happened the day I joined up with Philip and Alayna*. Something about good mates could make a person lose all common sense.

Out of the pack he pulled Alayna's two miniature crossbows— great for quick reloads—and all the bolts they had left. He handed them to her, and she caressed them fondly, gratefully.

"Time t' go, then," the gypsy-fairy said with a smirk of excitement upon his face. "Time t' steal a Collector from Collectors. Has there ever been a better heist than this?"

————

IT WAS UTTER DEVASTATION. The gates had been shattered and

were in pieces. Dead guards littered the entryway to the compound, and more bodies were strewn about the grounds in a steady trail leading toward the menagerie. Philip had left little more than carnage in his wake, and Alayna was suddenly beginning to wonder if perhaps they were more worried about him than they needed to be. She never would have thought him capable of overcoming even a fraction of the odds he'd faced inside these walls, even knowing what she knew of his powers. But *this*, this was shocking.

Beathan must have seen her wide-eyed gaze as they walked swiftly and stealthily toward the menagerie. "Ya' shoulda seen him when he thought ya' were dead. Somethin' in him snapped. He broke, and the beast in him made him stronger'n I ever seen before. Frightened even me."

"He can't stand up to the entire force at play within these walls, can he?" Alayna half asked, half stated.

Azir kept just to her right, maintaining a careful watch over her and everything around her. The vampire had snorted at the fairy's comment. It would take a mountain of proof to convince Azir that he should in any way fear the former Collector, someone Alayna knew he despised. How was she going to reconcile those two? Did she even want to? It was strange how she seemed to be thinking more clearly concerning Philip now that she had heard the truth of events from Beathan, now that she knew that he was close by.

They crept silently through the wreckage. They encountered Collectors a few times, but the three quickly dispatched of them. Alayna's miniature crossbows felt like familiar friends, extensions of herself. She hadn't realized how much she had missed them. She loosed bolts into the guards they encountered and Beathan and Azir mopped up after her. Unsuspecting, the Collectors fell quickly.

"We should pick a few locks an' release some more creatures. Add t' the mayhem," Beathan proposed as they began walking through the narrow dirt paths separating cages in the menagerie.

"It is not a terrible idea," Azir concurred.

Alayna shrugged. "I guess. But only those we can be certain won't attack us. Some are too dangerous to release now when our aim is to help Philip."

"Agreed." Beathan immediately began picking locks as they went, using tools that Alayna hadn't realized he possessed. The fairy was a thief, always had been and always would be, she supposed. She couldn't help but smile as she watched him in action.

A faun—normal, not a dark one—was released and thanked them with a quick nod. More creatures followed as they moved deeper into the menagerie. They released a werewolf in human form, what appeared to be a Redcap, and also a few minor witches—she assumed they were witches from the muzzles they wore. A few other creatures joined the ranks of the escaped, as well. It slowed them down somewhat, but Alayna agreed that, in the long run, the extra chaos would be an asset. It could be the difference between life and death, escape and capture. *And I will not be captured again,* she thought with steely determination.

They made their way farther in, and it wasn't long before Alayna realized she was leading them to her old cage. Somehow, instinctively, she knew that Philip would have made his way there. Sure enough, they found him. Not in her cage, precisely—no, her cell was ripped to shreds, the bars were warped, and the lock had burst. Philip was instead imprisoned in Azir's old cage. She saw him through the bars, bleeding from what looked like a hundred cuts and wounds, sporting a bruised face from having received countless blows. He was shackled with more than one set of manacles. The guards had left him lying on the ground with his wrists, forearms, and upper arms chained behind his back. The same was true of his legs. They feared his strength, and with good reason. However, in his current condition, he wouldn't be able to break from his restraints—not until he healed. Alayna prayed that he wasn't too hurt to heal. She was already slowing down from her own injuries sustained during last night's torture session; her adrenaline was wearing off. Blood trickled from a number of her own wounds which had reopened in a few of the skirmishes on the way into the menagerie.

As Alayna, Beathan, and Azir approached, the guards looked up from their posts and let out a cry of alarm. Apparently, they hadn't been as quiet as they'd hoped.

Ashford led the guards. There was a band of perhaps ten—many more than had surrounded her cell during her imprisonment. It appeared that Lady Helmsted had learned her lesson. High-priority captives were to be heavily guarded. *No matter*, Alayna thought. It would require more than ten Collectors to keep her from Philip now, when he needed her most. She was almost surprised by the sudden rush of emotion she felt surging through her. She hadn't felt that warmth toward Philip at all during the past month of incarceration. Perhaps it was due to the misconception she'd carried about her capture, about how she'd thought he had left her all alone in this place of his own accord. Seeing him now, a broken mess on the ground, seeing what he'd done to try and rescue her, she knew that nothing could be further from the truth. All of a sudden, she was aware of the residue on her mind, the dark spread on her consciousness emanating from her physical proximity to Azir. She wondered what part that connection, that mental link, had played on her emotions. It made her uneasy.

As the guards let out the call for alarm, Alayna and her two companions charged. No time to wait. They closed the distance and attacked full force. Azir carried no arms but needed none, his semi-clawed fingernails functioning in concert with his fangs as de facto weapons. Beathan was armed with his knives, and Alayna loosed bolts from her miniature crossbows as she sprinted into the fray.

She ducked a swing from one of the Collectors, dropped one crossbow, and pulled her belt knife—reacquired from her pack after rejoining with Beathan—to begin slashing. She disemboweled the guard in one swift duck, slice, and roll, coming to one knee in the swirl of conflict. Another weapon, a club this time, careened toward her face and she dodged again, sending up a mental prayer of thanks for the lithe speed and agility her Elfas nature granted her. With her natural attributes and Philip's training coupled with the mental and physical toughening she'd received while in the menagerie and the pits, Alayna was a force to be reckoned with. Even injured as she was, she still put down two more Collectors in quick succession. She hamstrung one and then slit his throat as he crumpled to the floor. She threw her knife into the chest of the second and retrieved it with a wrench, sending a fountain of blood spurting across her face. It painted her exactly as she felt.

She finally slowed to see and hear the skirmish around her. Beathan let out a fairy's mad laugh of exhilaration as he worked his magic, fighting with agility and skill in conjunction with spells. Azir tore throats and slashed with his nails. They were cutting a swath through the ten Collectors like they were little more than boys, regardless of their extensive Guild training.

And then there was just one left.

Alayna faced off with Ashford, the head guard who had overseen her captivity. He crouched in a ready stance, warily eyeing the three of them with a desperate half-snarl on his face. He knew the odds, knew that this was the end.

"Bitch!" he spat angrily.

"Ah, is that the best you got?" she taunted even as she felt her aggravated wounds flame with pain.

She flung up a hand and stopped her two companions as they prowled closer to take up the fight.

"No, he's mine. I'll handle him myself." She lifted her lip in a sneer and hefted her knife. Something about Ashford—perhaps his place of authority or his constant threats—whatever it was, it needed to be put to rest. She needed to prove to herself that this place hadn't broken her, hadn't damaged her. Or, at the very least, that if it *had* damaged her, then the damage wasn't irreparable, that it had also somehow made her stronger. She was going to do that by killing Ashford, by vanquishing him and what he stood for: this warped offshoot of the Collectors Guild.

"Come then, Elfas, you inhuman wench. At least I'll have the satisfaction of seeing you dead." They were the death taunts of a man who knew he was on his last breaths. She didn't deign to answer, just stalked closer and circled him while Azir and Beathan watched.

She darted in, taking the fight to him, but Ashford reacted more quickly than she had expected. He fought with a mace—a short, flanged, metal club that looked as wicked as the man who wielded it. He swung it with vicious strength and pace, and Alayna only barely managed to avoid it striking her face as she leaned back, just enough so that the weapon whistled past. She circled some more.

She had broken into St. Thomas and then broken out, fighting Deadbloods and Haunts in the process. She'd killed scores of Collectors like him over the past few months, had fought in the Night Pits and survived. She could handle Ashford. She told herself that, managed to convince herself of it as she fought. He lunged this time, swung the mace with one hand and then whipped it back up in a backhand strike with lightning speed. She managed to deflect the blow with her knife and land a punch on his face. He spat blood, and a tooth fell from his mouth. He smiled a bloody smile, an animal backed into a corner whose last hope was to take its hunter with it. He was at his most dangerous.

Alayna stalked closer, Beathan and Azir continuing to prowl around the outside of their invisible brawling ring, making sure that Ashford couldn't flee. She and her opponent exchanged blows and traded strikes until they were both bleeding from new wounds. Finally, Alayna saw her chance. The Collector swung a bit too hard, and as she dodged the blow of his mace, he over-extended himself just slightly, ever so slightly. It was enough to give her an opening. Patience, skill, and resolve had paid off. She darted in close, all dexterity and speed, and plunged her knife into his belly. She felt the shock hit his body, saw him involuntarily drop his weapon as the damage coursed through him. She tugged her blade up and then wrenched it to the side as she tore if from his guts, leaving him a bleeding mess upon the ground.

"I guess you didn't have what it took after all," she murmured, a parting mockery to the dying Collector.

His lips curled in a wordless grimace, but he was losing strength too fast to answer, in too much pain to form the words.

"Don't worry yourself, we'll be sure to tend to Helmsted, as well," she said as his life left him.

Beathan put a hand on her shoulder as she crouched. "Feel better?" His question was almost tentative, as if he were speaking to someone he didn't quite know. Maybe he didn't.

"I'll be better when Philip's awake and I've had the chance to hound every last one of these bastards into the great beyond! But for now...for now, this is enough."

Azir chuckled. "She is more fiery than you remember, Fairy. Not unlike myself." The vampire gave the dead man a kick for good measure. "You don't know what it was like in here, and this man was near the center of it."

They left him in the dirt then entered Azir's old cage, now inhabited by the semi-conscious Philip.

"Philip!" Alayna rushed to his side, tapping the side of his face gently to wake him. He opened his eyes, and she could see him trying to focus his bleary, pain-filled gaze.

Come on, love, you have to wake up. You have to heal and get up so that we can get out of here, she said mentally. Or, at least, she tried to, tried to access that mental connection, that link an Elfas could create with those with whom they shared a deep intimacy. But it was harder than normal, like trying to speak across a long distance or perhaps under-water. It felt more of a struggle than it ever had to put her words into Philip's mind. Again, her thoughts went to the residue on her mind, her connection to the vampire. She cast a glance Azir's way and saw the strangest look on his face. If she didn't know him better, she might have thought that it was jealousy or even hurt. Quickly, though, the look was gone and replaced by the condescending smirk he often wore.

"Yes, he's quite the terror," Azir said to Beathan with a sneer. The fairy ignored him.

Alayna tried again. She sent her words into his mind, focused on everything they had been through together, on everything she felt for him, her love, his devotion. And this time they pushed through, she could feel them being received by Philip's mind on the other end. His eyes flickered again and then opened all the way. Then, in the midst of all the pain from his wounds, he smiled. That smile lit a warmth in her that she had forgotten she needed. She smiled back.

CHAPTER TWENTY-FIVE

"I'm all right, really, I am," Philip protested as Alayna ran her hands all over his body, as if she couldn't stop touching him. She felt his brown hair which hung to his shoulders and caressed his lean face, felt his hard, wiry body. She touched his wounds and bit her lip with a worried gaze.

"I've rarely seen you so injured, Philip. How are you even sitting up, and conscious, no less?" Alayna disputed.

He winced gingerly as he adjusted himself into a more comfortable position against the cage's only solid wall. "I don't know. I'm... stronger now. And I think it's helping me heal more quickly than usual." He exchanged a glance with Beathan.

"She knows some of it, mate. I told her how ya' lost it for a while, went more monster than man. Not the worst of it, but some of it."

"Well, you can tell me the rest when we get out of here." Alayna sat back on her heels as she watched him. Philip still couldn't quite believe that she was alive. He'd thought that she was dead—twice, actually. It was like a miracle, a blessing, and a gift all rolled into one and magnified tenfold.

"I hate to break up the reunion, but since you are healing so quickly, might I suggest that we get a move on before more of your kind come." The vampire spoke with a slight bitter note to his voice, and Alayna looked at Azir with what Philip would have called a guilty face if he hadn't known better. He still wasn't sure what the vampire was doing here. They could sort it out later, he supposed.

Philip felt the wildness—the troll part of him—stronger than ever. He could practically feel his body healing, his wounds slowly closing as he sat up. He already felt well enough to struggle to his feet.

"Philip, what are you doing?" Alayna exclaimed.

"Azir's right—there's no time to waste. I'm feeling better already. But we aren't fleeing; we have business to attend to. I know who's in charge here. I recognized her voice giving orders right before they overwhelmed me."

"You mean Helmsted?" Alayna asked, slipping close to his side, hovering as if she didn't quite believe him when he claimed to be healing more quickly.

"That's right...you would know that, being held captive here," he muttered and winced again as he took a couple steps toward the cage door. "Well, she's high in the Guild. I'll not let her get away with this."

"Is it really your place t' question Guild practices an' ethics anymore?" Beathan asked pointedly.

Philip sighed. "Fine. We can call it revenge if you like, then."

"Suits me, mate. The difference is a technicality, but the world spins on tiny differences, eh?" the fairy said with a wink.

Azir's lips pulled back into a snarl. "Oh, I can certaintly get on board with revenge."

"Then it's settled. We go after her," Alayna agreed. "But not until you've had a few more minutes of rest."

Philip acquiesced. He stared into her eyes, drinking her in until his gaze couldn't hold any more. She looked back at him. Her eyes were the same, her features wounded and hurt but beautiful, radiant with her confidence and vivacity. He loved her more than he'd ever loved her before as he looked at her in all her strength and determination. This place, this pit of despair, this menagerie of shadow, had been cruel to her, but it had not been enough to break her.

Alayna's eyes took on a guilty look once more, and she cast a glance at Azir before opening her mouth to speak. Philip swallowed. He didn't want to think about what she might say, what might prompt that sort of look.

"Philip, I—,"

"Shh, Alayna, there will be time to talk about everything later, when we are far away from this place." He cupped her cheek in one hand. She shook her head, the guilty look remaining.

"No, I have to say this. I just have to get it off my chest. I can't bear keeping it in," she said.

Philip forced himself to fix his gaze on her, willed himself to forget the vampire watching their intimate moment. "All right, Alayna, what is it?"

"I am ashamed to admit it, but I have assumed this entire time that you abandoned me."

It hurt. It hurt more than he thought it would, and it had not even been the confession he'd been expecting. Philip had steeled himself for her to speak, but the words still felt like a blow to his gut, still made it hard to talk, to respond, as if the wind had been knocked from his lungs.

Alayna must have seen the pain in his eyes, because she immediately began stammering to explain. He cut her off: "How could you think I had abandoned you, how could you believe that I would ever do that?" His voice came out harsher and more pained than he'd intended.

"I—I don't know, Philip," Alayna said, and he heard the begging note in her low tone. He couldn't help but soften. He grabbed her hand and squeezed it comfortingly.

"I do. It's him. His presence does something to your mind, doesn't it? I noticed it back in England, and it would be no different here," Philip concluded with an angry look toward the vampire.

Azir sneered. "At least I was here, Collector."

"I don't know exactly what happened in me—*to* me," Alayna began. "I don't have answers. I just knew that I couldn't keep it from you."

Philip nodded. He smiled to assure her that they were fine, prayed that they actually were, that they would be.

Beathan cleared his throat. "I do believe we had somethin' to accomplish before leavin'." He stared at them pointedly. They all three cast similarly embarrassed looks at one another for wasting time with personal issues when pressing matters were at hand.

Alayna deemed that Philip had had enough time to recover, so they left the cage and made their way toward the manor. They passed bands of Collectors on their way out of the menagerie, some of whom attacked them and had to be dealt with. Others were too occupied with other escaped captives to notice or care about four more people, though. It was utter mayhem. More smoke than that usually provided by the bonfire in the corner of the premises poured upward from the grounds. Smaller fires dotted the entire menagerie. Philip, Alayna, Beathan, and Azir made their way toward the manor and finally reached it, climbing the back steps and opening the dark, walnut door to go inside.

The building was large, grandiose, even, but not unlike what Philip had come to expect from many of the private residences belonging to the Guild elite. High-ranking members like Helmsted—or Astori, before he had died—often had opulent homes. It was a flaw in many of their attitudes. The Guild was coached to blend in and conceal their identity from the world, and its members did likewise. Cover stories were created for Collectors as merchants or traveling performers, much as Philip and his old partner James had done. They had posed as a merchant pair on a ship sailing the Atlantic. Higher Guild members often posed as nobility or members of upper-class society, which gave them an excuse to build or buy extravagant homes. They couldn't reveal to the world their true purpose, but at least they could overwhelm society with opulence. Helmsted's manor was no different. As they prowled through the house, Philip noted mahogany furniture, gilt-edged sconces on the walls, and curtains made of the finest cloth. He'd burn it all down if he could, if it were his, just for another night of sleeping under the stars.

The manor was eerily silent, but Alayna took the lead and led them through the twisting halls and myriad rooms. "I think her study was this way," she volunteered as she limped to the fore, somehow still managing to move soundlessly.

They walked through a few more rooms before Alayna indicated with a nod that the one ahead of them was what they were looking for. From within, a few hushed voices spoke in hurried conversations as they crept quietly up to the study door.

"On my count," Philip whispered. "One, two, three." He burst through the doors with his companions at his back, and pandemonium broke loose. There were more than a few people in the room—at least eight Collectors and Lady Helmsted herself occupied its interior. A shouted command from Helmsted, and the guards rushed into the attack, pushing Philip and his friends back out of the study and into the room beyond. The fight was brutal and close-quarter. Fists and knives inflicted harm and drew blood. Philip struck down one Collector with a crushing blow and forced his way back into the study, trusting that his companions could handle themselves. He had larger prey in mind.

Lady Helmsted, her back to the door, was feeding papers into a fireplace, the flames quickly enveloping the dry parchment.

"Don't want any record of your operation getting back to the rest of the leading council at Guild headquarters, ma'am?" The honorific came unbidden, a reflex of a time now gone, and Philip's mouth twisted into a sour grimace. He wished more than anything to be able to take it back.

Helmsted spun around gracefully, a smug smile on her face even when confronting her possible demise. "I think the time is long past for titles between us, Philip. Unless, of course, you still wish to use them?" She gave him a searching look. He narrowed his eyes. What was she getting at?

"It's over, Helmsted. Your menagerie is in ashes, your captives on the loose, and we've come to deal with you."

"Have you, now?" Her hand strayed to the sword hilt hanging from a belt slanted across her dark green divided skirts. Philip strode forward carefully, tense and ready. He knew her capabilities. She was practically a legend with that blade and no less so with the pistol at her hip. If there was one credit to the Guild, it was that their high members earned the right to lead with their own prowess as Collectors. Helmsted was no exception to that rule. In fact, she was a shining example.

"What have you become? No longer Collecting to protect society —what are you now, a profiteer? I saw the pits and the breeding pens." He shook his head in disgust even as the sounds of continued fighting echoed into the study from beyond the walls. He prayed for his friends' safety.

Helmsted didn't deny anything. She merely smiled. "Indeed, I had my fighting rings. You might even have called it my own little coliseum."

Philip snorted with as much derision as he could muster and mocked, "Shall I call you empress? This isn't Ancient Rome, you know. You'll be held accountable for what you've done. I'll see to that."

Helmsted took a cautious step to the side as he approached, keeping as much distance between them as she could. "You know, I was wondering if and when you might show up. I've had cohorts throughout this entire region searching for you at the council's behest."

"I know. We've encountered them," he responded grimly. Philip barely managed to hold back the growl building in his throat.

"They are calling you the 'Deserter', as if you are the first ever. Isn't that positively theatrical!" She laughed, and her hawk eyes lit up with delight at teasing him.

"If I am a deserter, then what does that make you?" he retorted.

"You were a sailor, right? I'll speak in a language you can understand." The condescension in her voice was almost more than he could handle. Philip's jaw clenched as she continued, "The Guild is weak, broken by its Astoris and deserters. We shouldn't hide any longer. We should be doing more than protecting—we should be profiting from our sacrifices. A captain that leads her crew into the life rafts isn't a deserter. She's a savior. And, if she happens to lead them to a new ship, then she's a visionary, as well. She's *exceptional*."

"It sounds like insanity to me," Philip said coldly, "and I heard drivel like this spouting from Astori's mouth before I silenced him, so believe me, I would know. Besides, it looks like this ship is sinking, too."

"Innovation often does sound mad to the uninspired." Helmsted's sheer confidence in herself and what she was saying convinced Philip more than anything else that she needed to be eliminated. Not just for revenge but for the good of the world. She was a woman with power, skills, and authority, and she possessed enough self-righteousness to convince herself that the horror she inflicted upon others was just, right, and true.

He growled slightly in response.

"You know, you could join me, Philip. You were always such a solid soldier, a good Collector."

"I don't exactly think I'd fit in."

"Ahh, I see. So the rumors are true?" the Lady Helmsted queried with one eyebrow raised. "I should have assumed it so, I suppose, after seeing what you did to my compound."

It was Philip's turn to grin wolfishly with confidence. "You aren't the only one who's exceptional."

194

Helmsted's face turned into a grim mask. "But I am the only one of us that is human!" her voice surged as she drew her sword in a flash of metal and leapt into an attack. He should have guessed she'd initiate the fight as soon as she knew for certain that he was a hybrid. She might be rogue, or 'innovative' as she thought of it, but Guild principles still dominated her core, and she wouldn't align herself with a supernatural being. Helmsted in particular was well known for her hatred—or, at the very least, extreme disdain—for non-humans.

He drew his belt knife and brought it up quickly in defense. She was fast and as talented a duelist as they came, and he didn't even have a sword. As long as she kept him at bay with her blade, he was going to be at a distinct disadvantage. His belt knife clashed with the sword, and sparks flashed as the blades slid hilt to hilt. He grinned as his strength began to win out, their weapons still locked. Her skills were impressive, but his strength was supernatural. Her eyes widened in surprise, and he landed a solid blow to her ribs. She grunted painfully, but to her credit she spun out of the lock gracefully and whipped her blade across his shoulder, inflicting a thin, red wound on his sleeveless arm. He cursed in anger and tried to close again, but she got her tip up and wove it menacingly between them, slowing his approach.

"Nasty pair, aren't we?" she murmured, a sinister light blazing in her eyes. Like any warrior, she relished the challenge of conflict. "I've always wanted to face one of the rumored inhumans that infiltrated our ranks."

"Your wish is granted," Philip grunted as he lunged and then feinted with his blade, trying to draw her off balance as they circled one another. He had to get away from that sword or at least nullify it somehow.

He charged in close, deciding to risk it. Brawler tactics were always his strong suit. Her dueling sword came up and snaked its way toward him. He batted it away with his hand and then actually grabbed it near the hilt. The blade tore into his flesh, but he held fast. Helmsted yanked at the sword to loosen his painful yet vicelike grip, but still he would not let go. Instead, he landed a staggering blow to her face. A lesser warrior would have crumpled, but her training, her toughness, kept her standing. She abandoned a lost cause and dropped the sword, darting away to gain some distance with her back near the study door. He saw fear in her eyes for the first time. He relished it as he stalked closer, blood dripping from his gashed palm.

Helmsted whipped the pistol from her hip and fired a lead ball at him. It struck him in the shoulder, spinning him off balance, igniting agony in his arm. Of course she would keep it fully loaded and ready to fire; a good warrior was always prepared. She took the moment, seeing him unbalanced and wounded, and turned to flee. However, she did so just as the fighting from outside died down and Alayna, covered in blood, hair matted to her face with sweat, burst through the study doors.

"Alayna, look out!" Philip cried, but it was too late.

Helmsted might have been fearful of him, but she was a cool-headed fighter. She took advantage of the moment. The Elfas hadn't expected to be set upon so immediately when she entered the room. The Collector grasped her by the hair and had Alayna's own belt knife to her throat in a heartbeat.

"One move and I'll slit her throat."

Helmsted backed out of the study with Philip in tow. Azir and Beathan were just finishing off the guards. Azir snarled in rage at the sight of them, and for once Philip felt exactly the same emotion as the vampire, but he kept himself in check. A rash statement or movement wasn't worth what it might cost—Alayna's life.

"I'm leaving, and I don't want any of you to interfere. Otherwise, the fair little Elfas will be bleeding out on the floor," Lady Helmsted threatened. Philip knew she wasn't bluffing.

"If ya' kill her, ya' might as well slit your own neck, lass," Beathan growled with an uncharacteristic darkness.

"Well then, why don't we all make sure neither of those things happen?" Helmsted answered, equally grim. She backed slowly through the room and then through another as the three of them followed.

"I don't care what she does, I don't want her walking away from all this," Alayna practically spat with fury. Philip tried to motion her to silence. One wrong move from her, one split decision on her part that maybe it would be worth it to die if it brought down Helmsted would be enough to see it so. He couldn't abide by that, not when he had just gotten her back.

"You were already dead. I don't want to see it happen again, love. Just calm down," Philip pleaded.

"Listen to the deserter, Elfas," Helmsted agreed as she continued backing through the house and out of the building.

Philip continued to follow, shaking off the pain of his newly injured shoulder. Blood oozed profusely from the gunshot wound, but he knew that it would heal before too long. They followed Helmsted, her knife still at Alayna's throat, all the way around the exterior of the manor until they reached her personal stables.

Carefully, oh so carefully, with one eye on them and a tense hand holding her knife, Helmsted led her horse—the only one present—out of its stall and into the open.

"I'm leaving now. We've gotten this far without incident, so let's not ruin it," she cautioned. Philip saw the light of hope in her eyes. She was going to get away, and she knew it.

"I'm going to find you. I promise. I will make you pay for this," Philip swore his solemn oath to her.

"I've no doubt you'll try." She smirked and then, in one swift motion, flung Alayna away from her, leapt bareback onto her horse, clutched its mane, and dug her heels into its sides. It was well trained and immediately burst into a gallop.

"No!" Alayna yelled in frustration and fumbled to load a bolt into the one crossbow she'd kept hold of as Helmsted rode away. She drew it back, sighted, and released. The projectile flew true, but not true enough. Lady Helmsted was a swift rider and covering the distance between them and the gate at an alarmingly fast pace. The bolt punched into her arm and she nearly fell but managed to hold on at the last second and continued to ride, slumped over the horse's back. She was out of the gate and riding into the distance before they could do anything else.

"Do ya' think that shot'll bring her down?" Beathan asked, sounding more hopeful than convinced.

"If we know anything about her, it's that Helmsted is tough as steel and even more horrible of character. She'll survive," Alayna answered in frustration. Philip was about to agree with her until her glance toward Azir showed that by 'we' she meant herself and the vampire, not Philip. He swallowed his words, wishing that he didn't feel jealous over such an innocuous statement.

Azir voiced his agreement with Alayna. "I agree with you, my dear. Our time in the menagerie led me to despise her, yet I cannot deny that I have a grudging respect for her. She will no doubt make it to wherever she is going and somehow spin these events so that they work to her advantage. Maybe she will be the hero of this story, one of the few survivors of a despicable supernatural attack on a protected Guild compound."

Philip felt a surge of jealousy. If only he could disagree with the vampire, but he couldn't. Helmsted likely *would* spin these events. Philip just wished that there wasn't such a sense of solidarity between Alayna and Azir. If he was being honest with himself, it made him more uncomfortable than just about anything he could remember.

He opted not to speak on the subject. Instead, he turned his gaze to the compound around them. It was in flames. There was a chaos of creatures milling about, some fleeing, others feeding on the dead. A few Collectors, some injured, most of them terrified, were sneaking toward various exits, hoping to find a way to escape with their lives. There were more beings dead than he could count. Humans, of course—they had killed enough Collectors to fill a village cemetery—but there were more than that. Not all of the creatures Alayna, Beat-han, and Azir had freed on their way into the compound had escaped. Many had been cut down by the guards.

Philip saw a dead tree sprite and his heart sank. Helmsted had certainly been doing more than Collecting. Tree sprites were notoriously shy and never harmed a soul. A pity it had been murdered. He recognized a variety of other dead, some more deserving than others, their deaths more justifiable, such as a few crazed werewolves and a particularly nasty-looking Black Annis. He shuddered. He'd been on the receiving end of claws like that before, and he would not want to be again. He certainly wouldn't pity such a creature, dead though it was.

But the pitiable departed outweighed the deserving, and his jaw clenched as he stared at the scene. Strangely, and especially difficult to see was the baby troll—hardly bigger than a man—that was lying dead near a cage. He swallowed back a guttural cry of rage, forced it down. He was not a troll, he reminded himself. He. Was. Not. A. Troll. Nor would he be ever again. He was something in between. Philip nevertheless felt a kinship with the dead beast, and it was hard to look at it without growing restless and angry.

"We're going to make them pay," he declared forcefully.

"Who's that, mate? Most are already dead," the fairy quipped.

"Not these men—or not just them, that is. Think bigger."

Azir tilted his head as he looked at Philip, as if seeing him in a new light. "Are you saying what I think you are saying, Collector?" They shared a long look, enemies forced to work side by side toward a common interest. Philip nodded at the vampire.

"What do you mean? What is he saying?" Alayna asked.

Azir continued to stare at Philip as if he'd never seen him before, until finally the vampire said, "He is declaring war on the Collectors Guild."

THANK YOU FOR READING

Did you enjoy this book?

We invite you to leave a review at the website of your choice, such as Goodreads, Amazon, Barnes & Noble, etc.

DID YOU KNOW THAT LEAVING A REVIEW...

- Helps other readers find books they may enjoy.
- Gives you a chance to let your voice be heard.
- Gives authors recognition for their hard work.
- Doesn't have to be long. A sentence or two about why you liked the book will do.

―――――

Don't miss out on your next favorite book!

―――――

Join the Melange Books mailing list at
www.melange-books.com/mail.html

Subscriber Perks Include:

- First peeks at upcoming releases.
- Exclusive giveaways.
- News of book sales and freebies right in your inbox.
- And more!

In the midst of chaos and darkness, Elliyar and his companions fight a losing battle to defend their homeland, the fallen elven kingdom of Andalaya. They fight against a dangerous alliance of dark elves and human invaders. Arrows loosed from the shadows and violent ambushes characterize his people's existence. Yet the young elf, Elliyar, can't help but wonder if this meager resistance is really all that is left for them or if there is something more in store for his people.

It is in this war-torn land that an ancient power, a power that was thought lost for centuries, is rediscovered, and a primal evil begins to arise once more. Will Elliyar have the strength and ability within him to protect the ones he loves, especially the beautiful Miri, and shift the course of the war?

Dusk Runner is the story of battles and last stands, a tale of love and betrayal. It is the telling of one young elf who comes of age during the dusk of his people's existence and of his desperate fight for their survival. It is a story of the power of love to inspire and give hope even in the darkest times.

———

PROLOGUE

Djumair Silverfist had been a traitor for nineteen long years and a coward for most of his life. He was the most dangerous type of coward there was, a bold one. He reflected idly on his life as he awaited the final orders for his next mission. Djumair let his thoughts drift even further from the next task and more upon his own being. He was not someone to question the decisions of the past. They were gone and could not be remade, so why bother with them? However, he was not above succumbing, every now and again, to the self-reflective melancholy, one reserved for time spent sifting through memories over a goblet of wine and a good view. Djumair looked off the edge of the platform, not five feet from where he sat, at the plains interspersed sparsely with copses of trees beneath him. Even though he was alone, and had nobody with which to share his thoughts, he allowed his mind to continue its backward journey. He was a solitary person after all. In many ways, he preferred to be alone and it seemed fitting to reminisce by himself.

Permission granted, he continued to remember. Not for the first time, nor for the last, his mind pondered the curious tandem of cowardice and courage that was Djumair Silverfist. He knew exactly what was required of a person to be on the winning side of conflicts in life, and he did whatever was necessary to ensure that he never lost. That fact, in and of itself, was his craven fault. Yet it simultaneously lent credence to his arrogant understanding of his own dangerous competency when it came to vanquishing a foe. He feared the price of losing so greatly that he knew he was a coward to the very core of his being. However, he was bold enough to know which decision or action, in the right circumstances, would be enough to ensure that he avoided failure, pain, and any other unpleasant consequences of defeat. Sometimes those decisions were difficult, but he made them all the same. Therein lay his courage, the ability to make challenging decisions.

His mind flashed back to that fateful day nineteen years ago, when he unleashed the flood of water that burst open Verdantihya's fabled gates—ripped them open from within. Bleeding and broken, he had sacrificed everything to avoid death, to avoid losing. He had joined the winning side—that much was clear. While he now sat and sipped wine freely on a slaver's deck, his former kinsmen fought, died, bled, and were captured. He thought of them as 'former' because one couldn't really claim to belong to the very people who they had betrayed. This sense of un-belonging defined Djumair, but it was a fair price for his own freedom, though not without pain.

Djumair had spent the better portion of the last two decades fighting a war for a king who he did not love and a Grand Marshal who he did not respect, and it had all been by his own choice. Many long years ago, when he had first felt the icy fingers of fear twisting in his belly, he had chosen this path. The first invasion had been sudden and swift, and the humans had established such a strong foothold on the continent that he had known his people had no hope of triumph. He had done the only thing possible, he had defected to what he knew would be the winning side. It had been a decision motivated by fear, but the choice in and of itself had not been one that was without the need for courage. It was a strange internal parallel in which he lived; fearful enough to betray his people and avoid defeat, and brave enough to make the hard choices in life, the choices that cut ties to one's heritage.

He broke from his reverie as he watched a servant approach from across the open-aired room. The wind swirled gently, high up on the eastern most Pillar in the land. Djumair reclined in a lounging seat with a view. It was a seat reserved for the slave captains who frequented this last outpost before heading north to begin a raid, or heading east to deliver the latest batch of captives to the humans. The wind was a dry breeze billowing up from the southeast. It carried the scent of smoke from the Camps and the dust from the land further beyond them as it curled up over the edge of the platform, leaving the ground far below it, hundreds of feet down. It was still strange to Djumair, even after his long years in this southern land, that the air could be so dry. This wind had a strangely familiar smell to it, a scent for which he felt the inklings of recognition. However, just when it felt he was about to lay hold of the memory of that particular scent's origin, it slipped away from his mind's grasp. He didn't like that. Djumair couldn't shake the odd feeling of importance for whatever it was he could not remember. It never paid to forget important information.

He took another swill of the white wine that sat chilled in his goblet, the contents creating tiny droplets of condensation on the exterior. It was not the most popular of beverages among his southern compatriots, but it was light and tangy. It soothed his dry throat and reminded him of the pleasures of this land, pleasures he was not likely to forget seeing as they were, in large part, the reason he had chosen this course in life. Wine of this vintage had been impossible to find in the north even before the invasion, let alone now, with the northern people of Andalaya scattered to the four winds across their mountain lands.

The servant finally reached the small, stand table to Djumair's right. He carried a silver pitcher polished to perfection, full of wine no doubt, should Djumair require more. It was the joy, and the nuisance, of being important. People to do his bidding, and at the same time, those same people were the ones who often interrupted the few quiet moments he had to himself. The swallow of wine tasted sour as Djumair grimaced slightly at the bothersome servant. The boy should be able to see that his wine glass was still half full and in no need of refilling.

The servant was young and dark haired like all of his people, and as he drew closer, he must have seen the dangerous glint in Djumair's eyes. The boy hesitated as if considering retreat, but then continued once he realized that he had come too far to leave without offering more wine. Fear shone in the boy's eyes as he approached. Djumair knew the fright that his name inspired in others. Just because he knew he was a coward, didn't mean that others did. In truth, most people were cowards at their core; he was just one of the few who admitted it to themselves. He embraced it and let it become a strength rather than a weakness. He let his fear push and prod him until it became a source of ingenuity and boldness rather than a reason to run from a fight. But this boy didn't know he was a coward. Instead, this servant saw one of the most feared warriors in the land, someone known for chopping off his own hand in order to win a battle. It was good the boy feared him. He liked it that way.

Djumair Silverfist watched the boy's eyes glance down at the immaculately forged silver fist attached to the end of his left arm. It was sculpted to perfection to resemble the very likeness of a living hand closed into a fist. It lay, along with his left arm, on the armrest and it glimmered in the setting sun.

"Would you care for some more wine?" the servant stuttered, his black hair hanging down the back of his tan, brown neck. All of the boy's kinsmen were tanned and brown, courtesy of this southern sun.

For a brief instant Djumair felt bad for the boy. He was a servant, not a slave, but in this society of warriors and conquerors, once you accepted the role of servant, it was yours to fulfill for the rest of your life. The boy would never escape it. The pity was fleeting as Djumair remembered the boy's interruption of one of the few moments of solitary respite he had to simply enjoy the little things in life, like a sunset and a glass of wine.

He shook his head curtly. "Would you have me become drunk and susceptible to any sellsword who wishes to come my way?" He barked in response. "One glass of wine is enough for anyone who calls himself a warrior. Once you have had more than one, you cease the right to claim that title. You then become a drunkard and just another body for your captain to throw at the enemy." His words might have been a little harsh, but the boy had annoyed him.

"Yes, Silverfist, I mean, Sir," the boy spluttered quickly to repent, "what do I know of battle and fighting? Of course, you are right." He spun too quickly as he turned to walk away, and the pitcher flew from the tray, spilling its contents all over the ground.

The servant spun back to face Djumair, clearly expecting a tongue scathing remark at the very least, if not a command to the whipping post or worse. Djumair sneered slightly as he sat on the lounge chair, still reclining through the entire interaction, and watched the boy as he clutched the tray to his chest in fear, awaiting the consequences for spilling the wine.

His own image as reflected in the tray caught Djumair's eye, and he gazed upon his reflection as he pondered how he should punish the servant. From the polished, gleaming surface of the tray, light blue eyes stared back at him. Pale features, unlike the servant's, looked at him, and blond hair adorned the top of his head. The sides of his head were shaved in the manner of the warriors of the south, and his long, flowing locks of blond hair flowed off the back of his head just past his shoulders like a white-gold mane. It was not held in a braid, but it was gathered at intervals by loose, rawhide ties to keep it from getting in his way as he moved or fought. The hairstyle left the sides of his head clean, revealing ears that were pointed at the top, protruding in the manner of both his northern heritage and the servant's people. Dark or light of skin, the pointed ears were a common feature between the two races.

Djumair had a small, silver ring in his right nostril, but the most distinctive marks upon his face were the three blood red tears tattooed on both of his cheeks as if falling from the corners of his eyes. Traitor's Tears. They marked a person who had betrayed Andalaya in order to serve the King of the South. A decision Djumair Silverfist had made long, long ago. The tattoos were on his cheeks by choice. He had been the first to betray and had been the first to be tattooed. What was now required of the northerners who chose to give their lives to serve their new masters, he had pioneered as a twisted memorial to whom he had once been. In a strange way, everything about him was defined by choice, from the biggest decision to the smallest decoration on his body. Nothing had been forced upon him, and nothing would be.

He stood up slowly, faced down the servant with a penetrating gaze, and then backhanded him across the face as hard as he could. The boy dropped in a heap, and by the time he managed to pull himself together, Djumair had long since sat back down on his chair. He could hear the boy's sniffles, and feel the sting on the back of his good, right hand from the impact. It set his pulse racing and his blood buzzing. Even the slightest hint of combat made his whole body feel as if it were on fire. He was a warrior through and through. He feared death, but it did not keep him from the challenge of the fray. This however, was a simple disciplinary action and he calmed his fighting instincts.

"Go. Now. Get a rag, or better yet, remove your shirt and wipe up that mess," Djumair said flatly, as he gazed at the view before him. Maybe he could recapture some of the serenity that had preceded this unfortunate encounter—unfortunate for him, since it had interrupted his quiet. Djumair cared not a whit for the pain the boy was suffering. And suffering from the blow he was. Djumair could hear the pain in his voice as he responded that he would clean it up and intended do so immediately.

Djumair nodded at the boy's response but did not break his observance of the sunset painting the sky in front of him. He expected nothing less than immediate action when his commands were issued. This far from Dark Harbor and the Camps, he had the most power and authority of anybody on this Pillar.

Thoughts of Dark Harbor, the heart of his masters' domain, clouded his mind and he knew the peaceful moment from earlier had passed. He sighed to himself and let the worry, that he knew his thoughts of Dark Harbor would bring, come. What was Half-Mask planning? Something was in the works, some plan was being hatched, and Silverfist was not privy to the details. He hated not knowing. How was he to ensure the best possible outcome for himself if he did not know what was going to happen? True, his job was to follow orders. He gave them, as often as not, especially in a mid-point location such as this slave post—this Pillar was nearly halfway between Dark Harbor and the human forces, which were known as the Camps. However, when orders were issued by Half-Mask himself, even Djumair obeyed without question. Nobody frightened him like the Prince.

Footsteps, quick and quiet, approached and Djumair steeled himself for action, tensing his body in preparation to explode into action should the person behind him prove to be an assassin. It was not unheard of for people in positions such as his to fall at the hands of a sellsword ordered to kill them on behalf of a competing slave captain. Competition for honors in the land was fierce, and the higher your reputation among the slavers, then the higher prices you could charge at the auction block. A man such as Silverfist was always on guard.

As the person approaching him flickered into his peripheral vision, he relaxed. If it had been an assassin sent to kill him, the person would have attacked without allowing himself to be seen. Or at least he would have tried. If it had been an attacker, he would have been dead right now. Silverfist slipped the dagger that he carried tucked up the right sleeve of his silk coat, back into place before the person beside him could see that he'd had it out. It had slid into his hand freely, and the weapon returned to its place of concealment just as smoothly, with a quick flick of his wrist.

"So," Djumair drawled in a relaxed voice, "message from the capital, I take it?"

The soldier nodded his head and bared his teeth in a grimace of affirmation. Most people in these parts preferred fighting to running messages, and he, no doubt, had little reason to appreciate his duties as a courier. He was muscled and lean, with tan, brown skin and black hair. His head was shaved on the sides in the same manner, as was Djumair's, and his hair fell back from the top of his head in a tightly woven braid. His bared teeth were not a smile; it was more like what appeared to be a constant snarl, an expression with which he probably lived. The upper row of teeth in his mouth was filed to points that were sharp enough to rend flesh. It looked ridiculous to Djumair, and was one of the few affectations of this southern culture that he absolutely refused to adopt. He supposed that to some it might appear ferocious, especially when facing them in the heat of battle. The soldier's uniform was made of tight-fitting, forest-green pants and a sleeveless, black leather shirt. He was dressed for running, as a courier should be, and was only carrying a short axe at his hip and a long dagger tucked in one boot.

Djumair Silverfist eyed his opponent. They were almost certainly not going to enter into combat against one another, however, once you had fought in enough battles you ceased to allow yourself to be taken by surprise. It paid to be ready with a strategy to fight anyone, anywhere, anytime.

The soldier eyed him warily as well. He sneered as he looked at Silverfist, who was reclining in the seat with a view. Djumair, himself, was wearing tight, black hose and a well-cut, crimson silk coat. The coat hung loosely, unbuttoned, revealing his bare torso. He wore no shirt underneath, and the cool breeze danced lightly across his strong, toned chest. He tilted his head slightly as he watched the soldier appraise him, allowing a hint of menace to enter his expression as his own clear-blue eyes met the black ones staring back at him. He smirked as the soldier broke the stare first and looked away. It appeared that once again his reputation preceded him. Not many chose to fight him of their own accord. And of course, this soldier had no real reason to do so. The stare had merely been a byproduct of what happened when a war-like culture plunged headlong into the depths of conflict, chaos, and the continual hunt for slaves. Combat was natural these days even among allies, especially in times such as these when allegiances were shaky and often forced. It paid to be on guard.

"Well, what message have you for me?" Djumair waited after he spoke, allowing the messenger to produce a small scroll from his pocket. It was sealed with a crest in the shape of a face that was half covered by a mask. The seal of the Prince of Darkness himself, Half-Mask. Not a seal to be idly broken and certainly not one to be forged.

Djumair took the proffered parchment and reluctantly opened it. He had sworn allegiance to his current masters many years ago, yet he hated being sent on errands for which he was not given full information. Missions such as this, where he had been instructed to travel to this Pillar, the easternmost Pillar, and to await further information here, drove him to the furthest edges of his frustration. It galled him to no end to be kept in the dark. But he understood it. Djumair was accounted as a clever adversary by many and a dangerous ally by some. It was common for Half-Mask to keep him at arm's length, at least until he was ready to use Silverfist to achieve his own ends. Djumair Silverfist always got the job done, he was known for his competence, but even those who now owned his allegiance didn't trust him completely. Nor should they. After all, he had already switched allegiances once in his lifetime. In their eyes, that was reason enough to keep him at a distance. He knew they wondered whether betrayal might happen again.

The note was terse and whatever quill had been used to ink the words onto parchment had been pressed very firmly. It most likely signified the Prince's annoyance at having to send one of his most deadly weapons, Silverfist, on errands for the humans. Silverfist liked carrying out military objectives on behalf of the humans who had invaded his land as little as the Prince did, yet he knew it must espe-cially vex his royal master to have to succumb to the wishes of a race he deemed inferior to his own. Half-Mask hated the humans, yet he was forced to work alongside them; at least for now. For the present he, and subsequently Silverfist, would politely accede to the requests of their allies and bide their time, waiting for the day when their people would rid themselves of the yoke they had accepted nineteen years ago.

Djumair read the instructions silently. They told him to proceed to the northernmost camp of the humans and upon arrival, to follow the instructions given to him by the Grand Marshall. Half-Mask made reference to the fact that Djumair would most likely be dealing with a particularly vicious rash of raids that the Camps had been experiencing this spring. He was to make himself available, in what-ever way necessary, to the needs of the humans. Silverfist seethed quietly inside that he would have to obey direct orders from the human commander, but there was nothing to be done of it. For now, they held the tether. The sea of humanity that had arrived on the shores of this land years ago had swelled even greater in the years since their invasion. They were bolstered by new recruits from their distant homeland and had secured plenty of slaves, plucked from the rotting carcass of Andalaya to do the work deemed unfit for their human soldiers. They had entrenched themselves deeply along the eastern shore of the continent. The human military camps ran along the coast, from the fabled ruins of Akan Deraiya far to the south, all the way up the coast to where the East Mayn River met the sea. The mouth of the East Mayn, where it met the great sea known as The Fracture, was a perfect place for their northern camp. It was the last stop for ships sailing north, hugging the coast as they made their way toward Hope's End, the final staging point for slaves who were taken from this land and trafficked back along the Great Bridge to the home continent of the humans.

Silverfist crumpled the note in his good hand and tossed it aside to the floor in disgust. He was not pleased with the instructions.

"Something displeases you in what you read?" The soldier opened his mouth full of sharply filed teeth into an even wider grimace. "Should I report your displeasure to the Prince of Darkness when I return?" He threatened menacingly.

Silverfist snorted disdainfully. "I'll tell old Half-Mask myself when next I see him," he bluffed with a touch more bravado than he truly would have done if the Prince had actually been there to hear. His nonchalant words seemed to take the soldier aback. Not many dared speak in such a cavalier manner about the heir to the southern kingdom. He was without doubt the most feared person in all the land, the only exception possibly being the Prince's father. To be honest, they were both fearsome. The King of the South was midnight on a starless night. He was terrifying in the manner that only madness could steal the breath from your soul. But the Prince of Darkness was frightening in an entirely different way. He was what remained when light had been leeched away. Pure, unbridled darkness and terror. The King of the South had chosen darkness for his reign, but the Prince, Half-mask himself, had been raised in it. He had absorbed the darkness from the moment of his birth. And Silverfist served both of these dark masters.

However, Half-Mask's father, the King, had taken to seclusion for much of the time these days, and truth be told, Djumair had not seen him in years. It was rumored that the seeds of madness had recently sprouted in his brain. Djumair wasn't certain the seeds hadn't been there all along. Either way, like father like son, Half-Mask, or the Prince of Darkness as he was formally known, was concocting a plan.

And Djumair Silverfist wished he knew the depths of it. Oh, he had hints of the plan, glimpses of what might come, and the little that he did know left him feeling edgy.

Silverfist waved the soldier away as he considered his orders thoughtfully. He heard the soldier leave as quietly as he had come, the softly retreating footfalls barely heard above the whirl of the wind. A distant, terrified shriek from a slave from across the other side of the Pillar cut through the air. Even the minds of the hardiest of souls could shatter when faced with the reality of a lifetime of imprisonment and forced labor at the mercy of a cruel master. The holding cages of the slaves reeked of waste and fear. Silverfist was glad he was upwind from them.

He heard a noise behind him and he leaned forward then and stood quickly. He turned to give the soldier a tongue-lashing he would never forget for returning after he had been clearly dismissed. But fortune shined upon him as a knife held in a black-gloved hand slashed through the air where his head had been when sitting. The attacker, who was in fact not the messenger who had just left him, quickly righted his balance and pulled a second dagger off his hip, holding the two weapons lightly and easily in his well-studied hands. The assassin advanced slowly, calmly. He was dressed all in black, with a deep cowl pulled so low over his forehead that his face was obscured by shadows.

Silverfist's own dagger appeared in his right hand and he readied himself to defend. Not for the first time, he thanked himself for the wisdom of choosing to slowly sip a glass of wine rather than swill it down in a rush. Drunkards rarely survived long in this world and he had survived close to his fortieth name day. The two opponents circled each other warily, and from the corner of his eye, Djumair saw the corpse of the messenger lying in a pool of his own blood, his throat slit before he'd had a chance to react. *So, this assassin had some skill, did he?* Dispatching a soldier that soundlessly was not easy.

The assassin closed the distance between them suddenly and his two blades flashed as he spun them in an intricate dance, weaving and slashing towards Silverfist's face and neck. Djumair Silverfist blocked the attacker's first knife with his own dagger, and used his metal fist to knock the other from his would-be killer's hand. People always underestimated his silver fist as a potential weapon. Little did they know how dangerous it really was.

His attacker didn't give up at the slight hitch in his plan. Determination could be seen in his decisive movements of continued assault. He slithered his way nearer to Silverfist again and in a surprising flurry of fists and steel, he managed to close the distance between them enough to actually deliver a shallow cut on Djumair Silverfist's chest before Djumair crashed his metal fist into the assassin's face. The impact sent a spray of blood and spit flying across the room to splatter upon his wine goblet. Dots of red contrasted against the light of the setting sun reflected through the crystal clear surface and its pale-golden contents. The assassin was stunned for a moment, which allowed Silverfist to grasp and pull him toward the edge of the platform, before slinging him up over the rail and casting him off with a pitiful wail as he plunged through the empty air towards the ground far below. In truth, he had been just as dead when Djumair's fist had crashed into his cheek, as he would be from the impact of the fall, whenever he finally landed. Djumair had his metal fist crafted with tiny, sharp ridges along the silver knuckles. They were enough to break skin every time upon impact and were laced with a particular poison from the deserts far away to the south, beyond the Drylands. It was a convenient way to deliver a poisonous touch of death to an opponent's blood stream after striking them. It was a secret he kept as closely guarded as any other. Many looked upon his silver fist as a weakness. Only he knew just how truly lethal it could be.

The body finally struck dirt far below in a tiny puff of soil. It was a shame he couldn't be questioned, but Silverfist had no doubt that if he had been able to talk to the would-be killer, all that would have been discovered was that a rival slave captain had tried to thin the competition and drive up his own prices. Such was the price of fame and success. Besides, an attempt on one's life was needed sometimes to remind a person that he still lived and breathed. The racing pulse, the rush of blood to the head, it was a drug unlike any other, and Djumair Silverfist was no more immune to its treacherous grasp than any other warrior he had ever met.

He touched the long, dueling dagger hanging at his hip in remembrance. All battles could set the fire flowing in his veins, but only one fight had ever truly crossed the line into giving him real pleasure. His lips curved in a slight smile at the thought of that old victory.

North he thought. To deal with the raids and shadow tactics that his former brethren were using to harry the human troops and supply lines as the humans ferried their soldiers, slaves, and food stores between one staging area to another.

He knew he should feel frustrated with the Andalayan resistance. He was after all, being sent to deal with it. And deal with it he would. The resistance was shaky at best, disorganized, and lacking cohesion, and Silverfist always produced results. Yet there was a tiny part of him that felt glad they were giving the humans such trouble, that they were dealing just a small amount of death and destruction to the intruders—the humans. The emotion was not because of his lost heritage. No, he had given up every right to even think of himself as Andalayan long ago when he had chosen this traitorous course. He simply enjoyed the fact that the humans were having a difficult time of it. Whatever he was—whether he considered himself one of the pale-featured Highest from the shattered northern kingdom of Andalaya, or one of the dark-skinned Departed as his former people called their cousins to the south and who he now served—it made no difference. Even though for now, he fought alongside the humans and enslaved his former kin as part of the tentative alliance his new masters had struck with them, it changed nothing. Either way he was born of this land, and bred of its people. He was an elf and proud of it. He reached his hand down to feel the shallow wound on his chest. His fingers came away bloody, and he touched the tips to his tongue, savoring the metallic flavor of blood. He was a coward, and a traitor —there was no disputing that fact. But he was still an elf.

ABOUT THE AUTHOR

Mathias Colwell grew up in far Northern California exploring redwood forests and cloudy beaches. He loves God, his family, and friends. Mathias has been a writer for most of his life, drafting his first stories as young as eight years of age. His desire to write fantasy was inspired by such authors as J.R.R. Tolkien, David Eddings and the late Robert Jordan. He is an avid traveler and all-around adventurer, having visited or lived in 27 countries. His travels have led him around the world to five continents including stays in Siberia, Spain, and Chile, and he attributes many of his passions and goals in life to these experiences. In his free time, he enjoys reading, outdoor activities such as soccer, snowboarding and water sports. Mathias has a passion for issues pertaining to social justice and human rights and hopes to influence these areas in the future.

twitter.com/MathiasColwell
facebook.com/Mathias-GB-Colwell-225647397579547